W9-ALV-885

Outstanding Advance Praise for THE NINJA DAUGHTER

"If you love a heroine who's tough, brilliant, and never runs from a fight, look no further." **—Tess Gerritsen, *New York Times* bestselling author of THE SHAPE OF NIGHT**

"Remarkably fresh, intense thriller, and Lily Wong is one hell of a new hero. I want this Ninja on my side. Tori Eldridge is redefining the genre." **—J.T. Ellison, *New York Times* bestselling author of TEAR ME APART**

"Action-packed, devious, and with a lead character you'll truly care about. Highly recommended!" **—Jonathan Maberry, *New York Times* bestselling author of DEEP SILENCE and V-WARS**

"An exceptional first novel, offering readers a tense and fascinating look into a culture and a world that most of us have never seen. I loved this book!"
—Karen Dionne, internationally bestselling author of THE MARSH KING'S DAUGHTER

"An exhilarating thrill ride! Lily Wong is a champion to the underdog, smart, brave, and a powerful force to reckon with. I loved her!" **—Liv Constantine, internationally bestselling author of THE LAST MRS. PARRISH**

"Tori Eldridge has created a heroine to love... and to fear! Lily's quest to protect the women of L.A. left me breathless, and Eldridge's snappy, down-to-earth prose kept me flipping pages."
—Rachel Howzell Hall, author of THEY ALL FALL DOWN

"A real page-turner with action aplenty but also depth and heart."
—Zoë Sharp, author of the CHARLIE FOX SERIES

THE
NINJA
DAUGHTER

THE
NINJA
DAUGHTER

TORI ELDRIDGE

Copyright © 2019 by Tori Eldridge
Cover and jacket design by 2Faced Design

ISBN 978-1-947993-69-3
eISBN: 978-1-947993-93-8
Library of Congress Control Number: 2019951171

First trade paperback edition November 2019 by Agora Books
An imprint of Polis Books, LLC
221 River St., 9th Fl., #9070
Hoboken, NJ PolisBooks.com

For my parents—loved and remembered, always

My name is Dumpling, or, at least, that's the first name I can remember; there have been many—some given to me, some taken by me, but none that matter quite as much.

It was Baba who gave me the name. He would bounce me on his thigh, puff his cheeks full of air to make them look like mine, poke his finger in my baby-fat and laugh, telling me it was filled with delicious secrets like Mama's dumplings. I wonder—if he had known the secrets his daughter would keep, would he have still considered that to be a good thing?

Chapter One

"I don't give a shit," said the Ukrainian, glaring at me over blue-tinted glasses.

I snorted the blood dripping from my nose and glared back. Being five foot four, it wasn't something I could generally do. But since he had strung me up to a metal scaffold in some grungy, vacant building, and stretched to the tips of my running shoes, I was now as tall as him.

"I've never shared that story with anyone," I said. "You should feel privileged."

I meant it. I had spent the last fifteen minutes telling him a tale I had kept locked in a mental dungeon for years, hidden away from friends, family, even the police. The only reason I had shared the truth now was because I didn't expect the Ukrainian to live long enough to repeat it.

He should feel downright honored.

He backhanded me across the face. "Yeah? Well, I don't."

Fresh blood pooled in my mouth. If I lost a tooth over this, I was not going to be happy.

Once again, he tipped his head down so he could stare at me over his round, retro glasses. "Where are they?"

I spit the blood at his face, or rather I tried to. Most of it just trickled down my chin. "You're boring. You know that, right?"

He took a breath and exhaled as he flicked his hand and whipped the heavy knot of braided rope into the soft pocket beneath my breast bone. My lungs forgot how to breathe—a shot to the solar plexus could do that to a person.

Surprising, subtle, and devastating. The last time I had experienced this particular kind of pain had been from my teacher's palm. That lesson had been offered with a higher purpose, not out of anger. Sensei didn't lose himself to such emotions. But regardless of the intent, the result felt the same—every part of me tried to clench around the pain. Lucky for me, my current posture wouldn't allow it. The Ukrainian had unwittingly bound me in the best possible position for solar plexus recovery: arms up, chest open. Who knew hanging from the base of a platform with a metal cross support pressed against my back could be so helpful?

Still, it was hard to feel appreciative as I sucked air.

The Ukrainian spit and cursed.

"Kurva blyat!"

He had been saying that a lot, more so in the last hour. I didn't speak his language, but I had a pretty good idea what it meant. I didn't mind. He wasn't my favorite person, either.

"Crazy bitch. You want to keep this up? Fine."

He flicked the knot against the side of my bare thigh.

I forced a grin. I wasn't about to give him the satisfaction of knowing he had hurt me, not after hours of denying it. But when he headed back to his table of toys, I wished I had buried my pride and given him what he had expected to see.

That's what Sensei would have done.

Sensei had been teaching me the ninja arts since I was twelve, when I discovered him in my neighborhood park tossing grownups like confetti. By then, I had seven years of competitive Wushu training behind me. Even so, I had never seen anything so elegantly efficient as the Japanese art of the ninja.

I continued to practice Chinese Wushu in public, but I trained to become a kunoichi—female ninja—in secret. The first discipline rooted me in my Chinese heritage and gave me athleticism and grace. The latter gave me purpose. Unfortunately, as fully as I had assimilated some of my ninja lessons, others refused to stick, like burying my pride.

I had underestimated the benign-looking weapon and the capability of this ridiculous-looking man to wield it, and, as a result, had been unprepared. He didn't seem like the type who would spend hours honing a skill. And with forearms the size of my calves, I didn't see why he'd bothered.

"I'm sorry. Okay?" My words spurted out between gasps of pain.

He snorted and turned back to his table.

"Too late."

"Wait." Talking hurt, but at least I had gotten him to stop swinging the rope. Maybe if I engaged him in conversation, he'd forget about choosing another weapon. I could live with the rope. At least, I thought I could.

"I want to cooperate. Really. I'll tell you whatever you want to know." It was surprising how the words flowed when your life was at stake.

He took a deep breath that expanded his slinky disco shirt across his back. Then he turned around to face me.

I didn't know what kind of childhood this guy had, but I could imagine a two-by-four to the head on numerous occasions. He had that kind of attitude. The kind that begged to be beaten out of him. It was in the way he stood, with his stocky legs spread apart and his hands held low and out in expressive fists. The way he rolled his shoulders forward around a hairy chest, proudly displayed by

4

that open-collared shirt some designer had bastardized modern art to create.

Even if he had not hung me from a hook, I would have wanted to kill him.

"Bet you watch a lot of old TV shows. Am I right?" This wasn't the time for my snarky attitude, but I gave it anyway. "Or cheesy action films? Because you've done a bang-up job with the whole sexploitation thing."

"What are you talking about?"

"You know this is a cliché, right?"

I was gambling, but I needed time to coax my muscles into action.

Most people would never know the pain of prolonged traction. It began with resistance. The body tensed, the muscles flexed, the mind rebelled. Then came acceptance and relaxation as the vertebrae separated. Shoulders and hips released. Even the knees got a welcome break from their daily compression. It felt kind of good. But it didn't last. The human body was meant to be supported from the ground up, not hung from delicate wrists. The only factor that kept my predicament from feeling truly horrible was that I could ease some of the tension by standing on my toes.

Suffice it to say I had a new and profound appreciation for ballerinas.

The Ukrainian turned back to the weapons table and got sidetracked by a jar of peanuts. Apparently, capturing women who were trying to break into his employer's mansion and using them to recreate movie scenes while wearing '70s reject clothing made a guy hungry. I took advantage of his inattention to raise my legs. No such luck. My sore muscles wouldn't cooperate.

Once again, I thought of my teacher. *"Let your pain flow like water around river rocks—touching, moving, and, ultimately, pass-*

5

ing."

As my pain ebbed and my resolve strengthened, I knew the Ukrainian had failed. He had thought I would feel embarrassed to be displayed like a piece of meat; I wasn't. He had thought I would feel helpless hanging from a hook; I didn't. He had thought I would do anything to stop the pain and humiliation.

That time, he was correct.

Chapter Two

I couldn't blame the Ukrainian for what he was doing to me. Not really. I had been a monumental pain in his ass. At first, he had assumed I was a burglar breaking into his employer's house. But sometime between knocking me unconscious on the patio and thirty minutes ago, he had learned of Kateryna's and Ilya's disappearance. That's when my crime elevated from burglary to kidnapping. I knew this because I had heard Dmitry Romanko yelling it through the Ukrainian's cellphone. Ilya had not arrived at kindergarten this morning, and Romanko was killing mad.

That's when the Ukrainian began whipping me with the knotted rope. It wasn't sexual. It was more like a two-year-old's temper tantrum. He had gotten reprimanded by his boss and was taking it out on the only person within reach.

Lucky me.

But like most tantrums, the Ukrainian's had erupted and passed too suddenly for me to capitalize on it. So when I saw him grip the edge of the wooden table and squeeze it as though he wanted to crush it, I was glad. I needed him angry. I needed him to stop playing games. And when his ugly shirt stretched against flexed muscles, I knew I had succeeded. He didn't want me to give up. I had resisted for too long, disrespected his manhood, injured his fragile Ukrainian pride. He wanted satisfaction.

About time.

I needed him to do something reckless, like grab the hilt of the Fox 599 Karambit. Of all the weapons laid out on his table—pipe, brass knuckles, combat dagger, hatchet—the Ukrainian had chosen the most precise tool of the bunch. I knew because it was mine. I also knew it did not suit him.

I feigned a frightened expression as he swiped back and forth like a batter warming up for the plate. "Where are they?"

I looked away and muttered something I hoped was unintelligible.

"What's that? Speak up."

He had chosen the talon-like blade—my blade—to make a point. Bad pun? Sure. But hey, at least I had learned to accept new realities—like hanging from a hook while a sadist threatened me with my own blade.

The Ukrainian smirked. "Maybe I cut out little pieces. What do you think?"

What did I think? I thought he was ready. He had just begun shifting his weight to his left foot, freeing his right for the step that would bring the hooked blade to my chest. I didn't need to watch the knife; I got all the information I needed from the angle of his hips.

I raised my face, so he could see the terror he wanted to see, and waited for him to pause and breathe—the way he had before every previous attack. Then together, we inhaled. Only, this time, mine was a second shorter than his.

I clenched my abs, brought my knee to my chest, and snapped my leg out to the side. The edge of my shoe caught the nerve on the inside of his right wrist. The shock of the strike loosened his grip and knocked the knife from his hand while the friction of my skin against his tugged him forward.

As one leg finished its job, the other sailed over his head in opposition.

I arced my leg's descent just a bit, hooked his neck with my foot, and rotated him, face up. The Ukrainian's larynx crunched between my rising knee and my descending heel.

He wouldn't be calling me kurva blyat any time soon.

As he crumpled to the cement floor, with what I hoped was a fractured larynx, I grabbed the rope above me and began to swing. In spite of the metal cross support jamming my back, I managed enough momentum to pull my legs over my head and onto the platform above me. This should have knocked the rope off the hook, but it hadn't. So there I was, balanced on the edge of the platform like a pencil on a finger, with the wood digging into my hips, my back straining to hold its arch, my arms extended to their limits, and my fingers fiddling with the rope. If I allowed my chest to drop, even an inch, the balance would tip and down I would go.

Objects clattered below me as the Ukrainian struggled with his own dilemma. Maybe he'd suffocate before my back seized and I fell off the platform. Then again, maybe not. I tried not to risk my life on maybes.

By the time I untangled the rope from the hook, the trembling in my muscles had become a seismic event, which turned my neat gymnast dismount into a free-falling tumble. No ninja landing for me. Instead, I got caught in an awkward tripod of feet and bound hands.

The Ukrainian grabbed my hair and yanked me to my feet then stuffed my head under his arm and clenched. I tucked my chin like a turtle to protect my carotid artery and trachea, and to buy myself some time. If my wrists hadn't been tied, I could have snuck a hand around his arm and dropped him with the pressure of a single finger under his nose. However, since this elegant defense was not an option, I slammed my fists into his testicles.

Crude but effective.

I followed this up with a shot to his jaw, the force of which—unfortunately—caused him to fall back onto his table of toys.

This time, he went for the hatchet.

With only a second to decide, I moved in, down, and out—a combination of movements that would keep me safe from a downward, diagonal, or horizontal cut—then I slipped behind him, tossed my bound wrists over his head, and ground my forehead into the back of his neck.

Once again, I had his throat jammed between two precise and deadly forces.

I pulled until my wrists burned and the hatchet clanked to the floor. I pressed until my forehead molded into the back of his neck. I pulled and pressed until his heart stopped beating and his nasty soul skittered off to Hell. And then, I gave the rope one final yank.

He sank to the floor, and I collapsed over his sweaty corpse like an exhausted lover. My long dark hair clung to his pale dead skin. It was gross, no other way to describe it. I wanted to roll away, but I couldn't move. My back throbbed. My cuts stung. And sometime in the fight my tank top had ripped and I had begun to shiver—a clear sign of muscle failure.

I crawled off his chest and dragged myself forward like an inchworm to where the hatchet had fallen. By then, I was shaking so badly I nearly cut off my toes trying to secure the blade between my feet.

If I had grown up in North Dakota, like my Norwegian father, I might have had an easier time with the cold. But as a California girl? Not so much.

I visualized a hot sidewalk warming my bottom and legs and radiating heat up through my torso. It took longer than the river rock imagery had taken to rid me of pain, but it did the trick. My hands stopped shaking, and I was able to saw through the nylon without shedding any more blood.

I crawled back to the corpse. The sports bra I wore underneath my tattered tank top wasn't going to cut it. I needed something warmer. Even if it was butt-ugly and rank, it would not be the worst indignity I had suffered this day. I kept that in mind as I undid the buttons of the Ukrainian's shirt and freed a forest of curly black chest hair. The slinky fabric of his shirt stank of sweat, deodorant, and cologne.

"Suck it up, Lily."

I held my breath and slid my arms into the clinging sleeves and buttoned every button past my shorts and down to my knees. It had been ninety degrees in the shade earlier this afternoon. Where was that heat now?

My fatigued legs felt cold and stiff. I considered taking the Ukrainian's pants but was afraid of what I might find underneath. Hot pink briefs? A leopard skin thong? Nothing? Just imagining the possibilities made me want to vomit, which reminded me of what else I needed.

The Ukrainian had supplied himself with water, nuts, and a box of glazed donut holes, the remnants of which still sat on the table. I picked up the bottle and sniffed. The water smelled vaguely of donuts. I drank it anyway, backwash and all. The effects were instantaneous. My mind cleared. My energy boosted. The shivering stopped.

I had clothes, food, water, and a dead Ukrainian.

My situation had vastly improved.

Chapter Three

The Ukrainian had imprisoned me in a stalled renovation project in the Mid-Wilshire district about four miles from where I had left Dmitry Romanko's wife and son. If I had been thinking clearly, I would have used the dead man's cellphone to call a taxi. But the only thing working at full capacity were my feet. So once I took care of my physical needs, collected my karambit, and wiped down everything I could remember touching, I ran.

It wasn't fast, and it wasn't pretty. God only knew what I looked like, running down the sidewalk in an oversized disco shirt and my hair plastered against my face. But I made it to Aleisha's Refuge, staggered up the front step, and fell against the door. I didn't have energy left to knock. I was done.

A stern, but polite voice commanded me to step away from the door. Aleisha Reiner was a compassionate and welcoming woman, but running a refuge for battered women had made her cautious. I did as she commanded and tried my best not to fall off the step. I heard a squeal through the door, followed by the rattling of a security chain, and the clank of a bolt sliding open.

"Oh sweet Jesus. What happened to you, child? Are you hurt?" Aleisha's smooth, dark skin wrinkled into deep furrows as her generous mouth, so quick to smile, hung slack with concern. She rubbed her hands along my arms and around my head, checking for injury, then pulled me into a hug. "You're gonna be the death of me, girl. Do you hear?" I jostled against her bosom as she shook. "How you gonna help anyone if you get yourself killed?"

I muttered a response, lost in the pillows of her shirt, then pried myself away. "I'm fine. Honest. I just need to speak with Kateryna."

Aleisha shook her head. "She's gone."

"What do you mean? Did someone take her?" I pictured a gang of Ukrainians dragging Kateryna and Ilya out the door. Then something worse occurred to me. "What about the other women?" I pushed Aleisha away so I could examine her for injury. "Are you okay?"

Aleisha rubbed my arms as if she was calming a new arrival. "Hush. I'm okay. The women are okay. Everybody is just fine." The low hum of her voice and the soft stroke of her hands took the edge off my anxiety, but I still needed answers.

Aleisha shrugged. "She just took the boy and left."

I couldn't believe it. It had taken me three weeks to convince Kateryna to leave her husband and another week to help her gather the necessary documents, keys, addresses, and cash so she could stay hidden and start a new life. We had made arrangements with her cousin in Argentina. All Kateryna had to do was stay with Aleisha until we got her and Ilya on the plane.

"She went back?"

"Uh-huh. To Hancock Pack and that husband of hers."

I slid down the doorframe and sat, bare legs on cool tile, as the last of my energy rushed out of me like the air from an unknotted balloon.

Kateryna's dirt-bag lawyer husband worked for the Ukrainian mob.

I worked for Aleisha's Refuge, kept on retainer to rescue and protect. I didn't charge much, but what I earned kept my tech and weapons up to date.

Aleisha had assigned me to Kateryna's case because of the danger and complexity of the situation. Normally, I got the job done neatly and discreetly, using my kunoichi skills to investigate, rescue, and extract. Sometimes things got violent. More often, stealth, coercion, and misdirection sufficed. But this time? I left the question unanswered as Aleisha's husband hurried to the door.

"Is that Lily?" Stan's New York accent sounded more pronounced from alarm.

Tears welled in my eyes. Stan had that effect on me. He was shaped like a giant pear, topped with a freckled bald head. He had white fuzzy whiskers and soft shoulders that sloped to a squishy belly and a comfortable lap that was always ready for a sleepy child.

"Why is she on the floor?"

Aleisha must have given him a look because he didn't ask another question. He simply scooped me up and carried me to the couch. Once I was safely planted, he rustled through a cabinet for a first-aid kit and began tending my wounds. Aleisha went to get food. She must have known I wouldn't be staying long because she brought me a tamale, still partially wrapped.

I held the corn husk and smelled the steaming cake. "Asadero cheese, fresh roasted corn, and…barbecue ribs?" I took a bite of the heavenly cornmeal and groaned in ecstasy. "And you could open your own restaurant." Everything Aleisha cooked had a dash of soul and pounds of love.

She rolled her big brown eyes and patted her hairline, where cornrows pulled back into a tight bun. "I have enough people to cook for as it is. What would I want with a restaurant?"

I could have given her several reasons if I hadn't had my mouth full of sweet savory goodness.

She patted my knee. "You drink that water, and I'll get you a bottle of tea to go." By the time Stan had finished speckling me with bandages, Aleisha had returned with the tea and some folded clothes. "I thought you might like something else to wear." That something turned out to be a pair of dark gray sweatpants, cuffed tight at the ankle, and a matching hoodie. Both were several sizes too big but a welcome improvement from the Ukrainian's slinky shirt, which I tossed in the trash as soon as I got to the bathroom. Once I had washed the grime from my face, I looked and felt almost normal.

I slipped back into my shoes and braided my hair into a long rope. It hung nearly to my waist, so I wound it into a bun and knotted the end. Then I pulled up the hood of the sweatshirt. I could have been anyone.

Unless someone got close, they wouldn't notice the high cheekbones I had inherited from my Hong Kong mother or the strong nose of my North Dakota father, or the haphazard way the rest of their genes had muddled together to give me such an identifiable face. I don't know how it had happened, but Baba's Norwegian genes had made my Chinese features uncomfortably excessive. My brows arched too high, my nostrils flared too wide, and my lips were pouty and fuller than they needed to be. Even my eyes looked less like Ma's classic almonds and more like a startled cat.

No one would notice any of that in the dark with the hood of Aleisha's sweatshirt around my face. They'd see a short person in baggy clothes somewhere between ninety to one-hundred thirty pounds of unknown gender, age, and race. With a description like that, I could walk up to a witness and flick their nose, and they'd never realize I was the person they had seen.

Feeling better than I had all day, I went to say goodbye. Stan wrapped me in his arms and squeezed the air out of me. "You be careful. It won't take much to open that wound." He was referring to the gash above my left cheek he had anchored together with a butterfly bandage. "And find yourself a good doctor. You may need stitches."

His hug crushed me, but I didn't want it to stop. "I'll be fine, Stan. I promise."

Mollified, he stepped back to Aleisha. They made an odd couple, a sturdy black Baptist from Compton and a soft, pear-shaped Jew from New York. But they also made the perfect pair. They devoted their lives to helping others, had cheerful natures, and loved to eat. No wonder we all got along.

"You want a sandwich to go?"

I laughed. Typical Aleisha. "I'll be fine. With any luck, I'll be back later tonight with Kateryna and Ilya."

"You sure you don't want Stan to drive you?"

"Nope. Taxi will do. I'll pay you back tomorrow."

I never charged for transportation. I didn't see the point. I lived cheap and traveled on my feet, bike, or mass transit. If I needed something fast and private, I borrowed our restaurant delivery car or ordered a ride. Of course, that required an app. Which I no longer had because the Ukrainian had crushed my phone with the heel of his boot. Had—as in past tense. The Ukrainian was dead.

I didn't want to think about what I had done. Not now. Maybe not ever.

Stan tapped my forehead. "You don't worry about that."

He was referring to the money, not the Ukrainian, but the command still helped. I'd have ample time to mull over the ramifications of my actions, to replay the scene a hundred times until I was certain that what I had done was, in fact, inevitable and just.

But what if it wasn't?

Stan placed his hands on my shoulders and hunched so he

could peer into my eyes. "You did what needed to be done. Now you need to let it go."

I squeezed back the tears. Like before, he didn't know, but again his words were a comfort to me. I just hoped I deserved them. It hurt my soul to end a life, no matter how justified. Maybe that was a good thing. Maybe my tortured conscience would keep me human.

"I'm going to pay you back."

He nodded. "Of course you are."

Stan and I had traveled down this road before. He would pamper me with the taxi tonight, and I would deposit money into his account in the morning. He got to be fatherly and I got to exert my independence. Compromise and balance.

Maybe one day I'd also learn to bury my pride.

Chapter Four

Dmitry Romanko lit his family room like a stadium and kept his backyard dark, which made it easy for me to spy on him as he lounged on his couch watching television. I could hear the soccer match and commentary through the screen door. And I could see little Ilya kneeling on the carpet.

If I hadn't already known this family's dynamic, I might have thought I was witnessing a Hallmark moment: Dad sitting on the couch watching the game while his five-year-old son colored in a book on the coffee table. I might have felt envious of the peaceful-ness of their lives. I might have respected the way father and son could be themselves in each other's presence. But I did know, so I didn't believe.

Dmitry Romanko had a brutish demeanor he attempted to el-evate with metrosexual fashion. He favored tight V-neck tees to show off his pecs, squeezed his muscular thighs into pencil-thin pants, and wore his designer loafers sans socks. He flaunted a heavy gold bracelet and an even heavier gold watch. I had seen the marks of that watch left on Kateryna's bruised face. But no amount of styling gel, jewelry, or designer clothes could hide his working-class roots.

Ilya, on the other hand, reminded me of a bunny—soft, gentle, and alert.

Romanko slammed his hand on the table. "Pass, you idiot. Did you see that? Shevchenko was wide open. These stupid kids don't know what they're doing."

Ilya held still, ready to bolt.

"Pass, you motherless—" Romanko grabbed an accent pillow from the couch and hurled it at the television. Ilya ducked. Romanko didn't notice, or if he did, he didn't seem to care. He jumped to his feet and unloaded an angry stream of Ukrainian, like a coach chewing out one of his players for making a boneheaded pass. Except he wasn't on a field. He was in his home, watching television. Scaring his boy.

As Romanko reached across the table to grab a handful of candy from a crystal bowl, Ilya cowered. Did he expect his father to throw it at the screen or at him? I didn't know, and it didn't matter. The fact that Ilya expected something bad to happen was a clear sign of domestic abuse. All of this was lost on Romanko as he leaned back on the couch and tossed the candy, piece by piece, into his mouth.

If he had done nothing other than this, I would have hated him. But when I saw little Ilya's eyes soften back to their sad half-moon shapes, I wanted to cry. He loved his father. I could see it in his expression and the slight protrusion of his chin, as though he wished his dad would cradle it with his fingers and plant a loving kiss on his nose. My heart broke.

I backed away from the sycamore tree. Time to find Kateryna.

A narrow strip of lawn ran along the side of the Tudor Revival house, bordered by a row of cypress trees and a wooden fence. All of the balconies and dormer windows faced the courtyard or one of the two corner streets. This side of the house was stark, with rough-hewn brick and only a sliver of a bathroom window.

Great for privacy. Lousy for climbing.

It would have been easier to leap and swing my way up to the roof, but the yard was too narrow for generating momentum and the cypresses too flimsy for rebounding. So I dug my fingers between the bricks, wedged a foot onto the corner stone, and began my grueling ascent. Finger climbing required considerable strength. I could do it, but not for long. Using the protrusions of corner stones and gripping the side of the wall helped. Even so, I was trembling something fierce by the time I hooked my heel over the storm drain and pulled myself onto the slate tiles.

Once I recovered, I scampered across the steep grade, past one of the stone chimneys and three of the dormer windows, built into the peaks like tiny houses on cliffs. When I got to the fourth dormer, I slid down its short roof and crawled to the front. As was her custom, Kateryna had left the double windows cracked for ventilation. I reached in and cranked them open. I dropped onto her Persian rug and crossed to the king-sized bed, covered in a plush merlot quilt and dollops of whipped cream pillows. Stylish and comfy.

Sounds from the soccer match floated up from the family room below. Hopefully, Dmitry Romanko would stay put long enough for me to talk some sense into his wife.

I pulled back the hood of my sweatshirt and sat on bench at the foot of the bed, trying to look harmless as I waited for her to come out of the bathroom. Women my size didn't usually inspire fear. However, Kateryna had become as skittish as her son.

"Lily," she said in a hoarse whisper.

She had the decency to look abashed, but after the ordeal I had suffered, I wanted a tearful apology. "Why'd you leave?"

She checked the hall then closed the door. "You can't be here."

"And yet, here I am."

"No. You have to go. I've changed my mind. I don't want your help."

Kateryna was a lovely woman with a long, slender neck and delicate bones. She stood taller and weighed less than I did, but still managed to have more curves, as evidenced by the slinky nightie she was wearing. She had what I called a zipper figure: one you could see from the front and back but so thin it seemed to vanish when viewed from the side.

Next to her, I was a crayon.

My waist did not disappear from the side, nor did my thighs. And while her weight went to full breasts and a wide-hipped bottom, mine went to muscle. I had inherited broad Norwegian shoulders, narrow hips, and the limb proportion of my Asian mother. I would never grace the pages of a fashion magazine. Then again, Kateryna would never be able to scale a building.

Her golden ringlets bounced around her face as she tugged me off the bench. "You have to leave." Plucked and penciled brows raised in high arches. Her lips—lined, painted, and glossed—pursed with tension. Kateryna had other plans for her bed tonight than sleep.

I thought of Ilya in the family room, flinching at every move his father made, and wanted to slap some sense into her. Didn't she know? Didn't she care? I glanced down at her lacy nightgown. "What's going on, Kateryna? You and Dmitry making up?"

She flicked her hand in the dismissive way I had seen her husband do many times, then busied herself picking up his things around the room. "Thank you for your help. But I don't need it anymore." She folded his newspaper and set it neatly on the table near the open window.

I wanted to rip it to bits. "Maybe you don't, but Ilya does."

That stopped her. "Dmitry would never hurt Ilya."

"You sure about that? Because in my experience, a man who

beats his wife today, beats his kid tomorrow."

She dropped the act, and for a moment, I thought she might change her mind. Then she shook her head and sent her hair into a bouncing golden frenzy. "You don't understand. He will find us wherever we go."

"He didn't find you at Aleisha's."

"He would have."

"But he didn't."

She clicked the tips of her acrylic fingernails. A nervous habit.

"Why did you leave, Kateryna?"

The clicking stopped, and the tears began. "You said you would only be gone an hour, just long enough to get our passports."

I couldn't believe she was blaming this on me. "I gave you a list of important documents to put in your escape pack."

"I was scared."

I sighed. It had been a long day and was proving to be a frustrating night. I needed to calm my own emotions before I could hope to calm hers.

"Of course you were. You were scared—for Ilya," I added, wanting to spark her maternal courage. "But that doesn't explain why you left."

She wiped her tears and sniffed. "You didn't come back."

I wanted to grab her shoulders and shake those golden ringlets right off her head. Instead, I took a breath, reined in my anger, and tried my best to sound reasonable. "I ran into traffic." It was a plausible lie. I couldn't tell her the truth, could I? That her husband's thug had caught me trying to break into her house and knocked me upside the head? No, I wouldn't be telling that story to anyone. I felt embarrassed enough just knowing I had let it happen. In fact, I planned to lock the whole shameful incident in the vault with the rest of my unpleasant memories.

"I called him," she said.

"Wait. What?"

"Dmitry worries. So I called him. I told him I was leaving and taking Ilya with me."

My gut clenched. "Please tell me you didn't use Aleisha's phone."

"I called from my cell."

"Oh, thank God."

"Why?"

"Aleisha's home is a refuge. Strictly word of mouth. You can't tell anyone about it. Ever."

I saw the familiar bland veil of disinterest descend over her face and grabbed her arms. "I'm serious, Kateryna. You can't ever tell Dmitry where you were. You'd be putting other lives at risk. Tell me you understand."

She pulled out of my grip. "I understand." She rubbed her arms, inadvertently wiping away a bit of body makeup. A purple spot the size of a man's finger tainted her creamy skin. I imagined three more next to it and a thumb-size spot on the other side—all hidden by a foundation with some romantic name like Alabaster Ivory or Porcelain Nude.

What was I doing? I was supposed to protect women, not bully them.

"I'm sorry. I shouldn't have done that." When she nodded, I continued in a gentler tone. "When you called…what did he say?"

"That if I did not bring Ilya back, he would find us and send him to Ukraine without me."

"To his family?"

She nodded. "I would never see him again." The tears flowed. She blotted them with the back of her delicate hand. "I am not even Ukrainian citizen anymore. Dmitry said I could not be both.

But he is." She sniffed her runny nose and dabbed under her eyes.

It annoyed me that she still cared about her makeup until I noticed the bruises appearing under her thinning foundation. They were fresh. Dmitry had done this to her *today*.

I stepped back and sat on the bed. I didn't know what to do. I had worked for Aleisha long enough to know that decisions about when to leave an abusive partner had to be made from the inside. Well-meaning people, like me, could exacerbate a situation and endanger the lives of those they were trying to protect simply by forcing an action at the wrong time.

Was this the wrong time? Kateryna seemed to believe it was. Who was I to say otherwise?

As I struggled with my dilemma, Dmitry bellowed for Kateryna.

She startled like a deer, eyes wide, body tensed for danger. Then she grabbed a silk robe from her vanity chair. "I have to go." She covered her negligee and tied the sash around her tiny waist. "Please leave the way you came in."

I lingered at the window and listened to the soccer commentary that carried up from the family room. Ilya would still be coloring when Kateryna answered the call of her wife-beating husband. The situation sucked, and there was nothing I could do about it.

I planted my hands on the table and closed my eyes. When I opened them, I saw the picture of another blonde, blue-eyed woman staring up at me from the folded newspaper—Mia Mikkelsen.

I recognized her from recent news reports on television. The cocktail waitress had been attacked in her home by a customer, and the press was having a field day maligning her reputation and fawning over her alleged assailant, J Tran. The photos they had chosen confirmed their bias. The shot of Mia made her look like a slutty puffer fish. The photo of Tran looked like the cover for *Peo-*

ple Magazine's Sexiest Man Alive.

I sighed. "Bet you could use a big sister, right about now, eh, Mia?"

In addition to working for Aleisha's refuge, which was funded by Stan's previous vocation as a New York stock broker and a few celebrity angels, I did what I liked to think of as ninja pro bono work. I watched out for women getting harassed, shamed, or abused and stepped in when no one else would.

If I helped Mia tomorrow, would it make up for my failure today?

I thought about Kateryna's makeup-covered bruises and wished I was back in that warehouse with the Ukrainian—I could have used someone to punch.

Chapter Five

"Okay to take Washington?" the taxi driver asked.

"Sure," I said. "All the way to Overland." It was a straight shot southwest. Nothing to screw up. I could just sit back, enjoy the night breeze, and let my muscles cramp one by one.

Now that the adrenaline had worn off, I felt every bruise and strain. At least the Ukrainian hadn't broken anything. He had tried to kill me. I had stopped him. Period. End of story.

That's what I kept telling myself.

But was it the truth?

Had he *really* been trying to kill me? Or had he been trying to subdue me long enough to hang me back on the hook? Probably the latter, but he would have mutilated me for information. Kateryna would have been found. Aleisha's Refuge would have been at risk. So, no, it didn't matter.

But I had also told the Ukrainian my story, the one I had never shared. Because I knew he would not live to repeat it.

I had entered into the story gently enough. I mean, what did I care if some Ukrainian thug knew the origins of my nickname or how Baba had bounced me on his knee? Why should anyone have had to die just because they knew my father had thought my baby belly was stuffed with secrets like Mama's dumplings?

Besides, that wasn't even the truth. They weren't Mama's

dumplings at all. They were Baba's. He learned to make them to ease her homesickness.

But I hadn't told the Ukrainian any of my parents' secrets; I had only told him mine. And not just secrets, either. I had opened the door to my shadow world. I had given him a reason to fear me.

It was easy to fool people when you showed them what they expected to see.

I had spoken those exact words while telling the Ukrainian my story, and in so doing, had told him exactly how I would use his arrogance against him. Was it my fault if he had been too short-sighted to understand? Had I been giving him a chance? Maybe. All I knew was that once I had begun telling the story, the story wouldn't let me stop.

It had happened two years ago, in the summer before my twenty-third birthday. I was sitting in a bar, nursing a drink, pointedly ignoring the people around me. I didn't like the way they could take one look at me and act as it they knew me, like they knew what I was about. It was profiling, but in my favor. They would take one look at my Asian-ness and assume I was this intelligent, ambitious college girl, struggling to find balance between the strict culture of my ancestry and the wanton opportunities of my youth. The stereotype.

Were they wrong? No. But that was not, as my father liked to say, the meat of the issue. As in my namesake, there were other mysterious ingredients that comprised a dumpling besides pork.

There was a man sitting beside me at the bar. I remembered him being surprised by the sparkling cranberry juice I had ordered. He had probably expected me to have a rebellious affinity for scotch or a predilection for chardonnay. I had friends who would have fit both of those stereotypes. I was neither. I was cautious.

I liked my mind clear, my wits keen, and my legs ready to run. And if I had been inclined to violence, which I wasn't yet, I would never have needed to be pushed by alcohol.

No. What I wanted most, at that moment, was to run my fingers over every beautiful angle of that man's stunning face. Wanted but didn't; I was far too disciplined for that. Instead, I leaned closer and let my hair do the caressing while I blathered about national security, privacy, and the right to bear arms.

Clearly, I had lost all of my good sense.

I remember laughing to myself as he struggled to ignore my hair on his arm and formulate a cogent response to my seemingly contradictory views, and liked him better for it. In fact, I liked him too much.

Everything about him put me at ease and teased me with hope.

So when he ordered a martini and offered me the same, I accepted. The taste was clean, the fruit tart and plump. I remember liking it so much that I considered taking a new name for the evening—put aside Dumpling and call myself Olive. But after hours of conversation, names had not been requested or shared. While normally this would have felt odd, on that night, it felt right and natural, as though there were far more important things to discuss than names.

He pinched the top of my toothpick and swirled the remaining olive, stirring up feelings I had only experienced once before. Was he congratulating himself on the conquest? If so, it was well earned because he had invaded my defenses and made himself at home.

So when he downed the rest of his drink, I did the same.

"We can go," he said, and waited for me to rise.

He followed behind protectively, like a gentleman. It had been a long time since I had allowed a man to do that.

His car was parked nearby—close enough to be comfortable

for me to walk if I had been wearing heels yet far enough to give him a chance to take my hand. It was an endearing gesture and one my compulsion for mobility would normally never have allowed.

At least I was wearing my sturdy boots; I hadn't forsaken all my good sense.

Although, with the sensual breeze and the warmth of his hand against mine, I was having a hard time remembering why I thought that might be important.

When we arrived at his car—clean, sporty, not excessively expensive—he opened my door and waited for me to fold in my legs. I could feel his admiration, and I understood it. My legs have always been my strongest feature. They might not be model-long, but they had an athletic grace that makes men think of passionate embraces—or so I was once told by a would-be suitor who never had the privilege of helping me into a car.

As we drove, I thought about how out of character all of this was for me: the bar, the martini, the car. I didn't date. And I definitely didn't accept invitations from men I had just met. But something about him made me want to give up my lonely quest for vengeance and take a chance on love. Or at least, that's what I thought was happening.

The more I tried to recall the moment of my decision, the harder it was to remember when I had actually agreed.

The leather seat felt warm against my back. My skin flushed with fanciful thoughts. And my mouth drooped in a dopey smile, betraying feelings I didn't understand. I looked out the window and tried to hide the thoughts I feared were playing across my face. I didn't want him to get the wrong idea.

What would have been the right idea?

The streets were dark. There were no neon bar signs, no cozy restaurants, no security-lit establishments. Everything seemed closed for the evening. We had ventured onto unforgiving streets with oppressive buildings and gaping alleys. Streets that were empty except for phantoms huddled near dumpsters.

"Where are we?" *And why did my tongue feel like a swollen slug?*

I looked over at the man of my dreams, and what I saw was death.

Everything about him had changed. His alluring scent had soured with sweat, and his breath carried ugly words. I searched for signs of that calm, sincere gentleman, and saw a psychopath.

The seat jarred back as he made space to mount me. And I did nothing.

Me, the kunoichi who was never out of control, sat immobile as he ripped open my blouse and hiked up my skirt. I didn't strike or scream or buck. He had me, and he knew it.

There was a metallic taste in my mouth that I hadn't noticed before, and it wasn't cranberries or vermouth. It was medicinal in a way that would have tainted pure vodka. As I struggled to move my unresponsive body, my mind honed in on that swirling olive. His hand had been cupped over my glass as his fingers twirled the toothpick. This monster had dropped something from his palm while I had been gazing into his eyes.

What had I allowed to happen?

My arms hung limp, one beside me and the other perched against the door, as he petted my hair and told me how long it had been since he'd had a China girl like me.

That's when I saw him—when I *really* saw him. He wasn't just a tall, blond hunk in a Hugo Boss suit. He was the *same* well-dressed predator who had fooled my sister and ended her life.

My numb hand hovered near my necklace, a long silver chain with a dagger-shaped phurba. No one ever commented on it. Why would they? It was just some odd talisman with a carved face on a ceremonial-looking dagger. It was barely four inches long. It wasn't even sharp. Just a harmless Buddhist artifact. And yet, there it was within reach of my determined, nimble fingers.

As he unfastened his pants, I walked those fingers across my collar bone. As he maneuvered his hips, I folded the carved face of the phurba into my knuckles. And as he shoved his pants to his knees and fumbled with the feeble barrier of my panties, I gripped the base of the dagger.

Make me strong, I prayed.

And then I struck.

He dropped onto my lap, and slapped my face on the way up to clutch at his throat. But there was nothing there to grab. I had removed the dagger to continue my attack. I was gaining control over my arms and used them both to distract and deflect, making it hard for him to understand which hand was inflicting the damage. He could have smothered me with his weight if he had remained calm; instead, he panicked, and a lucky fist hammered my sternum.

The pain was stunning.

I grabbed for my chest as if to hold it in place so the broken plate wouldn't move. Crazy, I know, but that's how it felt: as if the only thing holding me together was my hand on my chest. So I kept up the pressure until I was sure nothing would move and my sternum felt solid and secure. Then I stabbed him in the face.

With every strike, I yanked and ripped, tearing his flesh into dog meat with the three-sided dagger. I didn't need to see the damage. I just kept striking until his strength gave out and his body expired. Then I opened my door and fell onto the curb.

It took several minutes before I stopped shaking, before I had quieted my sobs and spit away all traces of his blood. It took a few more to crawl to my feet, where I swayed until my drugged body grew accustomed to standing. My clothes were ripped. My face and torso were covered in blood. But I was alive.

I was lucky.

I had spent years trolling for the man who had raped and murdered Rose, with only scant descriptions from eyewitnesses to guide me. I knew my fifteen-year-old sister had used a fake ID to get into one of the clubs that catered to the eighteen-plus crowd. I didn't know if she had done it before.

Had she gotten scared? Had her friends ditched her? Was that why she had texted me? To come and get her?

I'd never know. I'd never responded.

I had abandoned Rose when she needed me most, and all I could do after her death was hunt down her murderer. I played bait in every underage haunt I could find and searched for the tall, blond twenty-something man with the strong jaw, predatory eyes, and out-of-place suit the witnesses had described. I had felt certain I would recognize his ill intent when he came to prey on me.

I was wrong.

I had fallen for his charms, just as my sister had, and had come close to suffering the same fate.

As I staggered away from that car and into the alley, covered in my sister's killer's blood, I made a promise to always remain vigilant and never accept what was presented. I would look deep and jump slow. And I would question everything. It would keep me alive. More than that, it helped me keep others alive.

There was no mention in the news of anyone killed that night in that vicinity. Nor could I find any man fitting his description in any of the nearby hospitals. So he had either somehow driven away, or I had suffered a horrifyingly visceral hallucination that had somehow drenched me in blood. Either way, it left me feeling incomplete.

I would never know for sure if Rose's killer was dead or alive.

***

I leaned my face out the open window of the taxi and let the breeze dry my tears.

The version of the story I had told the Ukrainian had been simple and to the point. The more profound recollections and personal revelations were only now invading my mind. I had told him just enough to relieve my heart of its burden, but not enough to send him running in fear of his life. I had given him reason to respect me but not enough to fear me.

I had given him a chance.

But after sharing my darkest secrets, the Ukrainian, whose death had been burning a hole in my conscience, had only said one thing: "I don't give a shit."

Well, if he didn't, why should I?

Chapter Six

I lived in Culver City just past the Sony Pictures lot, where Culver and Washington Boulevards kissed and parted to follow their own jagged trajectories. It was a commercial area filled with everyday stores selling essential products and services for urban survival—auto parts, furniture, dentists, hair salons—plus colorful non-essentials like tattoos, bongs, and bubble tea. We also had several ethnic eateries, which included Wong's Hong Kong Inn, a restaurant named for my mother and run by my father. I lived on the second floor.

I pulled the sweatshirt hood over my head and hobbled into the alley. Anyone who noticed would assume I was heading for a cardboard bed behind a garbage bin. And if my legs gave out on me, they might be right. However, I was actually heading toward the twin golden dragons emblazoned on the side of our delivery car. I liked to think these dragons, along with the giant version of them that covered the front of our building, protected our family from ill-intent and unexpected disaster.

I could have used some dragon protection today.

I shook off my doubt and limped toward the steps to the kitchen entrance, scanning the alley as I went. No lurking Ukrainians this time, just a bunch of produce crates, flattened cardboard boxes, and trash containers from the smoke shop next door. I punched in the key code and opened the door to a blast of garlic, ginger, and grease. My stomach growled. I hadn't eaten much today. Maybe Baba had left me a treat.

Sure enough, a couple of savory pastries waited for me on the prep table. He had also left a bamboo steamer sitting on a wok at the end of the long cooking station. The fire was out, but the pan still radiated a little warmth, so he couldn't have been gone long. I opened the lid and found two char siu bao and one zòngzi wrapped in bamboo leaves. Char siu bao were pillowy buns filled with barbecue pork. Zòngzi were little presents tied with husk that hid yummy treasures embedded in sticky rice. Sometimes Baba filled them with ground chicken or a paste of sweet red bean. Tonight, I hoped for lap cheong, a ridiculously greasy sausage. My body craved fat, and after the day I had just experienced, a handful of nuts were not going to cut it.

I put my steamed treasures on the plate with the pastries, filled a couple zip-lock bags with ice for my bruised muscles, and headed for the stairs that ran along the back of our narrow building.

Baba had grown up on a North Dakota farm before catching the cooking bug. He liked wide open spaces. So he turned the back third of our building into a kitchen. Fortunately, our takeout business made up for the small dining room and paid for the expense. But while we all benefited from the spacious kitchen, only Baba and I were permitted upstairs.

I glanced at the seventeen-pound Merida road bicycle suspended at a slant on the staircase wall. My legs ached just looking at it. Climbing the stairs felt worse.

I remembered another tiring ascent five and a half years ago when Baba and I had carried my mattress up these stairs for my first night in the apartment. He had been sad. I had been relieved. We had left my furious mother at home to sulk over my "foolish" decision to move away from home for the second time.

The first came just before my eighteenth birthday when I moved into a college dorm. While only an hour from Arcadia, living on the UCLA campus had felt like living in another country. I was free of Ma's scrutiny and in absolute control over everything I did, where I went, and how I walked in the world. Ironically, I ended up doing many of the same things I had done before, but I did them because they pleased me, not her. I dove into my studies, met new friends, and joined the Wushu team. I kept myself so busy I rarely came home for a meal, let alone a weekend. I even took a holiday retail job so I would have an excuse to stay on campus during winter break. I met Pete, went on dates for the first time, fell in love, and forgot all about Rose.

After Rose died, I moved back home and pulled away from my college friends, especially Pete. My first experience of making love would always be linked to my sister's rape and murder. How could I be with Pete? I couldn't even speak to him. I deleted his calls and messages, dropped out of school, and put all my energy into training in the park with Sensei. But after living in a college dorm for a year, moving back home was intolerable. Rose's spirit clung to every square inch and flooded me with memories—here we sat, there we fought, around the corner we hid. Every space reminded me of Rose.

Had she forgiven me? Had Pete? Five and a half years later, I still wrestled with my ghosts.

Chapter Seven

A faint glow from Baba's office guided me up the last few stairs. He left the door open and a light on, supposedly to help me find my way to the washer and dryer we kept in the back. I suspected the real reason was because he didn't like me traversing stairs in the dark. I laughed. Even when he wasn't with me, Baba could brighten my mood.

I glanced from his empty office, open and inviting, to my closed and locked apartment door. That pretty much summed us up.

It wasn't always this way; I used to be fun. I signed up for the dorm activities committee my first week at UCLA. And I always had a ton of friends. Ma used to complain that I spent too much time with friends and not enough time studying. Never mind that I only saw those friends during Saturday Cantonese class, Wushu practice, or school functions. She didn't care about that. To her, any time not spent actively studying in my room constituted gross indolence. Fun and happiness took a back seat to diligence and duty—the back seat of a very long bus.

I balanced my plate of food and tucked the Ziplocks of ice under my arm so I could punch in the key code. I had convinced Baba to use electronic locks because I didn't like carrying jagged objects in my pockets—who knew when I'd have to roll off a scaffold? The staff liked the convenience. Baba liked the ability to change access codes. Everybody won.

My apartment was almost as dark as the stairs, with only a faint glow dripping in through the glass doors at the far end. I hit the master switch and illuminated the long apartment like a diorama—I'd had enough of shadows for one night.

First came my entrance hall with a cubbyhole bench for my shoes and a wall that separated the entry from a walk-in closet and bathroom. Next came my sleeping quarters, sectioned off by a long Chinese chest of drawers and an antique wooden folding screen on the side of my bed that partitioned it from the living space beyond. A gifted craftsman had carved the top and bottom of each of the six panels with typical Chinese designs and used fabric inlays to portray herons standing in a garden of flowering reeds and wisteria. Each night as I lay in my bed, I found new images in the carvings. Each morning, I discovered new secrets in the garden. When I stood in the entry, as I did now, the soft light from my living area shone through the carvings and dappled my bed with lovely designs.

I slipped off my shoes and padded down the hardwood floor, glancing at the treasures I kept: meditation malas, a brass singing bowl, my silver phurba necklace, a porcelain figure of Quan Yin, and photos of Rose and my Chinese ancestors, around which I had placed offerings of incense, rice, and salt. Despite these accoutrements, I didn't think of myself as religious. I practiced Buddhism; I didn't worship—a distinction I took great care not to debate with Ma. She saw Buddhism as a religion. I saw it as a philosophy. Sometimes the two overlapped. Sometimes they didn't. The same could be said of Ma and me, although our differences more resembled the hardwood of my entry-sleeping quarters and the firm mat of my dojo.

Yep. I had a martial arts studio in my apartment. How cool was that?

It occupied the middle portion of my home, which meant I had to cross over the slightly raised platform of interlocking squares in order to travel from one end of my apartment to the other. The squares had been painted to resemble tatami mats, giving the twenty-by-twelve space the appearance of a Japanese room in an otherwise Chinese-American home.

Baba once asked why I used the Japanese rather than Chinese name for my training studio, but the answer felt too involved for me to explain. In the end, I just told him it was a martial arts thing. But that wasn't the truth. Dojo meant "place of the way." I used that name because my "way" changed when I discovered the ancient art of the ninja.

The wooden folding screen didn't just separate my dojo from my bedroom, it served as a cultural partition between the Japanese art I studied and the Chinese-Norwegian heritage of my birth. On the dojo side, I could honor my martial way and follow the Shinto practices related to the art. On the other, I could honor my Chinese Buddhist ancestors then wrap myself in the Norwegian Rosemaling quilt my father's mother had stitched for me. The screen helped me compartmentalize. Even so, there were times when each of the three cultures pulled so strongly, I couldn't figure out who I was. So instead, I focused on who I aspired to be: a protector of women.

I paused in front of the Vermilion wall of my dojo. I had painted every other wall of my apartment, except for this twelve-foot section, the soothing shade of the palest green to remind me of nature and inspire harmony. The Chinese red at the head of my dojo served another purpose. Like most things related to Asian culture, color was symbolic. Vermilion had the dual meaning of prosperity and danger. When I looked at it, I thought of firecrackers exploding in the streets of Chinatown.

Hóng, hóng, huǒ, huǒ! Red, red, fire, fire!

It was a wish for our lives to prosper and expand while at the same time cautioning us of danger. That caution hadn't helped Rose, but it helped me protect women like Rose who might need a big sister to look out for them.

Red fueled me with the passion to fight. Green reminded me of the harmony I needed to survive. To this end, I turned my home into a vast field of fragile new grass with one dangerous spark of fire.

Why so much green and so little red?

Because fighting was easy. Tranquility was hard.

Chapter Eight

I woke to the sticky feel of plastic against my stomach and my face mashed into a cushion. The couch? I cracked open my eyelids and got a close-up view of a rust-colored world. Definitely the couch. I rolled back, peeled the zip-locks from my skin, and inched out of the borrowed sweatpants. Dry clothes waited at the other end of my apartment, but no article of clothing merited forty steps.

I swung my bare legs over the edge of the couch and stared out at my view. The restaurant signboard took up the whole second-story face of our building, so I was basically looking at a wall. Or would have been if Baba had not applied his Midwest ingenuity to creating a balcony paradise. I couldn't see much blue, but I saw a whole lot of green. I even had a chaise lounge for the fleeting minutes when the sun passed directly overhead. I didn't indulge often. Every time I sat out there, I could hear Ma's voice telling me to stay out of the sun.

I shook my head. I didn't want to think of Ma this early in the morning. I'd much rather have a cup of tea. And since my tea station was seven steps away on the office side of my living space, I could have it.

My left thigh trembled as I stood. The Ukrainian had favored a forehand swing with his right hand, so the whole left side of my body felt tenderized. I hadn't looked, but I imagined a colorful pattern of knot-sized bruises emerging. No big deal. My body and I had an agreement: I kept it strong and healthy, and it tolerated my abuse.

I hobbled to the border of my dojo and office where my electric kettle sat on a tiny fridge under a shelf of whole-leaf tea tins. Loose or sachets, never bags. I detested those flat relics that crushed tea into dust. Leaves needed room to expand or they brewed weak. The same might be said for people. It certainly applied to me.

Beside the kettle, on the balcony side of my office, stood my water cooler and an enormous wall map, care of the of Los Angeles County Metropolitan Transit Authority. The Metro map showed the color-coded routes of every bus, rail, and subway—most of which I had memorized. To the left of this, was my L-shaped computer desk, cabinets, and shelves. With tea in hand, I fired up the computer.

I had been out of contact for almost twenty hours, which was a long time for any millennial. Even me. Not that I did the whole social media thing. Not anymore. I didn't want people knowing my business, and the stuff my old friends posted annoyed me. Every smile, hug, and cheerful status reminded me of how things used to be. It had been cleaner to sever the ties. However, while I no longer had my own accounts, I did troll social media to assist others—not just the women I tried to protect but Baba's web-clueless friends.

Every morning, I checked the pertinent sites to make sure no one was ruining their brand or disclosing personal information that could put them in danger. A lot of harm could be done with a carelessly worded phrase or an ill-framed photo. And that didn't include location tagging and timestamps. People shared so much more than they should.

Fortunately, Ma had set up Internet ground rules for me as a child that made erasing my web presence as an adult easier than it might have been. The number one rule was that I had to use an alias. I chose Rooster, my Chinese zodiac, and used an ink-brush watercolor of the bird as an avatar. I thought it was cool, so I didn't mind. But her rules about photos were aggravating. I was the only kid I knew who wasn't allowed to post pictures of herself. And if any of my friends posted a group photo with me in it—from Wushu or school events—they had to list me only as L. Wong, the Chinese equivalent to J. Smith.

A Google search for L. Wong led to forty-three million hits.

And those hits weren't just for women. Even if someone managed to track down a group photo with me in it, they'd have a heck of a time matching the androgynous name to all the likely candidates. Over seventy percent of Arcadia High School students and California Wushu competitors were Asian. Figuring out which Chinese kid was me would drive someone nuts.

In theory.

If Ma had considered the patience of a tenacious stalker, she would have kept me off the net entirely. When Violet Wong set the rules, she expected them to be followed. Any school or organization that had the temerity to print my first name, got an immediate and caustic message. Ma's temper was legendary in Arcadia. Lily Wong could not be listed, and Rooster and L. Wong could never meet. Not ever.

Rose got off easy. By the time she came of age, Ma had mellowed. Or perhaps it was a case of second child syndrome. Either way, Ma got it wrong: Rose had been the wild child, not me. Not that I was shy. Like any person born under the dynamic sign of the rooster, I gravitated to the spotlight. I had the kind of magnetism that drew attention and got people involved. Baba claimed I had come out of the womb crackling with energy. Ma remembered it differently: "*You were born vain, Lily. The first thing you did was wipe the gunk from your face so you could flirt with the doctor.*"

All that changed after Rose died.

For the first few months, everyone in my life tried to cajole me back to my former Rooster self. The Wushu team, my dormmates, the UCLA orientation committee. Everyone missed my enthusiastic participation. So regardless of how boastful Ma claimed I was, some of it must have been merited. Of course, they all gave up trying to get me back when I dropped out of college, including Ma. So I disappeared.

I killed my Rooster accounts on social media, didn't do anything newsworthy, and let my Internet presence get buried beneath the weight of two point eight billion users.

Everything I took from me, I gave to Baba, turning him into a local star and making his restaurant website the envy of our hodge-podge community. Customers flocked to taste the authentic dishes prepared by Hong Kong Vern—a big-boned, big-hearted, Viking farmer from North Dakota. Wong's Hong Kong Inn thrived, and Baba gave me the credit.

It was all very ninja, just not in the way most people imagined. But, of course, that was the point.

I hadn't trained in the shadow arts to become an assassin. I had done it to help, empower, and protect. Even at the age of twelve, when I had first started training with Sensei, I had a feeling that, one day, life would try to beat my family.

I needed a way to fight back. I needed a way to win.

Chapter Nine

My inbox held an assortment of newsletters and notices, which I'd probably delete unopened, along with five emails from Ma that I might, or might not, read later in the day. I also had an emergency email—marked with a yellow exclamation mark no less—from Debbie, our neighborhood hairdresser, who "desperately" needed to embed a celebrity's tweet in her blog.

Seriously? *That* was an emergency?

I took a fortifying sip of tea, sent Debbie a quick explanation and link to an instructional YouTube video, then moved on to what I really cared about: Monday's SMG notices.

Each of the special mailing groups notified me of new activity concerning court cases I followed via PACER, a government site that offered public access to court electronic records. The Federal Judiciary service gave me—and anyone else who wanted to register—access to court dockets, transcripts, and electronic case files. PACER allowed me to track the progress and outcome of trials involving the women Aleisha had hired me to help and anyone else who piqued my interest—like the cocktail waitress getting vilified by the press.

The first notice that popped up was for Mia Mikkelsen. It had to be a sign.

Like any good Chinese, I paid attention to cosmic communications. Did that make me superstitious? Probably. But my intuition, or whatever people wanted to call it, had saved my ass on too many occasions to ignore. Right now, the signs were telling me to attend the preliminary hearing. I checked the clock. If I hurried, I could get there in time to see a scumbag brought to trial.

Or so I had hoped.

By the time I had changed into paralegal-type clothing and caught a rideshare to the Los Angeles Airport Courthouse, the prelim was done and the sidewalk swarmed with protesters and news crews. One crew in particular had a sweet setup in front of the building's architectural centerpiece: a ten-story, green-glass cylindrical stairwell.

As I approached, three reporters raced out of the building. The one leading the pack was a pretty blond in an electric fuchsia dress. She stormed through the protesters toting signs denouncing victim-shaming, and headed straight for the two-man team in front of the stairwell.

"Prelim's over. You set?"

The cameraman nodded. "Just need you."

His partner dashed into the electronic news gathering where I could see him donning a headset in front of a control panel and video screen. The reporter checked herself in the mirror, blotted her pancake makeup, inserted an earpiece, brushed her tresses so they fell artfully in front of her shoulders, and took her position to await her cue with a frozen smile.

"Thank you, Randy. I'm standing in front of the Los Angeles Airport Courthouse where the People v Tran preliminary hearing just ended in a shocking dismissal. As you can see from the signs behind me, this case has sparked strong emotions concerning what these protesters are calling 'victim-shaming'. For almost two weeks, defense attorney Curtis Pike has used the media to paint alleged victim Mia Mikkelsen as a promiscuous, jilted woman out for revenge. Today, he also cast doubt on Mikkelsen's friend—who claimed to have seen a man of Tran's height and size in motorcycle leathers fleeing Mia's bedroom—by arguing that Tran did not own a motorcycle nor did his boot fit the print left in Mikkelsen's garden. In the end, Judge Michelle Bulman ruled that while there was enough evidence to suggest a crime had been committed, there was insufficient evidence pointing to Tran as the perpetrator."

I headed for the courthouse entrance without waiting for the back and forth between reporter and anchor. I had heard enough. Not even a trial? Are you kidding me?

Unlike the judge, I didn't need sufficient evidence to keep an eye on Tran. And I sure as heck didn't buy the boot defense: shoe sizes were easy to disguise.

For me, it came down to whether or not I believed Mia.

I did.

Her story seemed plausible. Her suffering felt real. And her conviction had never wavered, even in the face of public ridicule. She could have dropped the charges and been forgotten in a month. Instead, she had held fast.

Mia needed a big sister now more than ever.

I entered the building and sailed through security. No one cared about the sharp wooden spike securing my hair in a tidy bun. I collected my satchel, repositioned my scholarly, prescription-free glasses, and went in search of the docket. People v Tran was assigned to courtroom three eleven. After a glance at the crowd in front of the elevators, I opted for the stairs. I didn't want to miss catching Mia, and since I looked as though I belonged, I wasn't concerned about getting caught in the news team's background footage.

Despite my hurry, I paused before exiting the stairwell. Barging out the door was a sure way to draw attention. So, I took a breath and walked out of the stairwell with purpose, another paralegal heading for a courtroom. Normal. Expected.

I found Mia staring out the wall of windows as her attorney, a rather severe-looking woman in her mid-forties, tried to engage her in conversation. I moved close enough to hear.

"I understand if you don't want to make a statement down there, but *I* need to." When Mia didn't respond, the attorney shrugged. "Call my office if you have any questions. I'm sorry this didn't work out as we hoped."

Mia continued to stare out the window as though someone in that vast expanse might be able to tell her why she had lost. I didn't expect her to find an answer anytime soon, so I looked back the way I had come.

Although J Tran had his back to me, I recognized him from his stance. This was the other reason I believed Mia's story: he stood like a fighter.

I had noticed this before in video coverage, when reporters were clamoring for a statement. Tran had stood just as he did now—feet spread apart, arms hanging loose at his side, and utterly still. While his defense attorney swayed and gesticulated, Tran occupied space. He didn't rock or shake his head. Instead, he held his back straight, his shoulders broad, and his head canted slightly as though he might be looking down his nose.

But it wasn't just his posture, it was the way his suit fit—as though it were tailor made—and the way his long hair hung in perfect waves.

He intimidated simply by being.

If I hadn't known who he was, I would have guessed him to be a celebrity athlete of some kind, a welterweight boxer perhaps, or maybe a quarterback, or even an actor—God knew there had been enough of them tried in this courthouse.

I glanced at Mia, still gazing at the view. The giant Dane didn't fit with either of these men. She had a generic Scandinavian appeal with a curvaceous figure and tremendous height. Even in modest two-inch heels, Mia dwarfed every man in sight.

I stood at the window, using her for cover as I watched Tran's reflection. Would he opt for a quick elevator ride, a dramatic descent down the glass stairwell, or a back staircase escape?

Mia must have felt my energy because she turned to see who was rude enough to invade her privacy. What I saw changed my assumption. She wasn't annoyed; she was defeated.

"Sorry about the dismissal."

She blinked her sad blue eyes. "I thought it would go to trial."

I nodded. "Me, too."

She stared up at the sky as if the angle might stop her tears. It didn't.

I gave her a moment of privacy and checked on Tran. He and his lawyer had parted ways. Defense Attorney Pike took the glass-encased stairway, where the camera crews could record his grand entrance. Tran did what I would have done: he escaped down the back.

Down below, Mia's attorney addressed the reporters.

"What do you suppose she's saying?" Mia asked, more to herself than to me.

"Whatever paints her and the district attorney in a good light. I wouldn't worry though; she won't say anything negative about you. She'll blame the loss on victim-shaming."

"And him?"

Defense Attorney Pike had taken center stage.

I shook my head. "You don't want to know."

Mia turned away in disgust. "Do I know you?"

"Nope."

"I didn't think so. But you obviously know me. Then again, who doesn't, right?"

I shrugged. "The media hasn't been fair to you."

"Ya think?"

"I don't think, I *know*. I've been following your case since the story hit the news."

She snorted then heaved a long and frustrated sigh. "So who are you?"

It was a good question. I thought about which name to give. Lily Wong had done a lousy job saving Kateryna and Ilya. And Rooster, my social media avatar, was dead. It might be time for a new name. I thought of Baba.

"Call me Dumpling."

Mia laughed. "Seriously?" She seemed about to say more but waved it away. "So, Dumpling, what do you want? I mean, no offense, but why are you even talking to me?"

"Why wouldn't I?"

"Well, in case you haven't noticed, I'm not too popular anymore." She made the pronouncement then turned back to the view. The LA basin went on forever, until the buildings shrank to dots and the dots blended into the horizon.

For a large woman, Mia suddenly seemed very small.

"That's why I'm talking to you. You're alone at a time when you shouldn't be."

"Funny how that worked out."

I ignored the attitude. "What about the eyewitness? She's a friend, right? Why isn't she here with you? Or your boss from the Siren Club? I would have thought he'd have a vested interest in all this."

"I don't work there anymore."

"He fired you? And the protesters don't have his head on a stick?"

"They don't know. And he didn't fire me. I quit, with three months' pay."

I understood. People were distancing themselves from Mia to avoid the taint of crazy. It made me angry.

Mia shrugged it off like it didn't matter. "Did you see where Tran went?"

"He took the back stairs."

She ground her fists into her temples and moaned. "Great. What if he's waiting for me in the parking lot? What if he comes back to my apartment? It's not like I can call the cops, right? I mean, what's to stop him from attacking me again? What the fuck am I supposed to do?"

Mia wasn't looking for answers. She needed to vent until all her fears had been expressed and her emotions exhausted. Without a friend to listen, I became the receptacle for her angst. The more she dumped, the more she trusted.

"That smug bastard can do whatever he likes. The cops aren't going to help me. And the judge dismissed the restraining order. Everyone thinks I'm a vindictive bitch. Even my friends at the club won't talk to me." She choked out another laugh. "Like I'm going to start accusing everyone I know of rape and murder. Give me a fucking break! I'm the victim, and they're all treating me like a goddamn criminal." Snot trickled out of her nostrils as she sniffed and gasped herself back into control. "I'm sorry."

"Don't be."

"I think I'll just stay here awhile."

"Would it make you feel safer if I walked you to your car?"

She sniffed. "It might." The realization made her laugh. "Isn't that pathetic?"

"Not at all. Tell you what, if you like, I could even drive home with you, check out your place, make sure he's not around."

That's when she gave me the look.

Not the one that said: Are you a psycho-stalker planning on torturing and killing me in my own home? That would have been intelligent. No. Mia gave me the other look, the one that took in my sex and small stature and discounted me. I tried not to feel insulted.

I held out my empty hands and shrugged. "Just offering."

She back-pedaled so fast I thought she'd fall off her two-inch heels. "I'm sorry. Of course. You're just being nice. And I'm feeling bitchy."

"Understandable."

"Look. I don't mean to be ungrateful or anything, but I still don't get why you want to help."

I took a breath. Mia's question was bigger than she imagined.

"Forget I asked," she said, letting me off the hook. "Beggars can't be choosers, right? But do me a favor, will you? If he tries to kill me again, could you at least get a good look at his face?"

I laughed. "Mia, if J Tran tries to kill you, getting a look at his face will be the least I do."

Chapter Ten

Mia glared as if I had run over her dog—twice.

"I thought you were going to walk me to my car." Her voice trembled.

"I will. But first I want to check out the garage. Okay? But don't worry, when you come out of the elevator, I'll be there." She didn't believe me, but I continued as if she did. "Don't acknowledge me. Just walk to your car, get in, and lock the doors. Then I want you to check your emails."

"Why should I do that?"

"Because I want you to have a logical reason to wait. When I feel it's safe, I'll get in, and we can go."

"And if it's not? If something happens?"

"Then drive to the nearest police station." I held up my hand. "I know. They don't need to believe what you say, but you do need to go on record as having said it." I waited for her nod of acceptance. "One more thing, where are you parked?"

Armed with a description and location of Mia's car, I headed for the back stairs. On the way, I pulled out my cellphone. It was a backup that I had bought a year ago just in case some Ukrainian asshole crushed mine beneath his disco boot—okay, maybe not that exact scenario, but something equally unexpected. I also grabbed an empty soda cup that had been left on the rim of a trash can—it couldn't hurt to have another prop. I had a phone, a drink, an over-stuffed satchel, and black-rimmed glasses that kept slipping down my nose.

When I entered the garage, I looked like an over-burdened, unobservant paralegal, scrolling through her phone. In actuality, I had positioned the screen in front of my face so I could scan the garage.

Several cars drove through the aisles. One woman in a parked car checked her appearance in the sun visor mirror. Five people exited the elevator and split in different directions. And one fit-looking couple left their Jeep and headed for the stairs I had just come down.

No sign of Tran.

Mia drove a bright red Ford Focus, so it was easy to find. I was glad to see an affordable compact, well within my paralegal's budget, parked next to her on the passenger side. When I got there, I put the cup on the roof and dug into my satchel as though I were hunting for keys. I wasn't. I just wanted time to check the interior of Mia's car, which appeared to be empty.

I feigned dropping my keys and looked underneath. No sign of feet.

I grabbed the drink off the roof and headed for the elevator.

This time, I had my phone in the satchel and the strap positioned securely on my shoulder. Anyone watching me would have already made their assumptions. I wanted freedom of movement in case things went bad.

Every garage in Los Angeles had a trashcan near the elevator. The courthouse was no exception. As I approached with my cup, the bell chimed and the doors opened. I saw Mia but pointedly ignored her. Instead, I dumped my drink in the can and let my gaze roam aimlessly around the lot. Not only did that give me the appearance of bored disinterest, it helped me keep a soft focus. I noticed more when I wasn't searching for something specific. There was a life lesson in that, but now wasn't the time to consider it.

When Mia moved, I followed at a distance close enough to intercept a knife attack, stop an abduction, or possibly shove her to cover if I spotted a gun. If Tran used a sniper rifle, she'd be screwed. But short of that, I had everything under control.

When Mia got to her car, she did exactly as I had instructed: she locked the doors and scrolled through her phone. No one seemed to care. Then I noticed a car backing out of a parking space a few lanes away. Nothing unusual in that, except the vehicle was a Mustang GT. Drivers of muscle cars liked to flex their power, especially in parking garages where their rubber tires could squeal against polished cement. So why wasn't this guy expressing his inner Vin Diesel?

I slowed my pace until I had stopped behind Mia's car—feigned digging for her keys and not paying attention to whomever she might be inconveniencing. The GT stopped as well. Not a good sign. I looked around, as if suddenly aware that I might get run over. During that brief scan, I checked on the driver. The tinted window obscured his face. I offered a vague, apologetic wave and stepped back toward Mia's driver's-side door, eliminating any clear shot the driver might have had.

Could I have gone on the offense and confronted the guy? Sure. But if this was Tran, I didn't want him to know Mia had someone watching over her. I also didn't want to blow my cover in case I needed to follow him later. So instead, I brought out my phone and pretended to answer a call, which gave me a reason to wait and an excuse for adjusting my position. People rarely stood still while on the phone. I used that tendency to shield Mia, conceal my face, and check on the GT—which is why I saw the door open.

The man exited in a hurry and headed for his trunk. I still couldn't tell if he was Tran because he kept his body stooped and hidden behind his driver's side door; nor could I see if he held anything in his hands or what he might eventually pull from his trunk.

Too many variables. Too much unknown.

I dropped the phone into my satchel and looped the leather strap around my wrist. Armed with a swingable weapon, I charged. When I glimpsed wheat-colored hair, I realized my mistake. With a tilt of my wrist, I guided the whirling satchel over the man's head and allowed the force of the arc pulled me off balance.

He rushed to my aid, reaching out a hand to help me off the cement. "Are you all right? What happened?"

I twittered with feigned embarrassment and waved away his proffered hand. "I'm fine. Really." I struggled to my feet in a most inelegant fashion. "I must have slipped on grease." I repositioned my glasses, searched the dry cement for the culprit, and finding nothing to blame, offered a goofy smile. "Guess I'm just clumsy."

The guy chuckled. Not only was he not Tran, he was as clueless as a college movie frat boy, the kind who downed Jell-O shots, scored easy hookups—and drove muscle cars. Even if I hadn't been dressed as a mousy paralegal, a guy like him wouldn't have been interested in a woman like me, as evidenced by the way he turned to shut his trunk without so much as a glance down my blouse.

"Just be careful, all right?" he said with a smirk. "You might hurt someone." His tone sounded so patronizing he might as well have patted me on the head.

I laughed it off and added a couple of snorts for good measure.

"Who, me?" I shook away the ridiculous notion and headed back toward Mia's car, grateful for the guy's condescending dismissal. Had he been a tad smarter or mildly observant, I would have had a lot of explaining to do. Regardless, I still felt good about my decision to attack. If the frat boy really had been Tran with a gun, I wouldn't have had time to react, and Mia and I would be another LA shooting statistic. So when I got into the passenger seat and the frat boy gunned his GT—as I had expected him to do from the start—and peeled off with a squeal of rubber so loud Paul Walker could have heard it in racecar Heaven, I smiled.

Mia cringed. "I hate that sound."

"Really?" I watched the GT speed around the corner. "I find it kind of comforting."

Chapter Eleven

Mia tossed her bag and sweater on the bleached-wood table near the front door and strode across the Mexican tiles. "You want something to drink?" She disappeared into the kitchen before I could answer and came back with two opened bottles of Corona. "I don't know about you, but I need something stronger than a Coke."

I wandered toward the bedroom, encouraging her to leave mine on the coffee table. The only drink I wanted before noon was tea. And not the generic Lipton's that I'd no doubt find in her cupboard; I meant honest-to-god tea. I chuckled as I thought about Baba. Sometimes, nothing said it better than one of his North Dakota expressions. *Honest-to-god. Period. End of story*—the list went on and on. *See about* was another. I'd definitely have to see about a cup of Dragonwell after I left Mia's.

I shook my head. The lack of sleep was taking a toll. I felt punchy, which of course made me think about yesterday's beating. Punchy. Beating. I snorted back a laugh and covered it with a succession of coughs.

Mia came to the doorway, beer in hand. "Are you okay?"

"Yep. I'm fine." I needed to get my errant mind under control, so I focused on the decorative white bars on the window. Nothing amusing about them. Urban Los Angeles had turned security bars into a fashion statement. Too bad it hadn't been more effective.

"Just the one bedroom?"

"Yeah, I live alone. No roommates."

"What about your friend who interrupted the attack?"

Mia shook her head. "We were plastered. She didn't want to drive home."

"Huh. I'm surprised that didn't come up in the prelim."

"Oh, it did. Pike painted us both like a couple of drunks."

I snorted in disgust but didn't comment. We didn't have time to dive down that rabbit hole, I had an apartment to assess.

Mia lived in a second-story unit of a Spanish-style fourplex in the moderately upscale Fairfax District. The street was well lit, the windows secured, she had reason to feel safe. "How long have you lived here?"

"Almost a year."

I nodded—long enough to grow complacent. "No burglaries in the neighborhood?"

"None that I know of."

When I returned to the living room, Mia had plopped herself onto the couch, kicked off her sandals, and propped her feet on the table. I opened the balcony doors. "He came through here?"

"That's the theory. Nice, huh? Just my luck to get stalked by Spider-Man."

The balcony extended a few feet beyond the exterior walls of the building and hung over the lower unit's picture window. Wavy horizontal iron bars covered the front and sides of the balcony box and anchored into decorative stucco corner pieces. The combination was reasonably attractive and offered a bit of privacy without affecting the view, but no amount of style could keep this place from feeling like a prison. At least, not to me. Did Mia feel the same? Perhaps on a subliminal level she did because the balcony furniture had a thin layer of dust as if she hadn't used it in a while.

I checked the floor. The path from the corner to the door seemed a little cleaner than the area around it. Could it have been brushed with the sole of a motorcycle boot? Very likely.

"Any other theories?" I asked.

"That he came in through the front door."

"Wasn't it locked?"

Mia gave me another one of her looks.

I held out my hands in peace. "Just asking."

"Sorry. Let's just say that there was some question as to whether or not I let him in."

"Oh."

"I didn't."

"Okay." I held out my hands again. The gesture was becoming redundant. Mia had her offense-o-meter on a hair trigger. I couldn't blame her. Unless, of course, Pike was right about her being an obsessed nut case. I didn't want to consider that possibility. Not yet.

I searched the balcony for the easiest access with the least street visibility. The landlord kept the landscaping trimmed neatly and the branches of the coral tree sufficiently distanced. No opportunity there. Jumping from a neighboring structure or climbing down from the roof would have been too visible and needlessly risky. That left the side yard. A rain gutter ran along the bottom of the balcony then angled down on the building. I pointed to a gate. "He probably climbed up from there."

"What about the spikes?"

"If his soles were hard enough, he could have stood on them with no problem. And if not, he would just need enough space between them for the toe of his boot."

"So much for security."

I shrugged. "Spikes on walls and gates are mostly a visual deterrent. They won't stop a determined climber." I didn't mention that I knew this from experience. "Aluminum gutters are generally too flimsy to hold a man's weight, but if you look closely, you can see that this one is bracketed to the wall just below the base of the balcony. That makes it more likely to stay attached, especially for the short amount of time that Tran would have needed to reach the lip of the balcony floor."

She took a swig of beer. "Well, isn't that just peachy?"

I ignored the comment and leaned over the railing to check the yard. "I heard something about a boot print?"

"Yeah, next to the gate. But they said it wasn't his." Mia snorted her opinion of that likelihood, finished off her beer, and pointed to mine. "You gonna drink this?"

"Go ahead." The last thing I needed was alcohol. "It might not have been his boot, but I'd say whoever attacked you climbed up from that gate."

"Oh, it was his boot, all right. I could feel the hard soles of them digging into the sides of my legs while he tried to strangle me with my own fucking nightgown."

"And you're sure it was Tran?"

Mia glared. "I'm sure."

"And I'm just asking, remember?"

"Sorry. I'm tired of being called a liar."

"I get it."

I sat on the chair next to her and took off my glasses so I could rub the tired from my eyes. Then I pulled out the wooden spike that held my hair in place. There wasn't any need to perpetuate my paralegal image, and the tight bun was giving me a headache. I shook the hair down my back. It added to the heat of an already hot day, but I didn't care: the relief felt wonderful.

"So, Dumpling…you never did tell me that story. What's your

deal?"

I shrugged. "Just someone trying to help."

"Someone who knows how to break into a second-story apartment? I don't think so."

She deserved an answer, but since I didn't know which to give, I pulled a Joe Friday and stuck to the facts. "I've been following your case ever since the attack hit the news. I came down to the courthouse to see if it would go to trial."

"But why would you care?"

I paused. Should I tell her about my dead sister? Not much of a selling point. Or maybe I should tell her about the signs—the article I saw in Kateryna's bedroom and the first case of the first SMG notice first thing in the morning. Or I could just come clean and tell her I needed a pro bono win to make up for my professional failure.

Yeah. Maybe not.

"You're a woman who needs help," I said. "Isn't that enough?"

"No. It isn't. I let you into my car and my apartment because I was scared, but now that I'm home, I'm starting to worry more about *you* than him. So if I'm going to trust you, I need more than 'You're a woman who needs help.'"

There was steel in Mia's gaze that hadn't been there before. She demanded the truth.

"I lost someone to violence," I said, "If I'd been there, I could have stopped it."

"What makes you think you can stop whatever's happening to me?"

"Training, experience…sheer force of will? I don't have a résumé for this sort thing. But I guarantee you'll be safer with me than without."

She thought about that for a moment, took a swig of my beer, then shrugged. "Okay. What have I got to lose?

I gave her a long, hard stare. "Unfortunately, quite a lot."

Chapter Twelve

The best way to help Mia was to learn more about Tran. So I caught the Metro Rapid Bus Line to Culver City, transferred onto the C-1, and ran the last block home. It took me forty-five minutes—only ten minutes longer than it would have taken me to drive and park.

And Ma wondered why I used mass transit.

Once I got back to my place, I changed into biking clothes and called a friend at the DMV. Aleisha had hired me to talk some sense into the woman's violent ex-boyfriend. He got the message, and the woman continued to show her gratitude. I pocketed the address and headed for the Valley. If Tran wanted to hide where he lived, he could have used a P.O. box for his driver's license address like I did. So either he had nothing to hide, or he believed nothing could be found. I wondered which.

An hour and a half later, I found myself on a quaint street with welcoming paths and storybook houses. Except for Tran's. No wild roses for him; just an unremarkable ranch house and a barren rock garden.

The property next to Tran's offered the perfect opportunity to stash my bike. Their front yard overflowed with a tangle of twisted junipers, honeysuckle shrubs, and unruly bougainvillea. Inlaid stones cut a winding path to the front door, adding several feet to the distance and giving the approach a lost-in-the-woods vibe. There was even a wooden plaque with an etched warning to "stay on the path." They even had the requisite gnome.

I snaked my bike through the shrubs to the narrow channel that ran along the house. I barely had room to park, stretch, and guzzle a liter of water. Fifteen miles and the steep grade through Benedict Canyon made for thirsty work. Still, it felt good to work off the tension. Sensei had taught me breathing techniques to release extra energy, but I had yet to master them. Physical exertion, however, always worked; it just took longer.

I shrugged off my slim backpack and dug out a hand towel. Whoever had said men sweat and women glowed had never met me. My tank top had darkened from light gray to near-black, and my face was a sweaty mess. I carried a change of clothes in my pack, along with a brush and some tools for the trade, but I didn't change. Women habitually wore tanks and shorts in a valley neighborhood like this. No one would notice me.

Just to be sure, and because I hadn't seen any signs of life through the gnome house's front windows, I decided to approach Tran's house from the privacy of their backyard. Unfortunately, this involved traversing another maze of brambles and thorns.

Tran's yard looked quite different. It had a pepper tree bordering the back of a kidney-shaped pool and one saguaro cactus. That was it. No brambles. No cover. I climbed the fence and landed as quietly as I could on the pebbles. No signs of life. Not even the chirp of a parakeet. I sighed with relief. I had already noted the absence of water bowls and dog feces, so I didn't expect any barking. But if Tran didn't have a guard dog, he would likely have a security system.

I crept behind a built-in barbecue and scoped the place through the glass doors of the main room. Ranch-style houses were shallow and long, so I had a clear shot across his living room to the front door. As expected, I saw a telltale code box on the wall. Although a friend had begun teaching me the basics of alarm-disarmament, I wasn't ready to trust my skills. I'd have to stay outside.

From what I could see, Tran kept his home neat to the point of stark. No rugs softened the hardwood floors and not a single painting adorned the taupe walls. His living room furniture had square lines and tight cushions. None of it looked inviting or trendy; nor did it look cheap. Tran had not found these items in a discount store. The same applied to the furniture in the adjacent dining area. Everything I saw had an austere kind of elegance that defied category but implied an Asian influence.

His place wasn't like mine, with panel screens and ornate chests. And he certainly didn't have a dojo in the middle of his living room. Even so, the feeling persisted—J Tran's ancestry lived in the spaces in between.

I wondered about his ethnicity. Tran was a common Vietnamese surname. However, it could have been adapted from Chen or Tan. So even if his family had come from Vietnam, they might have been Chinese. And that didn't discount some Japanese or Korean blood added to the mix. He also had an unusual combination of wide and angular features with high cheekbones and a dark complexion that could easily have come from a Polynesian, African, Native American, or Middle Eastern ancestry.

When I looked at the empty spaces of his home, I saw place markers for the tokens and symbols of a possible heritage. Corners remained barren where most people would have put a standing lamp, a display cabinet, or an indoor tree. Walls that begged for a couch or chest had nothing. Tables that could have displayed framed photographs or a vase of flowers didn't. This wasn't minimalist. It was calculated. As I looked around, my imagination filled in the blanks.

The far corner of the room would have been a perfect spot for a Buddhist altar and would have explained the round cushion that sat alone on the floor. Why else would Tran have placed it there, separate from the seating area, if not for prayer or meditation? Track lights pointed at a blank wall in specific directions as if to light a collection of missing art. Tribal masks? Calligraphy scrolls? Certainly something other than a wall of taupe paint. And what about the shiny table? Who polished a table until it gleamed and didn't use it to display something precious? I might have been projecting my own inclinations onto him, but to me, J Tran revealed more about himself by what he hid than what he showed.

Since I couldn't break into his house without setting off the alarm and nothing more could be gained by snooping through windows, I turned my thoughts to the other reason for my visit—surveillance. I had intended to place a spy cam in a central location, but after seeing my target's fastidious nature, I changed my mind. A man like Tran would detect the slightest deviation.

I shook away my budding admiration. While Tran had some professional qualities I could appreciate, that didn't make him someone to admire; nor did his sex appeal make him less of a scum.

Sex appeal? What was I thinking? I definitely did *not* need a spy camera focused on this guy's house. Besides, watching him in this sterile environment would drive me nuts. Much better to track where he went.

I hurried across the patio to the other side of the house and followed a narrow walkway up to the front. From there, I scaled the wall and landed behind a pair of trash cans. I rolled one of them under a small window and climbed on top to have a peek.

Since I hadn't seen or heard anyone in the house, I didn't expect to find a car in the garage. However, I did expect to see *something*: if not the motorcycle his attorney claimed he didn't own, then at least some storage boxes, tools, or exercise equipment. All Tran's garage had was more empty space.

I hopped off the trash can and checked the front yard for a realtor's sign. Nope. He didn't appear to be selling. Maybe he had just moved in and the rest of his stuff hadn't arrived. Or maybe he had a compulsion for neatness, or an aversion to material possessions, or maybe he didn't live here at all. Whatever the deal, I found it mighty peculiar.

I shrugged off my backpack and sat against the wall behind the cans. I had time to wait. It would give me a chance to check my messages and see if Debbie had managed to embed the celebrity tweet in her hairdressing blog.

I snorted.

If I hadn't taken down the surveillance camera I had hidden in Kateryna's yard, I could have done something truly important and checked on Ilya. The last time I had seen him, his sweet face was tensed like a frightened bunny with nowhere to go. While I respected Kateryna's decision to stay with her wife-beating husband, it didn't stop me from worrying about her son.

"Let it go, Lily. There's nothing you can do." I took out my phone and pretended not to look for Kateryna's name in the missed calls and found three from my father. I hit redial. "Hey, Baba. What's up?"

"Well, Dumpling dear, I just wanted to make sure you were coming to dinner tonight. You hadn't replied to any of your mother's emails. She's concerned, dontcha know."

I hadn't even opened them. Dinner? No wonder she sent five. "Of course. I'm on my way."

"Uh-huh. I figured as much, but I just wanted to check."

"Got it covered. But thanks for calling."

Baba chuckled. "Your mother hired a caterer for the evening."

"You're kidding."

"Nope. French cuisine. Dinner's at seven, but she's planning cocktails at six."

Holy crap! I checked the time: five thirty. "Sounds great. I'll see you soon."

I ended the call and tapped the phone against my forehead. How could I be so stupid? I was just about to sprint to my bike when I heard the garage door opening. Tran had returned. I did the math: thirty miles from Van Nuys to Arcadia would take three hours by bike, two hours by Metro rail, or forty-five minutes by car. Even if I yanked Tran out of his BMW, stole it, and drove now, I'd be at least fifteen minutes late. Five more minutes wouldn't make a difference.

I took out the tracker. I had made my decision.

As Tran paused in the driveway, waiting for the garage door to raise, I shouldered my backpack. No matter what happened in the next thirty seconds, I would need to run, either for my bike or for my life; I wouldn't have time to collect any possessions.

When the car rolled forward, I fell in behind and attached the GPS tracker under the bumper behind the wheel well. If the car had moved just a little slower, I could have darted away before it stopped. Instead, I got trapped on the side of the car. If I ran, the sensor would trigger, the door would stop, and I'd get caught. If I hid until he entered the house, I'd have to open the garage door to escape, and he'd know someone had been there. Since neither option appealed, I dove above the sensor lights at the floor of the garage and rolled onto the driveway.

I half expected gunfire to riddle the metal and tear into my flesh before the garage door finally closed, but that didn't happen.

Nor did it reopen as I hauled ass to the gnome house next door. In fact, the only thing I heard was the sound of my own breathing and the crunch of brambles under my shoes.

Did I feel silly? You betcha. But just to be sure, I strapped on my helmet and ran the Merida through the junipers, jumped on the moving bike, and raced up the street.

Better to be foolish than dead.

Chapter Thirteen

Ma looked like she"d bitten into a thousand-year-old egg. Not a good sign. Her smooth almond skin was puckered from her lacquered lips to her plucked brows. Then, as if catching herself in dangerous wrinkle-promoting behavior, she relaxed, and Violet Wong became Cover Girl perfect once again. "Good of you to join us, Lily."

"Sorry. The driver got held up in traffic."

"Driver? You're pushing a bicycle."

I looked down at the Merida. After bolting out of Tran's neighborhood, I had ordered a rideshare on Ventura Boulevard. Normally, one would have come within five minutes in such a populated area, however, I had needed a vehicle with a bike rack. The wait had slowed my departure by another ten minutes, making me fifty-five minutes late. Much as I hated to admit it, Ma had good reason to be angry.

"I really am sorry. I didn't mean to keep you waiting. Are we celebrating something special? Baba said you hired a caterer. Wait. Is this a party? Is that why you came to the door, to warn me?"

I shut my mouth before my babbling could reach epic proportions and waited for her to answer. In the meantime, I schooled my features into an expression of contrition and did my best not to slouch as Ma appraised my appearance. She didn't do anything so overt as panning down and up my black track suit. She used peripheral vision. I knew because I had spent years emulating the action. It was harder than it seemed. Her inspection took no more than a couple of seconds, but given a choice, I would have taken another hour with the Ukrainian, especially if it would have spared me the impending argument.

Ma's brows lifted and fell with her sigh. "We are not having a party, I just wanted to give your father a break from cooking. And I came to the door because I wanted to know why you were late. But now that I see your state of dress and that bicycle you insist on riding, your tardiness is not only clear, it is predictable. Honestly, Lily, everyone in Los Angeles owns a car. Why don't you?"

I shook my head. The question had been asked and answered more times than I could remember. "If I had it, I'd use it. And since I don't need it, I don't want it." I held up a hand to forestall an argument. "Besides, most of the time, I can get a rideshare faster than I can get to a parked car. And traffic is the same no matter who's driving."

Her sigh could have blown out a candle. "You're here now. That's all that matters."

I opened my eyes wide but said nothing. Since when was my presence all that mattered? I thought about asking then changed my mind when I saw Baba amble out the door.

"There's my Dumpling. I told you she'd make it."

I managed to squeak out a hello before he squeezed me into a hug.

"You feel hot. Do you have a fever?"

"Uh, no." I looked around as if he should be able to see the heat radiating from the driveway. "It's ninety degrees."

Ma tilted her head. "You might have felt more comfortable in a dress." There was something odd about the way she delivered this bit of criticism, as though she was disappointed yet trying to avoid a quarrel. Something was going on. That's when I noticed how nice they both looked.

Ma always dressed impeccably, but today she looked even more elegant than usual. She had on a sleeveless cheongsam-style cocktail dress that fit snuggly enough to show curves and a flat tummy while still looking classy. Instead of having slits up the sides, the stunning purple dress fell just below the knee where it drew attention to graceful calves, tiny ankles, and heeled pumps of the same rich color. Her silky black hair had been bound into an artful chignon and secured with a purple and green cloisonné fan. The green of her hairpin matched her dark imperial jade earrings, cut in marquis cabochons with platinum and diamond accents, just like her wedding ring. The only other jewelry she wore was a jade bracelet divided into rounded segments and connected by platinum links. Of all her jewelry, the Sì Xiàng bracelet was the dearest.

My grandfather had given it to her before she came to the United States to attend college. He wanted her to remember her heritage and to feel that she would always have the Sì Xiàng—mythical creatures from the four celestial divisions—to watch over her when he could not. Each jade segment had been carved to resemble one of the four guardians: Azure Dragon of the East, Vermilion Bird of the South, White Tiger of the West, and Black Tortoise of the North. Together, they represented the Sì Xiàng. While each of the mythical creatures had its own color, all of Ma's had been carved from the same dark green imperial jade.

No matter how annoyed I got with my mother, I could never deny that Violet Wong was a stunning woman.

"You look beautiful, Ma."

"Oh?" she faltered, surprised by the compliment, then ran her manicured hands along her hair and hip as though some rebellious element might have miraculously sprung out of place.

"Everything's perfect. Really. You too, Baba."

If my mother resembled an exquisite doll, my father looked like a bear. And not the chubby teddy kind. Vern Knudsen was a blond grizzly.

He stood at a respectable six feet, with broad shoulders, sturdy limbs, and powerful hands. When Rose and I were little, he used to balance my baby sister on one meaty paw while doing bicep curls with me dangling from the other. He had turned fifty in May, as Ma would in August, but the silken strands of his vanilla-blond hair had already begun to silver. He had a proud nose and kept his wide face smoothly shaven. His thin lips were quick to smile. His teeth were large and straight. And his eyes were the color of cornflowers on a bright summer's day. So maybe he was more of a Disney grizzly. Either way, he was my Baba, and I loved him.

I took in the ivory Hawaiian shirt and tan slacks. "Why's everyone so dressed up?"

Ma made an exasperated sound. "I knew it. She didn't read any of my emails."

"She could have brought it with," he said, leaving off the "her" as was his Midwest custom. Then he turned to me. "Got a change of clothes in that bag of yours?"

The only items in my pack were the spy cam I didn't use, the brush I used before I buzzed the gate's intercom, and the empty space where my pants and jacket had been. The only reason I was suffering to wear them over my tank and shorts in this heat was to cover the bruises and scratches on my thighs and arms.

Ma gave my pack a disapproving look. "I doubt she could fit a decent pair of shoes in that thing, let alone an outfit."

"Oh, I don't know, Vi. The dresses young women wear today

seem pretty tiny to me."

"Anything would seem tiny to you. Trust me, Vern, an outfit worth wearing would take more room than that."

I rolled my bike toward the left-hand garage—there was another on the right—and leaned it against the side wall in the shade. The wrought iron gate had closed behind me, so I wasn't concerned about theft. Mostly I wanted to avoid standing in the heat while my parents talked about me like I wasn't close enough to hear. When I returned, I grabbed them by the arms and steered them off the stone paving and onto the cool white marble tiles of the entry hall.

"Sorry I'm underdressed, Ma. But right now, I could really use some air conditioning."

Ma kept the house, a wedding present to her from my grandfather, at a chilly seventy-two degrees, regardless of the season or time of day. I used to beg for heat in the winter, but she wouldn't hear of it. "California is so hot," she would say—even if it wasn't. Today, I had to agree. "Do you have any iced tea?"

Ma patted her chignon for the second time and offered me a polite smile. "I'll see. No promises."

The heels of her pumps clicked as she strode across the marble, past her home office on the left and the formal parlor on the right, and in front of the *Gone with the Wind* staircase that swept up to the second-floor balconies and bedrooms. While growing up with Rose, the mansion had felt like home. Without her, it felt cold.

When Ma was out of hearing, Baba touched my chin with his giant thumb and turned it to the side. "What happened to your cheek?"

"Huh?"

"Your cheek. There's glue on it."

I had forgotten about that cut. I had replaced Stan's butterfly bandage with tissue adhesive after getting home from Kateryna's.

A slim red line could still be seen. "I caught it with a fingernail. The glue's a liquid bandage. You know, so it wouldn't alarm Ma." I gave him a conspiratorial wink and hoped he would drop it. He didn't.

"Last I checked, you kept your nails trimmed shorter than mine."

I shrugged. "Hangnail. Doesn't take much." I took a few steps. "You coming?"

"Uh-huh."

I ignored the skepticism in his tone and kept walking. "Good. Because I'm thirsty."

He'd follow or he wouldn't. At this point, I wasn't sure which I preferred. While Ma scrutinized me with a critical eye, Baba observed everything without judgment. As a result, he tended to see things most people missed. I didn't think he suspected what I did when I wasn't helping in the restaurant or assisting his neighborhood friends with their oh-so-urgent internet needs, but I couldn't be certain: Midwesterners held their cards pretty dang close to the vest.

When I reached the kitchen, Ma handed me a glass of iced tea and motioned me toward the dining room. "Dinner is about to be served."

I looked back, hoping for a glimpse at what was simmering on the stove. "Oh my gosh, is that Coquilles Saint-Jacques? It smells heavenly. But don't tell Baba I said that."

"I heard you," he called from the dining room.

"I was just being polite," I called back, shaking my head at Ma so she would know I didn't mean it. Then I whispered to the chef, "It smells delicious." He nodded his appreciation and went back to stirring the sauce.

Ma smiled and patted me on the back. I had praised her caterer. All was forgiven.

"Why are the best cooks men?" I asked.

"Because they're the ones who like to eat."

"Ha! Speak for yourself. I love to eat."

A corner of her mouth curled as she launched into one of our infamous, silent exchanges.

"I know you do, dear."

"There's nothing wrong with food, Ma."

"I never said there was."

"And I exercise plenty."

"You exercise too much."

"What are you saying?"

"Who says I'm saying anything?"

"I am."

"Then you'll choose my meaning for me, won't you, Lily?"

Even the conversations we didn't speak exhausted me.

She inclined her head toward the dining room. "Shall we?"

Was it my imagination, or did she look smug? I couldn't be sure. While Ma and I had a secret language that thrived in silence, it didn't mean I always understood her thoughts. She had a door in her mind that she either opened or shut. Sometimes it swung back and forth so quickly the communication broke into disjointed bits I found hard to follow. I tried to explain it to Baba once. He called it a mother-daughter thing and told me to enjoy it.

Right.

Weren't mothers and daughters supposed to go shopping or gossip about past and future boyfriends? That's how it worked on television. Not that I wanted those types of interactions. Shopping with Ma made me feel like a short-legged, chubby street walker. And the one time I tried to tell her about my college boyfriend, a brown-eyed California boy, she spent the next hour flipping through Hong Kong magazines, pointing out all the good-looking Chinese movie stars. As if Andy Lau or Huang Xiaoming were going to leave their spouses and marry me. And who was she to judge? She ran off with a Norwegian from North Dakota.

I inhaled a calming breath and thought of Rose. It had been different with her. Ma and Rose gelled in a way Ma and I never did. She was always easier on Rose. Tight jeans became chic, short dresses stylish, and high school dating acceptable. The world turned upside down, and no one but me seemed to notice. Was it any wonder I didn't enjoy the mother-daughter thing?

Ma interrupted my thoughts. "What are you looking at, Lily?"

"Huh?" I had stopped in front of a family photo hanging on the wall. It showed all of us together a few months after Rose had been born. "She was such a chubby baby."

"Ha! Rose was fat."

I laughed. "Cute though."

Ma stroked my arm. Even through the fabric, I could feel the gentleness of her touch, as if she wanted to say more. I could have pried, but she wouldn't have appreciated it. Rose's murder had affected each of us in markedly different ways: Ma focused her frightening tiger mom energy onto all things Chinese, Baba poured his broken heart into me and the restaurant, and I became a protector of women and kept it from both of them. Who was I to pry into her motives? Instead, I gave her an out. "I can hear Baba's stomach growling from here."

She smiled, this time with both corners of her mouth. "Then we better hurry."

By the time we rounded the corner, I was feeling pretty good about the evening. My parents had forgiven my tardiness and casual attire, and Ma and I had shared a couple of truly genuine moments.

And then I saw him.

"Why is Daniel Kwok sitting at our dining table?"

I had clenched my teeth into a fixed smile, like an old school ventriloquist. Ma did the same.

"Because he is our guest. Now go say hello."

I gave her my adoring daughter look. "We're not done, you and I."

She raised her plucked brows high in feigned surprise. "Yes, we are, darling." Then she turned back to the men and entered the room like a queen.

I shook my head. It all made sense—the caterer, the fancy clothes, the barrage of emails I was kicking myself for not having read. This wasn't a family dinner; it was an ambush. Suddenly, I didn't feel so bad about my casual track suit.

Daniel stood as I approached. "Hello, Lily."

"Daniel." I spoke his name without inflection.

He lit up as if I had gushed it with excitement. "It's nice to see you again. You look terrific."

I could feel Ma gloating from across the table but refused to acknowledge her. If Mr. Kwok wanted to play the gentleman and seat me in my chair, I'd accept it like a lady. "Thanks. You, too."

I meant it: Daniel Kwok was a handsome man. He just wasn't my type—way too Chinese. I preferred Caucasians. No surprise there, considering that I adored my father. But after Pete—with his caramel hair and gingerbread eyes—Caucasian men reminded me of everything I had thrown away. I didn't deserve Pete's kindness and love. But did I deserve a perpetual reminder of my mother? I hoped not. Daniel represented everything I did not want to become—obedient, deferential, and ambitious.

He was the perfect Chinese son.

And in his fitted black jacket, charcoal jeans, and white shirt that hugged his tall model's physique like a celebrity in a Hong Kong magazine, he looked a helluva lot better than I did. No doubt

Ma was thinking the same thing.

"Daniel has just returned from Hong Kong," she said.

I glanced at Baba for support. He shrugged and cut a thick wedge of pâté for his bread. Apparently, he wasn't part of this subterfuge. Or if he was, he was keeping these cards close to the vest as well.

I looked back at Daniel. "Did you see my grandparents while you were there?"

"I did. In fact..." Daniel paused to take out a jewelry box from his jacket pocket. "Your gung-gung gave me this to give to you."

I stared at the jewelry box. "Well, this is awkward."

"Lily!"

"Sorry, Ma, but even you have to admit this is a little strange."

Daniel patted the air in Ma's direction and smiled. "It's okay, Mrs. Wong. Lily's right." Then he turned to me. "Your grandfather just wanted to save time and money on shipping. That's all. He told me to tell you he saw it in a shop and thought you should have one of your own."

I opened the box and found a barrel bracelet divided into four rounded segments of jade, very similar to Ma's. Each segment had been carved to represent the four celestial creatures of the Sì Xiàng, but unlike hers, each of my guardians had been carved on the appropriate color: bird on red, tiger on white, tortoise on black, and Azure Dragon on a bluish shade of green.

"It's stunning."

Daniel leaned closer. "The colors symbolize the seasons, directions, and—"

"Elements. I know."

"I'm sure you do. Your grandfather told me to tell you that when you put it on, your wrist would become Huang Long, the precious Yellow Dragon of the Center."

I gasped. That part hadn't occurred to me. But why would it? Yellow was the emperor's color. I would never have presumed to think of my skin in this way. But yellow also represented the Earth element: grounding, authoritative, immovable. Was Gung-Gung sending me a message? It certainly felt that way. I just wasn't sure exactly what he wanted me to know.

I glanced at Ma to see if she had been privy to this surprise. She hadn't. There was tension in her face as she struggled for neutrality. The only part of her body that gave away her emotions was the hand covering her own bracelet. Was she hiding it or reminding herself that she had hers first? Either way, I felt bad.

My mother carried a lot of baggage. Not only was she the only living offspring, she had the temerity to be born female. The fact that her stillborn and miscarried siblings had also been female had not lessened the affront in her father's eyes. Wong Shaozu would have no male descendants to carry on the family name, and more importantly, no sons to perpetuate the ancestral worship. His soul would forever roam without honor. The name Shaozu meant one who brings honor to his ancestors, but who would bring honor to him?

Baba motioned at the box with the remaining crust of his bread. "Put it on, Dumpling. Let's see how it looks."

I cringed. "I should be wearing something nicer than a running jacket."

Ma cracked a smile. "Actually, the black track suit might not have been a bad choice."

I smiled in return. It felt good to share another moment with Ma. Sometimes I got so wrapped up in my own family issues, I forgot about the pressure she had been under and the guilt she still carried.

If Ma had followed her father's instructions, she would have graduated from UCLA with a degree in finance, returned to Hong Kong, and attracted a worthy man from a family over-blessed with sons. That man would have been offered a financial empire as Ma's husband if had he agreed to be formally adopted as a Wong. This sort of arrangement would have raised all sorts of incest issues in America, but in China, before the one child law, it would have made perfect sense. Ma's future would have been secured, and my grandfather and his ancestors would have had a male descendant to honor them. Instead, Ma fell in love with an American agriculture student from UC Davis.

I slipped the bracelet over my left hand and fastened the clasp. It looked far more beautiful against the black cuff of my jacket than it would have against my bruised skin. My right wrist looked even worse.

I had intentionally crossed my left hand in front my right when the Ukrainian had tied them together, so the rope had scraped everything around my right wrist except the outside edge. It hadn't made any difference to him how I had chosen to cross my wrists, but the left-forward Jumonji no Kamae fighting posture ended up making a big difference to me. Having my left hand in front while hanging from the scaffold had caused my right side to hang slightly back. That had given me a couple more inches with which to generate power for my kick.

That was another reason I wouldn't wear the bracelet on my right wrist: the only jewelry I tolerated on my dominant side were the ones I could use in a fight. Gung-Gung's gift was far too fragile—such were the workings of a ninja mind.

Daniel leaned closer than necessary to peer at the bracelet. "It suits you," he said, beaming as if the gift were from him.

"I guess." The whole situation was annoying the hell out of me. Still, I couldn't deny the bracelet's stunning beauty. While the deep imperial green of Ma's Sì Xiàng personified elegance, the bold colors of mine radiated strength.

"Your grandfather knows you well," said Ma.

"Or he's sending me a message."

She grimaced. "Or perhaps he's sending one to me."

Could that be true? After all, although Baba had given Rose and me Gung-Gung's surname, he couldn't turn us into sons. Gung-Gung's soul would remain in jeopardy unless I made up for my mother's failure by passing on the Wong name to my future sons. Was that the meaning behind this gift? Had Gung-Gung given me a stronger version of the bracelet he had given Ma to empower me to succeed where she had failed?

As always, Baba rushed to rescue. "Well, I think it's beautiful. Just like you." Then he covered Ma's hand and gave it a squeeze. She smiled and glanced up at him. In that brief exchange, I saw the depth of their love.

I searched for a way to apologize that wouldn't make the situation worse, but that was the problem with careless words, they couldn't be unspoken. Meanwhile, Daniel fidgeted at my side. Poor guy was just an innocent messenger. I reminded myself not to kill him.

"Thanks for bringing me Gung-Gung's gift," I said, emphasizing my grandfather. Innocent or not, I didn't want Daniel expecting anything in return—at least, not from me. Whatever transpired between him and Ma was between them. My relationship with Violet Wong was complicated enough without getting involved with his.

Chapter Fourteen

As soon as the last fork was laid on the table, I made my excuses and left, claiming a need to ride off calories from a chocolate soufflé I had barely touched. Tension had killed my appetite. It also pumped up my adrenaline. I needed a release and figured twenty-seven miles on a bike would do it. I had just passed the halfway mark home when my phone started beeping like a garbage truck in reverse. It could only mean one thing: J Tran had entered my zone.

I had chosen this particular GPS tracker system for the customization features that allowed me to set specific sounds to a variety of actions. Birds chirped when the target arrived at its home destination. An engine revved when the target moved after fifteen minutes of inactivity. A door slammed when the target came to a stop that lasted more than ten minutes. Dogs barked if the target entered a hot zone. And a truck backed up if the target came within five miles of whatever wherever I was. The first two sounds shut off after the initial alert had been given. The last two kept going until I shut them off manually. Neither could be ignored.

I stopped at the curb, took out my phone, and silenced the alert, which brought up a map of Central Los Angeles. Tran's GPS marker showed him approaching just north of my route. I braced the phone against my handlebars and rode. If I hurried, maybe I'd discover what business J Tran had in Koreatown.

I found his car parked across the street from the Robert F. Kennedy Community Schools, a massive cement-walled complex that encompassed twenty-four acres and six independent public schools, kindergarten through twelfth grade. The whole complex, including the walled-and-fenced-in soccer fields, had been built over a partially subterranean parking structure. Since Tran had parked on the downhill side, the top seven or eight feet of this was visible through the chain-link fence, providing me a view into the garage like the windows of a house.

Directional lights, anchored high above, cast shadows down the wall and onto the street. Normally, I avoided such dark pockets. Tonight, I searched for the darkest spot I could find.

After chaining my bike and helmet to the fence, I took the karambit from my backpack and moved it into my right pant pocket. Then I switched my cellphone to mute and put it in the left pocket. Feeling sufficiently equipped, I slipped back into the straps of my pack. I was just about to cross the street to check out Tran's car when I heard voices echoing in the garage. Since the rest of the street looked deserted, I decided to investigate. And when I saw the broken lock on the service gate, I did so with care.

The voices sounded male, drunk, and Korean. I dropped down to the cement floor and made my way along the wall. The voices echoed from deeper in the garage, but I didn't want to cross empty spaces if I could avoid it. Besides, the perimeter offered good sightlines, which was how I spotted him.

Tran was standing behind a pillar with his back to me, looking in the direction of the voices. He wore a fitted jacket, matching slacks, and soft-soled boots all in the same charcoal gray. His wavy brow hair hung in a ponytail at the center of his square shoulders. He looked dressed for a night on the town or a meeting with important clients, not lurking in a garage.

What about these guys had captured his attention?

To answer that question, I needed a better view.

A sedan parked in one of the interior lanes provided the perfect vantage point, but I'd have to cross thirty feet of open space to reach it. I got my chance when one of the men yelled something in Korean that made the other guy laugh.

I sprinted for the sedan, staying on the balls of my feet and keeping my knees bent to lessen the impact and reduce the sound. As long as Tran's focus stayed on the men and they continued to make a racket, I'd make it. I jumped the last five feet just in case, redirecting my forward momentum into a crouch, and remained coiled for action. After several seconds of quiet, I lowered my cheek to the cement and peered beneath the undercarriage. Tran hadn't moved.

I inched my way to the front of the car where I could look in the direction of the voices. The men were definitely Korean, too old for students, too young for teachers. One was bald with tattoos climbing up from the collar of a green and yellow bowling shirt. The other had spiked black hair and muscles straining against a sleeveless black tee. Both wore baggy pants and high-top sneakers and stood in front of a bright green Hyundai decked out for street racing with spoilers, drag radials, and shiny chrome. No doubt I'd find the requisite nitrous oxide system and a turbocharged engine under the hood.

The guy with the tats and bowling shirt punched the muscle guy in the arm. "That's fucking hilarious, man. It just blew up? For real?"

Muscles shoved him back and laughed. "Fuckin NOS exploded. Peeled the skin right off his face."

"No shit?"

They laughed so hard they didn't see Tran as he left the pillar and began walking in their direction. He could have been a teacher on his way to his car, that's how little attention he paid the street racers. For all I knew, that might actually be the case. What did I really know about J Tran aside from what had been disclosed on television, what I had seen while watching him in the courthouse, and what I had deduced from the spaces in his home? Precious little. Still, he didn't move like any teacher I had known, not even Sensei. He glided in an unnatural and predatory way, with only a minimum of movement in his hips and arms.

I took out my phone and snapped some shots of the Koreans. The light wasn't great, but the images should come out clear enough. The tats on the back of the bald guy's neck might give me a clue as to which gang or racing club these losers might belong to and why Tran might be interested in them. If he even *was* interested. Now that he was on the move, he didn't so much as glance at the Koreans, not until Tat—as I now thought of the tattooed punk—took notice of him. Then he stopped.

"Check out this bink fool. What you doin' in K-Town, boy? You get lost? There ain't no South Central, Chinktown shit here. You in the wrong place."

Apparently, Tat didn't embrace Tran as one of his own. In fact, from the epithets he was slinging, he seemed to think Tran was of African-Chinese descent. Was he right? I didn't have time to consider it because the Koreans had shifted, giving me a clear view of their faces and the ink on Tat's throat and arms. I snapped more shots to examine later.

Muscles slapped his buddy. "Maybe he's East LA. That it, homie? You all dressed up for your mamacita? 'Cause you ain't gettin' no Korean pussy here, I can tell you that."

"Whatever the fuck he is, he don't belong in our hood."

"Got that right." Muscles whacked Tat on the arm, this time

hard enough to rock him, inciting an angry barrage of Korean. They were so involved in their argument that neither paid attention to Tran.

They didn't see the slim blade that shot from Tran's palm or the way he held it invisibly against his leg. They didn't watch as he glided forward on bent knees and supple feet with terrifyingly beautiful grace. They were too full with themselves to see any of it.

I took a breath to shout a warning, but it was too late. In the instant between my comprehension of the situation and my vocal chords' ability to formulate a sound, Tran had struck.

The muscled man's back arched in pain and shuddered as Tran withdrew the slim blade and stabbed two more times in quick succession. The Korean's bodybuilder strength was of no use to him now as he crumpled to the ground whimpering. I watched, stunned by the sudden violence, while Tran cruised by as if nothing had happened, as if he hadn't just punctured god knew what organs and sentenced a young man to a slow and excruciating death. Three quick steps later, the punk's tattooed friend reached behind his back, presumably for a weapon. But if he had a gun stashed in his waistband, Tran slit his throat before he ever touched it.

Death took its time.

Blood spurt through Tat's clutching fingers and rained down on his fallen buddy's face. Neither victim concerned himself with the other. Their worlds had shrunk to emptying veins and ragged breaths. And while they died, Tran wiped his blade with a cloth taken from his jacket pocket, like a professor cleaning his spectacles. His indifference to the dying men unnerved me almost more than the violence. He hadn't even checked for witnesses. He just folded the bloodied cloth and replaced it with care.

What kind of person did that?

I eased behind the sedan. Soon, Tran would check his surroundings. He wouldn't take kindly to a witness. But having hid from his view, I had also eliminated my ability to see. All I had left was sound. I wanted to bolt but didn't dare. Every scenario that raced through my mind ended with me dead and Tran wiping his stiletto over my corpse.

I had to get my fear under control.

I took one slow, centering breath and focused on the facts. The garage was too quiet for me to chance peering under the car because, although my backpack hugged my shoulders, the slightest movement could shuffle the contents. I could, however, arm myself with a weapon more lethal than a cellphone. I eased the karambit out of my pocket and rested my thumb on the quick-release switch. With the slightest twitch of my thumb, the hooked blade would spring.

I waited, poised for action, and listened for any hint of Tran's location. I thought I heard a scuff of rubber and the rhythmic pad of steps, but it might have been the thumping of my own heart. Sensei had been teaching me how to focus my hearing beyond my body's perimeter. I had yet to master the skill. As far as I knew, Tran could be standing on the other side of the car, ready to pounce. All I heard was my fear.

I took another slow, centering breath. The more relaxed I remained, the quicker I'd move and the more intuitively I would respond. I prayed that my thousands of grueling training hours and ninja intuition would suffice.

After endless seconds, during which Tran could have attacked a dozen times, I finally heard the scrape of metal against gravel behind me where I had entered the garage. I sagged with relief but continued to listen until I heard the rumble of an engine turning over. Even then, I waited until the car noise had receded before coming out of hiding to scan the garage.

No Tran. Just me and two dead Koreans.

Time to go. If anyone saw me, they'd assume I had witnessed the attack, or worse, committed the crime. I had to get out of there, but I also needed to get a closer look at the scene.

Tran had painted some kind of design on the Hyundai—and it looked as if he'd done it in blood.

Chapter Fifteen

I lowered the quilt onto my nose and cracked open an eye. Gentle morning light shone through the carvings of my antique screen. I smiled and fluttered back to sleep. Or I tried. Someone was knocking on my door in short, persistent bursts. No more dreams for me. Too bad. I had a vague sense they might have been pleasant for a change.

"Coming," I said, and padded to the door in bare feet and an over-sized tee. If Baba—because who else could it be?—wanted me out of bed, he'd have to take me as I was.

I opened the door. Sure enough, there he stood with a serving tray and a smile.

"Hey, Baba. Everything okay?"

"Yep." He raised the tray. "You didn't eat much last night."

I opened the door wider and motioned him inside. "Maybe I'm not fond of French cuisine."

"Uh-huh."

He wasn't buying the story, and I was too sleepy to sell it. Besides, I had more urgent concerns. The lacquer serving tray was a harbinger for prying conversations. In the five and a half years I had lived above the restaurant, Baba had only brought me breakfast three times: my first morning in the apartment, the morning after a horrible fight with Ma, and the morning after I had been attacked by Rose's murderer—although how he had intuited that last event remained a mystery to me. Each time, Baba had carried his offering on the black and gold lacquer tray. I knew it was silly, but every time I saw the thing, I felt nervous and defensive.

"Not like you to leave chocolate soufflé unfinished."

He had me there. Normally, I'd finish mine and then polish off his. If I didn't exercise as much as I did, I'd weigh two hundred pounds. As it was, Ma gave me flack about my weight.

I put a hand against my belly and sucked it in tighter. In my saner moments, I recognized the absurdity of checking for flab. I had less than sixteen percent body fat and my abs were ridged like corrugated steel. But when did logic have anything to do with self-image?

I glared at the lacquer tray. The damn thing had brought Ma with it. How was I supposed to eat with her specter hovering over my shoulder? *Are you sure you want to eat that, Lily?* Just thinking of her made me feel like a spud in a sack.

"Does she think that little of me?" I asked.

"Who?"

"Ma. Why did she invite Daniel Kwok to dinner? Does she think I can't get a guy on my own?"

"Nope. She's afraid you'll sell yourself short."

I snorted. "Really."

He raised the tray. "You want some breakfast? Hate to throw it to the hogs."

Whatever he had hidden under the cover smelled delicious and elicited a loud response from my belly. I stuffed my suspicions and focused on what was in front of me: food from a thoughtful father. That was it. No harbinger, no critical specter, no ulterior motive. Just food and tea.

"Sure. Give me a sec, okay?"

He nodded and headed to the front of the apartment while I went to the bathroom to splash some water on my face and take care of other morning necessities. When I emerged, I found my breakfast laid out on the patio table.

My stomach growled. "What you got there?"

"Jook with minced pork, ginger, scallions, and some Darjeeling tea."

"Yum."

I adored the soupy rice porridge, known in most parts of Southeast Asia as congee. Its bland taste provided a comforting base for sweet, savory, or umami flavors and just about any ingredient you wanted to add. Minced pork, ginger, and scallions were my favorite. With the plethora of Chinese dialects and transliterations, jook—a Cantonese word, commonly used in Hong Kong—could get a little confusing. But whether you called it congee, báizhōu, or zhōu—the pinyin transliteration of Mandarin—or you called it by the Cantonese name and spelled it as jūk or jook, the end result was always delicious.

I leaned over the bowl and inhaled the scent.

"Don't let it get cold."

"You're not having any?"

"Already ate."

I rolled my eyes. "Let me guess—at six?"

He shrugged. "Old habits."

I took a bite of the rice porridge and sighed in ecstasy. Jook was comfort food, and after what I had witnessed in K-Town last night, I could use some comfort.

"How come you never fix biscuits and gravy?"

"Why would I?"

"Isn't that what you ate for breakfast growing up?"

Baba laughed. "A very small part, dontcha know. I also had

93

stacks of pancakes, slabs of ham, a rasher of bacon, and at least five eggs. And don't forget the heavy cream in the coffee. But all of that came after milking the cows and mucking the stalls. By six o'clock, my brothers and I were plenty hungry."

I slurped the last bit of jook from the bowl and sat back while Baba poured tea into small clay cups. I picked mine up and held it in both hands, enjoying the warmth.

"If I ate everything you and your brothers did, I'd be as fat as a blimp."

He winked. "And your mama would never forgive me."

"There is that." I sipped the tea. "But seriously, why don't you ever fix me North Dakota comfort food? Why is it always Chinese?"

"I can fix you biscuits and gravy if you like."

"That's not the point. You absorbed Ma's culture. But what about your own? You even had us call you baba, like Ma calls Gung-Gung, instead of papa like you call your own dad. Why didn't you pass any of your Norwegian heritage on to Rose and me?"

"Ah, Dumpling dear. You know the answer to that."

"You were trying to appease Gung-Gung."

"I stole his daughter."

"You didn't steal her. She fell in love with you. And why wouldn't she?" I reached for his meaty hand. "Sometimes I think you're too good for her."

He squeezed my fingers gently. "Thank you, but it's not true. You're too close to her to see who she really is. And after your sister passed away—well, it's taken a toll on her."

"It's taken a toll on all of us."

"I know. But she's a mother. There's a difference." He held up a hand to forestall any argument. "My point is that you've never had a chance to know her as I did. Your mother is a complicated woman who cares deeply about family and honor. She's also a passionate person with sharp intellect and deep emotions." I must have looked incredulous because he continued. "It's true. Sometimes these qualities live together peaceably, and other times—"

"Like when she told her family about you?"

He nodded. "They create conflict."

"But you gave up everything."

He patted my hand and poured more tea. "I gave up very little. I've always had a roaming nature, and North Dakota is—how should I say—closely knit. If I hadn't met your mother, I probably would have traveled the world."

"See, that's what I mean."

He shook his head. "I didn't need to travel after I met Vi. Everything about her was exotic and exciting." He chuckled. "Although it might have been fun to explore my Viking roots. Who knows, I might have made a good raider back in the day."

"No way. You would have been a farmer."

He gave me a mischievous wink. "Oh, I don't know. There's something to be said for pillaging countries with beautiful women."

"Baba!"

"Anyway, my culture, if you can even call it that, felt bland compared to your mother's."

He caressed the Yixing teapot with fingers more suited for a plow than a tiny work of clay. The handle barely offered room for his thumb and index finger, but he managed to pick it up with confidence and grace. I watched him fill my cup before using the other pot to fill his own. Even in this gesture of courtesy, Baba followed Ma's customs. I tapped my fingers on the table in thanks.

"That doesn't explain why you gave us her family name. I mean, we weren't even sons. What good did it do?"

He shrugged. "Lily Knudsen? Why would I saddle my daughter with a name like that? Nope. It felt right to give you a Chinese last name. And if we ever had a son, everyone in the family would be the same."

"Except you."

"I don't need a name to tell me who I love and who loves me."

I shook my head in amazement. He might have adopted Ma's customs, but that didn't make him Chinese.

"What's the matter, Dumpling? You look like you're carrying the weight of the world." He glanced at my wrists. "And taking a beating for it."

I had forgotten about the scratches and bruises left from the Ukrainian's rope. The inside edge of my right wrist looked particularly agitated because of the bits of nylon that had wedged into my skin. Stan had used tweezers to dig out the ones he could see, but the finer threads remained. They would work themselves out eventually. But right now—only two days since I had showed up at Stan and Aleisha's refuge, beaten and exhausted—the threads were irritating my skin into angry red streaks.

"I scraped it on a wall."

"Uh-huh."

"It happens."

"I'm sure it does."

He sounded so reasonable. I didn't believe it for a second. "Go ahead. Spit it out."

He shrugged. "Those don't look like scrapes, is all."

He was right. The marks didn't encircle my entire wrist, but they curved enough to look like exactly what they were. I held up my left hand as well; if he had noticed one wrist, he had noticed them both. I crossed them right over left then raised them into left-forward Jumonji no Kamae so he could see how the marks lined up. He didn't say a word. He just sipped his tea and waited. Baba could outwait a rock. I needed to give him a plausible explanation, preferably without lying.

"You know I train hard."

He nodded.

"And that the training involves defenses against realistic fighting situations?"

"Yep."

"Well, there you have it."

I rested my elbows on the table and stared at him over the tiny cup of tea, just as he was doing to me. Neither of us said a word. We just sipped our tea and waited for the other one to flinch. Finally, Baba put down his cup. I did the same.

"You're done, then?" He glanced at my empty bowl, but I knew he wasn't referring to the jook. He was asking if I had said all I intended to say.

I nodded and watched as he picked up that blasted lacquer serving tray and left.

Chapter Sixteen

Having showered and dressed, I switched on the kettle and studied the giant Metro map on the wall as I waited for the water to boil. I did this often, which was why I knew all the bus and rail routes that ran, like arteries and veins, through LA County. I even kept track of the maintenance and expansion plans, like how the subway Metro wanted to build between Union Station and Cerritos. I liked the idea. Any rail line that took me through Chinatown to anywhere was a good thing.

The kettle clicked, and I made myself a cup of Dragonwell. Then I sat down at my computer and tried to make sense of the images covering the screen like a storyboard sequence for a detective show. Dark garage. Well-dressed man. A couple of gangster Koreans. What could go wrong? Except that what seemed about to happen didn't.

I bypassed the images of the Koreans bleeding to death while Tran wiped his blade. I didn't need photos to remember that scene: it would haunt me forever.

Instead, I selected the photos of the bald, tattooed Korean when he was still alive. There were two of them: one of his front and the other of his back. I chose the first and zoomed in on the tattoo emerging from under the collar of his green and yellow bowling shirt. No letters or symbols. Just a continuation of the same scaly design that snaked down his arms. I checked the other photo and zoomed in on the back of his neck. Embedded in the design were four capital letters: LGKK.

Interesting.

The Last Generation Korean Killers were a gang that had formed after their predecessors, the Korean Killers, had died out. As far as I knew, the descendants had succumbed to the same fate. Or had they?

Now that I knew the guy was—or had been—LGKK, I checked the photo of him lying face down with his shirt raised up in the back and saw a gun wedged into the waistband of his pants. I had been right: he had been going for it when Tran attacked. He just didn't have the experience to know it wouldn't work.

People liked to quip about not bringing a knife to a gunfight, but when it came to close quarter fighting, they had it in reverse. At twenty-one feet, an expert shooter would have a hard time getting his weapon drawn, sighted, and fired fast enough to stop a knife attack. This bozo would have been screwed at thirty.

I moved on to the last photo that showed the design Tran had painted on the hood of the Hyundai. Two Korean logograms. One resembled an upside-down funnel over a stubby letter L, and the other reminded me of a pagoda temple. Tran had used something waxy, like lipstick or crayon, but with a wider delivery system: stage makeup perhaps, the kind that came in thick sticks like a push-pop. He hadn't painted it in blood as I had previously thought, but the color matched the blood, which together with the chartreuse paint job, made the hangul characters look like a hideous Christmas decoration.

Most Asian languages were written in a common collection of logograms that stemmed from Classical Chinese. Over time, each culture also developed additional methods of writing. The Koreans used an alphabet system called Hangul that grouped letters into blocks of syllables. It had a simpler, rounder look than any of the Chinese-based characters, which was why I recognized it. But that didn't tell me why Tran had known how to write it. The Koreans had not considered him to be one of their own. So, either they were wrong, or Tran had gone out of his way to learn these two blocks of Hangul. But why? Personal grudge? Gang enforcement? Hired hit? I needed to know what the characters meant. Since I couldn't copy and paste from the photo to an online translator, it took some doing.

When I finally deciphered them, I sat back in my chair and sighed.

Obey!

That was the extent of Tran's message.

"Huh."

I pulled up a news report about last night's murder to see if there might be a clue about what Tran had meant. Nothing. Although the article did mention the LGKK gang tattoo on the back of the bald guy's neck and offered a bit of history.

"The last known generation of Korean Killers disbanded in 2000 when their leader got deported back to South Korea. So, it is unlikely that this crime had anything to do with the LGKK. Although we will still investigate that possibility. At the moment, it seems more likely that the execution-style killing was a part of a recent turf dispute between Asian street-racers."

I understood their deductions; I just didn't agree with them. It seemed more likely to me that a new generation had resurrected the Korean Killer legacy and tread into another gang's territory. Although that still wouldn't explain why Tran had assassinated those kids.

Kids.

The Korean punks would have been Rose's age if she had lived. I shoved my chair away from the desk and my computer screen full of death. The cops hadn't found Rose's murderer; I had. And they sure as heck wouldn't find Tran.

I hadn't reported the crime last night, and I wouldn't report it today. What would be the point? A forensics team wouldn't find any DNA samples under the Koreans' nails or footprints on the cement floor. And if my eyewitness account led to a search warrant, no one would find anything in Tran's house. I had seen the place. Tran didn't even keep mementos of his life. He certainly wouldn't keep incriminating evidence. Nope. If I reported this crime to the police, it would come down to my word against Tran's, and after observing the prelim fiasco with Mia, I had a good idea of who would win.

Chapter Seventeen

I found Mia at the old Farmer's Market section of The Grove eating beignets and jambalaya in front of a Jewish pastry shop. She had been asleep when I called on the phone and looked as if she had hung up and rolled into yesterday's yoga sweats, which were now dusted in powdered sugar. I waited for her to glance up at me then slipped into the seat beside her.

"How you doing?" I asked.

She held up a donut, dipped it into the stew, and stuffed it in her mouth. Apparently, Mia was an eat-through-your-misery kind of gal.

"So, what did you want to talk about?" she asked while chewing. "You sounded kind of bent on the phone."

I had practiced numerous ways to approach this conversation during the bike ride from my place to the market. None of them felt good. I didn't want to frighten Mia any more than I assumed she already was, but I no longer believed Tran had tried to kill her. After witnessing his deadly efficiency, I couldn't see him botching a simple strangulation. In fact, I couldn't see him choosing that method at all. Unless it had been personal.

"Well, I thought if I got to know you better, I might find a connection between you and Tran."

She shrugged. "I only know him from the club."

"Right, but there might be another way he knows you."

"Uh, that's kinda scary."

I gave her a reassuring smile but didn't argue. She was right; Tran was scary as heck. "So are you involved in any social groups?"

"Like what?"

"Singles networking, square dancing, running, that sort of thing. I'm just trying to get a feel for what you do when you're not working at the Siren Club."

She laughed. "Well, not any of those, I can tell you that. And it's past tense, remember? I don't work there anymore. But to answer your question, I guess I like to hang out, shop, eat..." She motioned to the market. "Normal stuff. Nothing weird."

"With your friends from work?"

She shrugged. "Used to. With Therese mostly. But I don't think we'll be hanging out much after she bailed on me."

I nodded. While Mia's friend had testified on her behalf, she hadn't offered much in the way of emotional support. I wondered if anyone else had. "Dating anyone?"

She brushed the sugar from her fingers and picked up the coffee cup beside her plate. "No."

Touchy subject. I pushed it further. "Is that why you were interested in J Tran?"

Coffee spewed back in the cup. "What the fuck does that mean?"

I sat back and watched as she patted the dribbled liquid off her chin. "Well, according to the statements from your coworkers, you were really into him." I held up my hands to forestall her objections. "Hey, I'm not judging, honest. Tran's hot, no doubt. I get it."

She glared at me for a moment then huffed and began picking at crumbs and flicking powdered sugar off the table. "How was I supposed to know he'd go all psycho killer on me?"

"No way you could." I meant it. Even I, who lived a secret and often violent life, had been shocked by the savagery I had witnessed in the Koreatown garage. Was that where *I* was heading? Was J Tran the male version of future me? I shuddered and shut that door before something really scary could jump out of the closet, and got back to a safer subject. "You testified that Tran had flirted with you at the club. Did he ever ask you out?"

Mia tore a corner off a napkin and rolled it between her fingers. "Not exactly. But he danced around it, if you know what I mean."

"Did he ever ask about your hobbies, background, the people you knew?"

"Just where I was from and if I was an actress. The usual pickup topics."

I watched as Mia rolled the paper into a tiny spear, which she used to poke at the clumps of sugar. "What did you tell him?"

"That I grew up in Vegas, wanted to be a showgirl, but wasn't tall enough." She nodded at my disbelief. Compared to me, Mia was a giant. "I'm five eleven," she said. "That's tall but not *showgirl* tall. Besides, I was a lousy dancer."

"Did you tell that to Tran?"

"Hell no."

We shared a laugh. "So what was it like growing up in Vegas?"

"Hot." She smiled. "And boring. I lived in a trailer park with my mom, so we couldn't afford a whole lot. Just the basics—school, booze. Lots of booze."

"What about the acting? Is that why you came to LA?"

She shrugged and tossed the paper spear at a roaming pigeon. "Turns out I suck at that, too." She held up a hand. "And no, I didn't tell Tran."

"Did you ask about him?"

She rolled her eyes. "Ye-ah. I mean, you've seen him. His life had to be more interesting than mine. He's certainly better looking."

She had a point. While Mia had a generic Scandinavian appeal, Tran had the dangerous exotic thing down pat. "What did he tell you?"

"Nothing. He kept turning the conversation back to me, like he had read somewhere that women like men who make them the center of attention, or some shit like that."

I chuckled. Mia and I were in firm agreement about that garbage, but I still wasn't any closer to understanding her connection with Tran. I tried a new direction. "Do you have any Korean friends? Any links to their community?"

"That was random."

"I know. But it might be relevant. Do you?"

She shook her head. "I've had Korean barbecue a couple of times. Does that count?"

"Probably not."

"So what does any of this have to do with Tran?"

I shook my head, wishing I knew. "Just examining possibilities, that's all. In the meantime, be careful, okay? Keep your doors locked, turn on your security alarm as soon as you enter your apartment, and draw your curtains at night."

She bit her lip. "You're scaring me."

"Just looking out for you, that's all."

The judge had dismissed her case, the police had a city full of perps to catch, and any friends Mia might have had before the incident had faded into the background. If I didn't look out for her, who would?

Chapter Eighteen

As I unchained the Merida from the tree, I wondered where I should go next. My conversation with Mia had offered some insight about her but nothing that connected her to Tran. If I wanted to know more about him, I'd have to get it directly.

I checked the tracker. Tran's car was still parked at his residence. Was he sleeping in after a hard night's work, dark muscular body sprawled across white sheets…

What the heck, Lily?

I shook the image from my mind. Six years had passed since my one and only sexual experience. I didn't appreciate the pornographic fantasy.

If you have that much energy, go clean your room!

That's what Ma use to say when I got boy crazy in high school. I hadn't really understood it then, but now it made perfect sense. I laughed, startling an old man as he ambled through the parking lot in my direction. I pointed to my ear as if I had a Bluetooth hiding in my hair. He nodded with understanding but veered away just the same.

"Good going. Way to scare the locals."

I checked to see if the old man had heard that, too. If he had, he ignored it and continued across the lot to his parking space.

I clipped on my helmet, and started to leave when I saw Mia.

She was heading into the plaza toward the ritzier part of this development. Since I didn't know where else to go, I followed.

She stopped at a kiosk that sold colorful East Indian dresses and chose a lacy number with spaghetti straps, which she held against her baggy sweatshirt. On the rare occasions when I needed something new to wear, I found it online, or I tore through stores like a Marine on a search and rescue mission. I would no more amble through a promenade mall than I would feel myself up in public. Mia, on the other hand, seemed quite comfortable doing both.

Wait a second.

She didn't have any friends, and she wasn't dating anyone. So why did she need a new dress?

I once asked Rose the same thing. She called me clueless. And she was probably right. Why shouldn't Mia want a new dress?

Mia's cellphone rang, saving me from further ruminations.

"Freddy. Finally! Why haven't you called?" Mia sounded both excited and petulant; I gave her a ten for complexity and execution. "Yeah, but the press is gone now," she continued. "I'm yesterday's news. Trust me, no one cares about me anymore." She crossed her free arm under her breasts and made a fist beneath the one holding the phone. "Not even you."

For a woman who wasn't dating anyone, Mia looked an awful lot like a pissed-off girlfriend. Then her back straightened and she assumed a more assertive posture. She even unclipped and tossed her hair. "Then come see me. I'm at The Grove. Isn't that near you?"

She looked proud and strong, and I really wanted her to win. *Come on, Freddy*, I thought. *Get off your ass.*

Then her chin dropped and her back slumped, and Mia grew petulant again. "I seriously doubt we'll run into your wife. Doesn't she have a play date or something? Please, Freddy, I really need to see you." She listened for a moment then smiled. "Sure, that sounds great. Ten minutes. See you there."

Freddy had a wife? No wonder Mia had lied. At least she had the grace to be discreet. Although as I watched her march back to the kiosk, buy the lacy dress, and dash into a nearby coffee shop, I wondered if that discretion—along with her attire—was about to change.

Five minutes later, Mia emerged wearing the new dress and a determined expression.

She had brushed her blond hair into a silky cascade, and applied lip gloss that glistened in the sunlight. If Mia wanted to rekindle her romance, she looked well prepared. The fabric's buttercup-yellow flattered her fair looks, the artful lace accented her cleavage, and the flared cut of the skirt slimmed her waist and made her large calves look almost delicate. In five minutes, Mia had transformed herself from a frump into a vision. I should be taking notes.

I rolled my bike behind a booth selling cellphone accessories and waited for her to pass. Then I fell in behind a pair of chatty mothers strolling their babies. The kiosks disappeared, and the plaza transitioned into storefronts on an open boardwalk. There was a fair amount of morning shoppers to hide behind if Mia turned around, but I knew she wouldn't. Mia had told Freddy she would meet him in ten minutes. Eight of those minutes had already passed. She needed to hurry.

Mia followed the trolley tracks that ran through the center of the boardwalk, turned left at Gilmore Lane, and stopped just past the corner. Since this appeared to be the rendezvous point, I backed up behind a potted palm where I could watch. I had just taken out phone to open the camera app when I got a call. "Hey, Ma. What's up?"

"Just calling to say hello. You left so early last night."

"Right. Sorry about that. I was kind of burned out." I was talking to Ma, but most of my attention was on Mia, who was waiting anxiously on the street corner.

"From the heat?"

"Sure. The heat."

Mia's gaze shifted from one end of the street to the other. I checked the time. One minute to go. I hoped, for her sake, Freddy was punctual.

"Lily?"

"Hmm?"

"Will you go?"

"Go where, Ma?"

"Out with Daniel."

"Wait. *What?*"

Mia rose up on her toes as if she couldn't otherwise see the white car driving toward her on the empty street.

"Gotta go, Ma."

"But you didn't answer."

"Sure. Whatever. I'll talk to you later, okay?"

I hung up before she could respond and switched to camera mode in time to snap a wide shot of the Lexus. I zoomed in on the plate and waited for the car to stop, but it continued down the street. Poor Mia was left on the sidewalk with her hopes crushed and spine sagging in her cheery buttercup dress.

Chapter Nineteen

The man I thought of as a second father launched a punch straight at my nose, and I loved him all the more because of it.

While Mia had gone back to the Farmer's Market to dowse her sorrows in powdered sugar, I had gone to Sensei's new house in Los Feliz, where he had built a home dojo in place of a living room. My morning had frustrated the heck out of me, and nothing rid my mind of frustration like a good fight. If I didn't get my face broken in the next two seconds, I'd feel as clear as a summer sky.

I shifted my weight from the front foot to the back and rode out the energy of Sensei's attack. His was not the quick punch of a boxer, but a deceptively reaching strike he launched from his gut. I cross-stepped backward, wanting to stay out of his reach yet close enough to tempt another attack.

His next punch came harder and deeper to compensate for my retreat.

I evaded it by sinking and stepping backward with a longer, lower stride—a fluid Ichimonji no Kamae. This fighting posture and corresponding water element allowed me to absorb my teacher's attack while at the same time drawing energy for my own. Having taught me this technique, Sensei knew exactly what I was doing. He also knew I couldn't stay in this kamae for long.

His third punch drove me into an even deeper and longer retreat.

I could have veered off to a safer position, but where was the fun in that? We were playing a game of cat and mouse, and it was time for me to take control. When his punch fell short, I smirked. It was a cocky thing to do. I knew it. He knew it. And I did it anyway. I even opened my arms and flattened out my torso into Hira Ichimonji no Kamae to give him an irresistible path to my gut.

Sensei took the bait and launched a stomp kick right to my solar plexus, the same spot the Ukrainian had hit with his knotted rope. While the rope strike had taken my breath, Sensei's kick—if I allowed it to connect—would break my sternum.

I shifted left, to avoid his kick and position my hip, while at the same time raised my hand to intercept his face.

Everything seemed to be going as planned. Victory should have been mine. But instead of taking my teacher gracefully to the floor and securing his face beneath my knee and his arm in a painful lock, Sensei shifted his hip—ever so slightly—and reversed the throw.

My legs flew into the air, the room turned upside down, and I hit the mat with stunning force. His thumb dug into a kyusho pressure point under my jaw and pinned me to the floor, rendering me helpless. One point. One thumb. Such was Sensei's skill. Then the pressure released and nausea filled the void.

"Breathe, Lily-chan," he said.

I did as he suggested and tried not to vomit. Funny how the release of pain could feel worse than the pain itself.

"Better?"

"Hai," I said—the Japanese word was easier to grunt than yes—and crawled my way into a formal Seiza no Kamae seated position. Not only did I feel too deferential to sprawl, but kneeling with my heels under my butt kept my spine straight and helped me to breathe.

As Sensei walked across the mat to open a window, I marveled at his fluid grace. He was close to seventy, short, and stocky; yet he could jump to surprising heights, roll like a playful chimp, and bend as supplely as grass. I hoped to be like him one day, but after getting slammed on the mat, that goal seemed unreachable.

I'd asked him, twice, why he had taken me on as a student: once when I was fifteen and realized that he was teaching me secrets he didn't share with his other students, and again when I was eighteen and had committed myself to the path of a warrior protector. The first time I'd asked, he distracted me with a cool technique. The second time, I paid attention.

"I teach you seriously because you are a serious person, Lily-chan." Sadness had crept onto his face, but he banished it with hard resolve. "Partial learning leads to partial success. Now that you are committed to this path, I won't have your death on my soul."

He hadn't told me the whole truth, but I hoped, if I trained with him long enough, he someday would.

"What went wrong?"

I shook my head, not knowing where to begin. "Everything? I don't know. I thought I had control of the fight."

"And against a less skilled opponent, you would have."

"So where did I mess up?"

He breathed in the fresh air; I did the same. Then he turned to face me and spoke with quiet deliberation. "We must start with what you did right. You rode my energy close enough to keep you safe and me hooked. You manipulated my emotions and made me believe that if I extended just a little more, I would have you. And then, you belittled me with your smirk and teased me with your open posture. Everything you did would have worked against a hot-tempered assailant. But one in control of his or her emotions?"

He let the question hang unanswered.

I sighed. "He wouldn't have fallen for it."

Sensei's almond eyes grew a touch rounder. "He?"

I nodded.

He considered this a moment. "And this man threatens you?"

"Not me. One of my charges."

"Ah. I see. Then you must be better than good or this man will defeat you and harm the one you protect."

I shrugged. "I'm afraid so."

He pulled back and squinched his face with disapproval. "It isn't like you to be afraid, Lily-chan. Hold your center, and remember your training."

"But that's the problem, Sensei: this man disrupts my center."

"Ah. Well, that's a different problem. Why do you think this is?"

"I don't know."

He turned his back and returned to the window. "Maybe you should find out."

He had given me privacy because he wanted me to journey to the quiet place where I hid secrets from my conscious mind. So I closed my eyes and enacted the Goshinbo rituals to purify negative karma and protect my body and spirit from harm. Once I felt calm and safe, I invited my inner wisdom to provide me with the answers I had been too afraid to ask.

Those answers came in the form of a vision.

I saw J Tran standing in a field, staring in my general direction at something in the distance. He seemed relaxed, as though he knew whatever he waited for would inevitably come his way.

Next, I saw him on a hill, wind blowing streams of dark hair away from his stern face. His chest was bare and he wore drawstring gi pants, the kind made for martial arts uniforms only of

113

softer material that clung and fluttered with the breeze. I could see the cuts and shadows of his chest, stomach, and thighs. My hands wanted to feel. Instead, I kept my fingers entwined in my mudra and went through the motions of shielding my spirit once again.

The third vision brought us so close I could see my reflection in his cold, dark eyes.

My pulse raced. My breathing grew shallow. I chanted the mantra of protection, surrounded myself in empowering light, and waited for its brightness to burn away Tran's image. Then I took a series of deep breaths and focused on the training mat beneath my shins. When I felt sufficiently anchored to reality, I opened my eyes.

Sensei sat in front of me, a sword's length away.

"Did you find your answer?" he asked.

"I did."

He waited long enough for me to explain. When I didn't, he placed his hands on the mat and offered a slight bow. I beat him to it and held mine longer. When I returned to an upright position, he had moved closer.

"Take care of yourself, Lily-chan. And remember to guard your center." He drew a circle in the air in front of my torso. "Here." Then he touched my solar plexus, the seat of my emotions, and gave it a firm tap. "And here."

I bowed my head in acknowledgment. "I will," I said, and hoped it would be true.

Chapter Twenty

I arrived home during the peach and aqua prelude to a gorgeous SoCal sunset. The restaurant signboard and neighboring buildings walled in the sight from my apartment, but that didn't matter: my favorite viewing spot was on the roof.

So much of what I did as a modern-day kunoichi—a female ninja, who in my case, protected other women like Kateryna and Mia—involved me scaling buildings, swinging from high places, or otherwise getting from one point to another regardless of the obstacles. Those skills did not magically appear. They had to be developed and maintained. Our building and the ones surrounding it served as my outside dojo.

Whether climbing, leaping, rolling, or fighting, movement was movement—and the ninja way of moving transformed the ordinary into magic. It might look odd or feel awkward to an untrained observer or novice practitioner, but once mastered, Taihenjutsu felt natural and effortless. Usually, I trained on my roof at night in the shadows cast by urban glow. Today, I simply enjoyed the sunset.

I stretched out on the white gravel, pretended it was sand, and let my mind wander where it would. That direction turned out to be Mia Mikkelsen.

I had learned quite a bit about her this morning. She had

grown up in a trailer park in Las Vegas with her mom, tried and failed to become a showgirl, moved to Los Angeles to become an actress, and tried and failed again. She waitressed at a club, got involved with a married man, and lived in an apartment I doubted she could afford. Classic Hollywood tale.

But what did any of this have to do with J Tran?

Had Mia been looking to upgrade from a married sugar daddy to a bachelor hunk? Possibly. From the quality of Tran's clothes and his confident demeanor, Mia would have assumed he had money. But while I no longer believed Tran meant to kill her, I also couldn't imagine him feeling emotional enough to terrorize her. So why had he done it?

Unless this had something to do with Freddy.

I had witnessed Mia's desperation as she cajoled her lover into meeting her. What if she had taken it a step farther and threatened to expose their affair? Was Freddy the kind of man who would hire a killer to stop her? The obvious course of action was to ask Mia, but since she had already lied to me about not dating anyone, I couldn't trust her. Better to track down Freddy on my own.

I was pondering the best way to do this, when my cellphone rang. I didn't recognize the number. Could it be Kateryna calling from a train station on her way to freedom? I could hope.

"Hello?"

"Hi, Lily. It's Daniel." When I didn't answer, he added, "Daniel Kwok?"

"Right, of course." I tried to conceal my disappointment. "What's up?"

"Well, your mom called and told me you might be interested in going out on a date."

"Huh." When the hell had I agreed to a date? And then I remembered. Ma had been babbling on the phone when I was at The

116

Grove watching the white Lexus approach Mia. In my hurry to end the call, I must have agreed to go out with Daniel.

"I hope that's okay. I'd love to take you to dinner. I was thinking tonight? If you're free."

"Uh, sure. I could eat." My taste buds were primed for sunset-inspired lavender-lemon and strawberry-balsamic gelato, but I could adjust. "What did you have in mind?"

"République. Have you been there? It's a foodie paradise."

"Really? Sounds like my kind of place."

"Great. I've got an eight o'clock reservation, so how 'bout I pick you up around seven thirty?"

"Wait. You already made a reservation?"

"Well, sure. I figured I could always cancel if you didn't like the place or changed your mind about the date."

It sounded like something I would have done. But he didn't need to know that. Instead, I honed in on the last part. "You thought I'd change my mind?"

"Let's just say I considered the possibility."

I smiled. Daniel had just earned some serious brownie points. I liked a man who didn't take me for granted. Maybe this wasn't such a bad idea after all.

Chapter Twenty-One

The armholes of my black dress cut around my deltoids, the waistline hugged my abs, and the hem stopped just below the bruises on my quads to display chiseled calves—I looked like a freaking fitness advertisement.

But would I impress a date? Maybe I should break out the bra. My reflection shrugged. Apparently, she didn't know any more about dating than I did.

The bra in question was a sexy padded number from Victoria's Secret. Ma had gotten it for me during a rare shopping expedition a few years back. The adventure had begun well enough with lunch at a Beverly Hills bistro, sprinkled with a hefty amount of Arcadia gossip. "Did you hear that Joy Ching won Miss Kowloon?"

I remembered feeling annoyed. "And how would I have heard? Her family moved back to Hong Kong when I was still in high school."

Ma continued, unperturbed. "Well, I'm telling you now. She's going to run for Miss Hong Kong next. Her parents are very proud."

"I'm sure they are."

"You know, you could have done something similar. You're really very pretty, Lily. You just need to present yourself better."

"What's that supposed to mean?"

She sighed. "Don't be obtuse. It's in the way you stand, talk, dress."

"Oh, is that all?"

"Don't be flippant. This is exactly what I'm talking about. Everything about you is so…casual." She delivered the last word as though stamping me with some embarrassing degradation.

"What's wrong with casual?"

Her eyes closed and her face moved ever so slightly as if to gently dislodge any unappealing notions. "Nothing. Except you can't be that way all the time. Not if you want to get ahead."

"Who says I want to get ahead?"

"Don't be ridiculous, Lily. And stop being so resistant. I'm trying to help." She tapped her lacquered nails on the table, caught herself, and reached for a glass of chardonnay. "Part of this is my fault. I shouldn't have let you take Wushu at such a young age."

I gaped. "You're kidding."

"Not at all. Deep stances lead to big thighs, and big thighs shorten the line of the leg. And I'm sure twirling all those heavy staves and spears contributed to your excess upper body muscle, which undoubtedly stunted your development."

"My development? Oh my God, Ma. Are you saying I'm flat?"

"Don't be crass. Of course not. Your breasts may not be as big as mine or my mother's, but they exist. You just need the right lingerie. But I do think Wushu had something to do with it." She took another sip of wine. "I should have put you in ballet."

"Right. Because ballet dancers have such big breasts."

"No. Because they're feminine. Look at you. You have more muscles than a boy."

My mother's words echoed in my mind as I inspected my reflection. Nothing I saw looked boyish to me. Instead, I saw a strong, athletic woman. So what if my breasts weren't huge? They filled out my dress and balanced my hips. And if my legs didn't start at my armpits, they were long enough to leap over obstacles and run across town. I really didn't see a problem.

Except for the shoes.

I stepped out of the black pumps—another item purchased during that infamous shopping expedition which, like the padded bra, had remained buried in my closet. While I liked the length they added to my calves, they made me feel trapped. I preferred shoes that allowed me to run, climb, and fight—not that I was expecting to do any of that tonight, but I'd feel more at ease to know I could.

I returned the stilettos to their home, put the box in the closet next to the unopened Victoria's Secret bag, and brought out a pair of low-heeled, ankle-high boots. Between these, the bike shorts I wore under my dress, and the stretchy faux-leather jacket, I could do anything I might need to do. To finish my ensemble, I strapped the karambit to my thigh and hung the phurba necklace around my neck. While I didn't expect to need the three-sided ceremonial dagger against a physical attack, it might come in handy to pierce through delusions—this was, after all, a date.

I headed down the stairs, chuckling as I went. Daniel Kwok had no idea who he'd be taking to dinner.

He watched from the entryway of our restaurant as I wove through the tables. He looked as handsome as a Hong Kong fashion model in his brown pants, V-neck shirt, and slim-cut brown jacket. Like a delicious chocolate bar. "You look stunning," he said.

"Who, me?" I looked down to make sure my wardrobe hadn't magically morphed into something sexier than I remembered.

"Absolutely."

"Uh, thanks." I tried not to argue with a win. It sounded obvious when I first heard Baba say it, but the philosophy was more challenging than it seemed.

Daniel watched with interest as Baba's wait staff brought steaming dishes to the tables behind me. "You know, I've never eaten here before, but I've heard great things about your father's cooking."

Was he backing out already?

"I guess we could eat here, if you want."

"Honestly, Lily, it doesn't matter. I'm just looking forward to spending time with you."

His eyes crinkled into narrow slits and his mouth bowed into a heart-shaped smile, the kind that went up on either side of center like the Joker's. If I detected the slightest whiff of comic book psycho-crazy, I was going to kick him to the street no matter how many compliments he threw my way.

"That's a helluva line, Mr. Kwok. Did you go to school for that?"

He paused longer than necessary before replying. "No. I have a BA in business."

I couldn't tell if he was joking. "Well, I get a lot of my father's cooking. So what do you say we go check out the foodie paradise?"

Daniel beamed, obviously delighted with my choice. "After you."

He opened the door and held it while I walked out to the boulevard. Apparently, Daniel Kwok played the gentleman even when Ma wasn't watching.

I rolled my eyes and caught a glimpse of the full moon. It shone like the polished disk in my dojo temple, reflecting my ill-thoughts and suspicious nature. Could Daniel be the real deal? It wouldn't be the first time I judged someone more harshly than they deserved. Call it self-preservation. Rose had been trusting to a fault, and look what happened to her. Then again, nothing about Daniel seemed disingenuous, just literal. If I wanted to enjoy the evening, I'd need to rein in the snark.

And then I saw his car.

The black Lexus sedan screamed business exec so loudly I expected the license plate to read FUTRCEO. Fortunately, Daniel misinterpreted my pained expression for impressed surprise. "You like it? My father drives the same car in Hong Kong."

"Then it must be hard for him to get around." The comment slipped out before I could stop it. Daniel must have heard it because his head tipped like a puppy trying to figure out how the ball he had been chasing had suddenly disappeared. It was kind of cute. "I'm kidding. It's a beautiful car. Your dad has good taste."

Daniel grinned, and I was pleased to see it no longer reminded me of the Joker.

"My father's a smart man. Just like your grandfather."

I let his observation about Gung-Gung pass without comment. We had come to the first hurdle of the evening—getting into the car.

I didn't go out on dates often, but when I did, I always arranged to meet the guy at the destination. This allowed me to bail if things got weird and kept a potential stalker from knowing where I lived. It amazed me that more women didn't do this. Instead, they blithely gave out their home addresses and trapped themselves in confined spaces with men they barely knew. It made me want to scream. None of those women would ever get in a stranger's car, and yet they did just that every time they went on a first date. And not just the first date, how about the second, or the third?

How long did it take to detect a rapist or a psychopath? Weeks? Months? Ever?

Calm down, Lily.

I took a steadying breath. I had let Daniel pick me up because, thanks to Ma, he already knew where I lived and because our families knew each other. If he turned out to be a serial killer, Gung-

Gung would go on the war path and wipe out the entire Kwok family. Okay, that might be a slight exaggeration, but the point was, Daniel's family would lose enormous face, which would likely ruin them in Hong Kong.

I tried not to think of any of this as Daniel opened the passenger side door and waited while I did the whole leg-folding thing. It wasn't easy—not because of the knee-length skirt, but because of my nerves. If at that moment I had been given a choice between getting in Daniel's car and hanging back on the Ukrainian's hook, I would have chosen the hook. At least I'd know the score.

The last time I let a man get me in a car, the evening had gone horribly wrong.

Chapter Twenty-Two

A food critic once described République as a super-bistro on steroids. That seemed about right. The restaurant offered an elegantly rustic ambiance with an epicurean menu that would have satisfied the most discerning gastronome. And from the sights and smells that greeted me in the foyer, I'd say they'd nailed it.

"Can I just breathe in our meal?"

Daniel smiled, inordinately pleased, as if he had slaved in the kitchen himself. "But then we'd deprive our taste buds of the pleasure."

"Good point. We better eat." I gaped at the racks of meat displayed behind glass. "And I may need a steak."

Daniel laughed. He might not get my sardonic humor, but he seemed to appreciate my enthusiasm for food. He pointed at the bottles lined up in a temperature-controlled wine cabinet. "And a good merlot?"

"Sure. Why not?" I wasn't a big drinker, but that sounded like something I could get behind.

We followed the hostess past the gleaming modern bar and main dining hall, through a stone archway, and into a long room with vaulted ceilings and cozy alcoves tucked against the walls. Clearly, this was the place to be—away from the crowd and in sight of the open gourmet kitchen.

The hostess gestured for Daniel to walk up the kitchen side of the long central table and escorted me up the other. Then she stopped in the middle and offered me a seat with the perfect culinary view.

"Is this okay?" Daniel asked, glancing from the dignified couple on my right to a party of thirty-somethings on my left.

"Are you kidding? This is like house seats at the ballet. It can't be an accident."

"It could be."

"But it's not. Seriously, Daniel. When did you make this reservation?"

"Okay, you got me. I made it last week when your mom invited me to dinner."

"She invited you *last week*?" I wasn't sure which annoyed me more, that my date had presumed I'd accept his offer or that my mother had given him more notice to last night's dinner than she had given me.

He shrugged. "You're family. She knew she could count on you." I must have made a face because he looked surprised. "What?"

"I doubt she would agree."

"Of course she would. You're a good daughter, and good daughters always honor their parents."

I laughed. I had so many things to say about that comment I hardly knew where to begin. "And what about sons? Do you always follow your parents' wishes?"

"Yes."

"Wow. Not even the slightest equivocation?"

"Why does that surprise you?"

"I don't know. Because this isn't ancient China?"

"Traditions are the foundation of living, and what's more traditional than honoring one's parents?"

Was he for real?

To avoid answering, I snuck peeks at my neighbor's plate, triggering an embarrassingly loud growl from my belly.

Daniel laughed. "Wait till you see the menu."

République offered so many intriguing choices that we ended up ordering one entrée and a selection of appetizers and sides to share. As each delectable came and went, I took the measure of the man sitting across from me. He had asked about my interests, but when I danced around the topic, he seemed just as pleased to tell me about himself. I couldn't figure out whether he was self-absorbed or nervously trying to fill space. Either way, his monologue spared me from having to prevaricate and allowed me to devour more than my share of the Gruyère-potato beignets.

Daniel continued as though he had my undivided attention. "Please don't misunderstand. I'm pulling in a good salary, and I've risen faster than any of the other new loan brokers, but the company has a glass ceiling, and the top is exclusively white male. I don't see them ever promoting an Asian."

I popped a roasted Brussels sprout into my mouth and closed my eyes. Whoever had originally thought to pair these little cabbages with bacon deserved some kind of award.

Daniel watched as he sipped his merlot. "I've never seen a woman enjoy food as much as you."

"Really? Well, this chef is amazing."

"True. But still, you must exercise a lot."

I snorted. "Why's that?"

He made a face as if the answer were obvious. "Because you have the perfect figure."

I stopped chewing. "You've got to be kidding."

I thought of Kateryna Romanko's delicate femininity, Mia Mikkelsen's towering abundance, and my mother's classically proportioned elegance. Each of their body types seemed more desirable than my broad shoulders and muscular thighs.

And yet, my date seemed genuinely baffled. "Why would I kid?"

I thought about answering, but Daniel didn't need to hear my insecurities. Besides, I had already noted his personality characteristics. Gratuitous flattery was not one of them. Daniel said exactly what he meant. In my world, where deceit and manipulation obscured the truth, his unmitigated statements cut through like a beacon of light.

He took my hand and stroked the top of it with his thumb. Then, as if the gesture might be too intimate for a first date, he switched his attention to Gung-Gung's bracelet. "This suits you."

"Really? I almost didn't wear it."

"Why not?"

I shrugged. "Too fragile."

He took it as a joke. It wasn't. The only reason I had changed my mind was because I could tuck it under the cuff of my jacket if I ran into trouble. Besides, the platinum links went well with my silver phurba dagger. And there was no question about me wearing that.

Daniel tapped my hand. "Bold and unusual."

"I'm sorry?"

"That's why it suits you. A single color of jade would have been too safe, too ordinary."

As I floundered for something to say, our waitress came by to collect the plates. "Would you like to see our dessert menu?" she asked.

Her offer relieved one embarrassment and bloomed another. The dignified couple to my left had been nibbling at a fried croissant drowned in hazelnut chocolate for the last half hour. I desperately wanted to try it, but after Daniel's comment about my hefty appetite, I felt self-conscious. Once again, Daniel cut through the bullshit.

"I think we'll need a couple of those," he said, nodding toward the cornetti fritti. Then he leaned closer to me and dropped his voice.

I froze. If I as this transparent about dessert, what had I revealed about myself?

"I didn't think you'd want to share."

I didn't.

chapter Twenty-Three

Siren Club was a trendy place that catered to an elite crowd with deep pockets and an appreciation for top shelf drinks. It made sense that the bouncer, elegantly attired in black on black, paid more attention to the clientele than the head count.

"I'm glad I left my jacket in the car."

"Huh?"

I shrugged. "My dress looks sexier without it."

He laughed. "I don't think you have to worry about that. You'd look sexy in sweats."

The last time he had seen me, I had, in fact, been wearing a sweat suit, albeit a nice one. Maybe my fashion choices weren't so bad after all. I smiled. "Thanks. Although I wasn't fishing for a compliment; I just want to get into the club. But you look nice enough for both of us, so I'm sure they'll let us in."

Daniel beamed. Mr. Perfect had a streak of vanity.

"I still can't believe you suggested this place," he said. "You don't seem like someone who'd be into the club scene."

"I'm not normally, but a friend of mine used to work here. She made it sound pretty cool. Besides, the night is young and we're all dressed up."

"Don't get me wrong, it's a terrific idea. I'm just surprised, that's all."

Daniel wasn't wrong to be surprised. I hadn't visited a club since I had gone trolling for Rose's murderer. The only reason I had suggested it tonight was because I wanted to see where Mia had worked and maybe chat up some of her former co-workers. Slow nights, like Tuesdays, gave bartenders and waitresses time to work bigger tips by engaging with their customers. Also, I'd have more freedom on a date. A lone woman on an off night attracted the wrong kind of attention.

"Are you sure you're okay with this?" I asked. "Because we could always call it a night."

"No way. I'm having too good of a time."

"Me too," I said, and was surprised by how much I meant it.

The bouncer asked for our IDs, and I caught his gaze drifting to my bracelet and Daniel's watch.

"See. You look stunning," said Daniel as the bouncer waved us into the club.

I smiled, but I knew the truth: we had passed the bouncer's wealth-o-meter. Still, the warmth of Daniel's breath against my neck felt awfully nice. I brushed my cheek along his to whisper back my thanks and was annoyed to hear that my voice had dropped an octave.

"Lily? Are you okay?"

"Huh? Of course." I had blocked the entryway during my little interlude with Daniel's cheek, and the group behind us were getting impatient. "Just waiting to follow you in," I said—as if I ever waited to follow anyone anywhere.

Daniel smiled and led the way into the club. When he arrived at the junction between the dance hall and the lounge, I asked if he wanted to dance. I needed to burn up my hormone-induced energy before I could concentrate on intelligence gathering, and this seemed like the most expedient way to do it. Unfortunately, Daniel turned out to be a distractingly sensual dancer. It took a half dozen songs before I felt back in control of my emotions. By then, I was happy to follow Daniel to the bar. I felt even happier when I saw the mass of thirsty patrons waiting for their turn. It would take at least thirty minutes for him to maneuver his way to the front, catch the attention of a bartender, and pay for the drinks—plenty of time for me to go ask some questions.

I tapped Daniel on the shoulder and shouted near his ear. "I'm going to find a restroom."

"Okay. What do you want to drink?"

"Something with ice."

He gave me a thumbs-up and turned back toward the bar. I left him to it and set out to get some answers.

I didn't need to relieve myself, and I didn't care about washing away the sweat, so I wasn't sure what caused me to detour to the restroom; I just found myself walking through an exit and down a relatively deserted corridor to what the club euphemistically referred to as the Ladies' Salon.

As the heavy doors closed behind me and the throbbing bass beats deadened to a soothing pulse, I realized the salons were intended for more than pit stops. Clubbers could come here to primp in peace or enjoy a quiet conversation. They could even lie down on a couch and rest their aching feet. I doubted it ever occurred to the designers of the club what other actions soundproof walls might inspire.

Then again, maybe it had.

I didn't know about the Gentlemen's Salon, but the bathroom stalls in the Ladies' Salon had thick wooden doors and enough space inside for two adults to engage in all manner of sexual gymnastics. And from the thumping coming from the stall at the end of the aisle, I figured an adventurous couple was putting this to the test.

Until I heard crying.

"Quiet," a man whispered, followed by whimpers from a woman.

This didn't sound like an erotic nightclub hookup, it sounded like rape.

I raced down the aisle and pounded on the teak door. "Get out of there. Now!"

The woman cried for help, but her voice was muffled midway through the word. I yanked at the handle and pounded, again. "Security is on its way."

The thumping and whimpering continued. Whoever this monster was, he wasn't going to stop until someone made him. I jumped on the counter opposite the stall. Good thing I had opted for practical boots rather than sexy high heels or what I was about to do would have been a whole lot harder.

I grabbed the door and pulled myself over the top. My entrance wasn't as cool as Jackie Chan's dive through the casino cashier slot, but it got me into the fight—head first. I grabbed fistfuls of the man's hair, and twisted to send his face smashing into the opposite wall, which would have been wickedly cool if I hadn't conked my own head in the process and squished the woman into the gap beside the toilet.

Pain shot through my neck. My vision wavered. I grabbed at the man to pull myself up. He slammed me back down. My head missed the toilet bowl and smacked onto the tile floor. I tucked my knees to jam his punch and stomp kicked him into the teak door. The woman screamed. The stall that would have been roomy for one and cozy for two, had become a deathtrap for three. I had to end this fight.

"Stay back," I shouted, more to the woman than the man. I

needed her out of my way and out of his path.

Instead, she attacked, fists hammering in a frenzy of ill-targeted strikes. The man clubbed her with his arm. She slid to the floor.

"Sonofabitch," I yelled, and kneed his balls so far into his gut they wouldn't drop for a week.

He howled in pain—not just from his impacted testicles but from the zipper that had ripped his exposed scrotum from stern to stem.

Justice was a bitch. And tonight, that bitch was me.

I left the would-be rapist to his suffering and helped the woman out of the stall just as a bouncer charged into the ladies' lounge, followed by a couple women and their dates. The distraught victim crumpled into the arms of her girlfriends. The bouncer headed for the stall. The dates pressed in to help. No one looked at me.

I had become invisible.

It was a ninja trick. I focused my thoughts on something neutral and devoid of emotion—in this case, listening to the distant music—and in the process, I wiped my energy slate clean. No one even glanced my way as I slipped into the corridor and back to the anonymity of the club.

Chapter Twenty-Four

Once I had distanced myself from the scene of the crime, I took a moment to relax and reflect. The night wasn't even over and I had already beat the crap out of someone.

At least it wasn't my date.

I snorted a laugh and hurried to the cocktail lounge. I needed to take care of my reason for coming to this unlucky club before the cops shut it down for the night.

The Siren Club lounge was a glittery underwater fantasy with shell couches, seahorse tables, and cocktail waitresses costumed in sequined bikini tops and long, fitted skirts split up the center and fanned at the bottom like a tail. I followed one of these mermaids to the waitress station at the end of the bar and asked for a glass of ice.

"You want some water with that?"

I shook my head and immediately regretted it. "No, thanks. Just the ice."

She watched as I removed a sizable cube and tucked it under my hair where a lump was forming.

"You okay? Do you want to sit down or something?"

"Nope. Just hot. The dance floor was crazy crowded. Is it usually this busy on a Tuesday night?"

She shrugged. "Popular club."

"Yeah, it's one of my favs. I just never come during the week."

She studied my face as if trying to remember when she might have seen me.

"I'm usually dancing. But I come into the lounge now and then, mostly on Saturday nights."

"Oh, that's why I haven't seen you. This room gets packed on weekends."

I laughed in agreement. "Tell me about it. Hey, is Mia around?"

"Nah, she's not working here anymore."

"Oh no. I was hoping to hear how things went with Freddy. She was so excited about him."

"She told you about Freddy?"

I nodded. "We bonded over an asshole customer."

"Oh. Well, that would do it."

I shook the water from my hand and pinched another ice cube from my glass. "So, do you know what happened with them? Mia and Freddy, I mean. I got sucked into the drama, but I don't know how it ended."

Her eyes brightened beneath her glittery false eyelashes. "Oh my God. You didn't see her on the news?"

"The news? Why was she on the news?"

She checked to make sure the bartender was out of hearing. "Mia accused one of our customers of trying to kill her."

"No."

"Yes. But don't worry, Mia's a drama queen. The guy didn't do it. She just wanted attention."

I let my jaw drop to express the appropriate amount of astonishment. "Unbelievable. But what happened with Freddy? I feel like my favorite nighttime soap got canceled."

She shrugged. "I don't know, but she had a sweet thing going. Did you know the guy helped her pay for that apartment? I mean, he wasn't model gorgeous or anything, just a regular guy. Older, of course, and shorter. But Mia's tall so she had to be used to that."

I leaned in. This was exactly the kind of dish I was hoping to hear. "She dumped him?"

"Don't know, but she was definitely looking to trade up."

I shook my head in wonder. "If I had a guy like Freddy, I'd take good care of him." I gave her a sly smile. "I don't suppose he still comes around?"

"Nah. Once they got together, he stopped coming. Buttoned-down type. I don't think this was his scene. His last name's Weintraub if you want to look him up. Oops, table five's almost done with their appletinis. Gotta go. Nice talking to you."

If nature abhorred a vacuum, then so did nightclubs, because the instant the waitress left, a cologne-stinking sleazeball filled her place. "Can I buy you a drink, sweetheart?" he said, running a sweaty hand up my arm.

Bad timing.

I snagged and bent three of his fingers and drove him toward the floor until his ear was level with my lips. "Did I ask you to touch me?"

He shook his head and struggled to hold himself between the pain I was inflicting and falling on his knees.

"Sorry. I couldn't hear you."

"No," he croaked. "You didn't ask."

I increased the pressure. "And have I done anything to suggest I would *want* you to touch me?" When he shook his head, I did the same. "No. I did not. So maybe you should keep your clammy hands to yourself, you think?"

"Sure. Yes!"

I guided him back to standing and released his fingers. "Now go play nice. And keep your hands to yourself."

The sudden relief from pain made him bold. "You fucking—"

I held up my palm. "You don't want to push me tonight. Trust me."

He must have seen the truth in my eyes because he backed off.

I tried not to feel smug. Then again, maybe I had earned my satisfaction. Not only had I taught this guy a lesson, I had damn near castrated a would-be rapist, and gotten the full name and physical description for Mia's mystery man. Not a bad night's work.

Now if I could just figure out what to do about Daniel Kwok.

Chapter Twenty-Five

My troubled mind wobbled like a top at the end of its spin, laden with heavy thoughts, memories, and remnants of a disturbing dream. I knew I should get out of bed, make some tea, focus on something constructive, but I couldn't let go of my grandmother's quilt.

Farmor—which meant father's mother in Norwegian—had grown up in a coal town in North Dakota where she had lived in a two-bedroom house with her immigrant parents and five siblings. As the eldest daughter, much of the work caring for family had fallen to her, so much so that she dropped out of school shortly after turning fourteen. When my life got hard, I often thought of the way my father's mother handled every bump in the road with steadying grace.

I hugged the quilt and rubbed the swirling flowers against my face. Farmor had stitched the Rosemaling designs by hand, using vermilion and pale grass-green threads to match the walls of my apartment. She had even sewn the printed patchwork steps that bordered the quilt into auspicious groups of three. With this one loving creation, Farmor had honored Ma's Chinese culture while still sharing her own Norwegian heritage. All to comfort me after Rose's passing.

Passing.

Farmor's euphemism couldn't erase the violence. Nor could it ease my guilt for choosing to make love to Pete instead of answering Rose's text.

So why hadn't I dreamt of Pete and Rose—or even Daniel? Any of them would have made more sense than dreaming about Tran.

As with my meditation in Sensei's home dojo, Tran had been standing at the top of a cliff, gazing at the horizon, while I watched from the rocky beach below. He had seemed so contained up there all alone, as if he didn't need anyone or anything. I didn't believe it. Everyone needed something. Everyone had secrets. My dream-self burned to know his.

As I climbed, the ascent grew increasingly more dangerous. Soon, I was clinging to the underside of a ledge over jagged rocks and pounding surf. It was crazy. Why was I risking my life? I had no answer; but still, I kept going, digging my fingers and toes into sharp fissures, struggling to reach the top of the cliff. As I climbed, my thoughts wandered, and I pictured a silly image of a tiny Tran, clad in classic ninja garb, creeping across my god shelf to steal the giant polished metal disk from my shrine. He had stolen my reflection! I needed to know why, but when I grabbed the edge of the cliff, the rocks gave way, and I fell.

I woke before I hit, so I had no way of knowing if the fall would have killed me in my dream. If it had, would I have woken? Or did people die in their sleep because they died in their dreams? And if so, could we resurrect ourselves by the same device? Every question bloomed another until my thoughts chased each other as fruitlessly as a pug chased its tail.

Once again, I hugged the quilt and thought of Farmor. *Stop your silliness, Lily. There's work to be done.* She was right, as always.

I blew her a kiss. "Mange takk, Farmor."

I only knew a handful of words in Norwegian, but "many

thanks, Grandmother" were probably the most important. Unless my grandfather had a say, in which case he would tell me the most important word in the Norwegian language was bestefar, which meant best father. Bestefar took great pleasure in listing all the ways a grandfather was superior to a father, somehow missing what those arguments implied about his own parenting skills. I used to laugh at the absurdity of some of the brags until one day, when I was seven and visiting my grandparents' farm in North Dakota, Baba assured me—out of Bestefar's hearing, of course—that all the brags were true. Then I laughed even harder.

The three of us had been sitting in front of the fireplace on a cold autumn night while Farmor tucked Rose into bed. Bestefar and been sitting in his easy chair, me on the ottoman, and Baba on the hearth, poking at the fire.

"You know, Dumpling," Baba had said, "the only reason Bestefar had children was so, one day, he could be a grandfather and finally say he was the best at something."

"Hogwash," said Bestefar, nudging me with his foot. He had piercing blue eyes instead of Baba's more soothing cornflower, and his silky blond hair had long since turned white with age. "Don't you listen to him. Your papa slipped in on a sandwich is all."

"I did no such thing. I worked my butt off for you, mucking out stalls every morning before daybreak."

"Ah, that weren't nothin," Bestefar said. "I drove a wagon to school across the snow."

I tugged at his socks. "Did it sink?"

Bestefar smiled. "Nah. It had skis. And a coal stove in da center to keep the barns—that's what we called the kiddies—from freezing off their noses. They would huddle on the side benches while I sat up at the front, peepin' through a slit just big enough for da horses' reins and my own eyeballs. It weren't like a prairie wagon, you understand, more like a big wooden box with a peaked roof so the snow would slump. But as the eldest, it was my job to drive it through da snow. Couldn't see nothin' but white most of the time, dontcha know. But I always got everyone to school."

Then he winked. "Heck, your papa rode to school in my Oldsmobile with the guldarn heater blastin.'"

Spit sprayed from Baba's mouth. "Blasting? Half the time you had the window open."

Bestefar shook his head sadly. "See what I mean, Lily? Soft as a sow's belly."

"Soft?" Baba grabbed my foot. "Your grandfather had me driving posts in zero below."

Bestefar clucked. "And they never were straight."

"While he lounged in that very chair, drinking Akevitt and beer!"

"I never *lounged*," said Bestefar, thrusting out an arthritic finger. "Never once."

Baba waved away the preposterous claim. "Don't let him fool you, Dumpling. He lounged plenty, especially after one of Farmor's meals."

"Well. That is true, dontcha know." Bestefar patted my knee with his giant hand. "Your farmor fixes the best lutefisk in North Dakota, by golly—plump and flaky, white sauce smothered in bacon—best honest-to-god fish you ever tasted. None of this steamed black bean nonsense your papa calls cooking."

"Hogwash! You've eaten at every Chinese restaurant within forty miles of Walcott and you know it."

"Only because your mamma makes me, which she wouldn't do if you visited more often and cooked it yourself." Bestefar held out his hands and smiled. "So you see, Lily, I am and will always be your best father. Remember that when trouble comes knockin.'"

I smiled at the memory.

If Bestefar knew the kind of trouble I got into these days, he'd tie me to that crooked post and let winter freeze some sense into me. Not that it would help—I was stubborner than Baba and Bestefar put together. Or so Farmor had told me on my first trip to their farm.

Rose was only four months old, and I had hovered over her like a mother hen. When I found out that a calf, younger than my sister, had to sleep in the barn, I refused to come back in the house without it. I could still see my grandparents standing in the barn doorway, shaking their heads as Baba made a bed out of hay.

"Uff da!" said Bestefar. "If she wants to freeze, then let her."

Baba and I spent the night shivering next to the perfectly contented calf. The next morning, I conceded that animals belonged in the barn and spent the day wrapped in one of Farmor's quilts, drinking hot chocolate in her toasty kitchen.

"You're the best mother ever," I had said, wanting her to feel as special as Bestefar.

"No, barnebarn. You already have the best mother there is. But I'm your farmor, your father's mother, and that's special enough for me."

Although I might not see my grandparents often, I carried them with me in ways I was only just beginning to realize.

I released the quilt, smoothed it over my bed, and paused to admire its beauty. Then I padded toward the dojo for my morning meditation. I had missed it two days in a row: first, because of my mad dash to the courtroom and then, because of Baba's surprise breakfast. I wasn't about to miss it again.

My mind was an undisciplined mess. If I didn't remedy the situation, I wouldn't be any use to anyone.

I bowed onto the mat, walked to the center of my dojo, and

knelt into Seiza no Kamae. I could have brought out a cushion and sat cross-legged. Or I could have used the low meditation bench. Both would have been easier on my knees once I passed the ten-minute mark. But I wasn't after comfort. I needed to concentrate, tap into a higher wisdom, and get some answers. For that, proper sitting posture felt best.

The kamidana drew my attention, as it was meant to do.

Kamidana was the Japanese word for god or spirit shelf that served as an altar for a household shrine. Mine took the form of an actual shelf mounted in the center of my dojo's vermilion wall. The Japanese called this place of honor kamiza, or top seat. However, like most words in that poetic language, the meaning differed depending on the context in which it was spoken or the kanji used to write it. One meaning referred to the top seat reserved for a special guest or the most prestigious person in the room. Another changed the meaning to spirit seat. In my dojo, I liked to think of both the kamiza above, which held my Shinto temple, and the kamiza below, where Sensei would sit if he ever visited my home. So far, he had declined this offer. *Your dojo is the place for personal discovery. Mine is to teach worthy students like you.*

I placed my palms together in gassho and vowed to do my best.

The kamidana featured a miniature temple with a shimenawa rope of rice straw hanging across the top to ward off evil spirits. Paper lightning bolts dangled to purify the space. I had arranged various offerings on the shelf—rice, salt, water, plants, candles, incense, and a cloth ofuda that was given to me by Sensei. In the center of the temple, I had perched a shintai.

A shintai was a temporary repository where spirits could visit and rest. It could take the form of small objects like a stone, a wand—or in my case—a small metal disk polished into a mirror to symbolize a stainless heart and a truthful reflection.

I focused on the mirror as I began my opening recitation.

"To receive human birth is difficult, now I have received it. To hear the enlightenment teachings is difficult, now and here I hear them. If I do not take the path of enlightenment in this lifetime, when again in the future will I ever have the chance to do so?"

I continued through this and other affirmations to declare my intent, purify my thoughts, and dedicate my practice to the betterment of the world. It was a tall order—one that required daily renewed commitment. Fortunately, the process brought its own reward. Even if I never found enlightenment, I could honestly say my life was improved by the attempt.

This appreciation of process over outcome curtailed my natural impatience—which in itself required constant and mindful attention.

I brought up the vision I had seen in my dream—Tran on the cliff, as unfathomable as the ocean that had captured his attention. *Why are you here?*

When he didn't respond, I began my climb. As in my dream, the route grew progressively more precarious until I found myself clinging like a gecko to the underside of a ledge over a jagged coast that now seemed three times farther than it should have been. This was ridiculous. The cliff had already proved unstable, and I had no reason to believe J Tran would break his silence even if I did manage to climb up to his perch. Yet having begun, I felt compelled to keep moving toward the goal.

I pulled myself onto the ledge, climbed to the next, and stopped. The conditions had changed. The cliff was now as smooth as glass and the rocky shore a thousand feet below.

I had become so fixated on my quest I hadn't noticed. Instead of stopping to reevaluate what I *thought* I knew and changing my

144

course accordingly, I had foolishly forged ahead, moving farther away from where I needed to be. This was the wisdom I needed to receive. And it didn't come from Sensei or Farmor or Bestefar; it came from somewhere deep inside of me.

Never become so attached to following the path that you cease to question whether you should still be on it.

Chapter Twenty-Six

Half an hour later, armed with a clear mind and a cup of Darjeeling, I searched the Internet for Freddy Weintraub and found links for a film producer whose forty-seven projects included *Enter the Dragon*, arguably *the* quintessential martial arts film, and *The Curse of the Dragon*, a documentary about Bruce Lee. Baba had given me both of the films for my thirteenth birthday because, by then, his "ninja daughter" had amassed a room full of Wushu trophies.

I laughed.

Baba had proudly supported me without ever realizing the accuracy of his words.

No one did.

Performing a Chinese martial art with graceful moves and beautiful silks was not the same as training in the dirt with a strange Japanese man. I hadn't understood the intricacies of the difference, but I had known that much. So I practiced Wushu in the training hall in full view of my family and friends, and learned Ninjutsu in the park when everyone thought I was at the library.

Until the night Rose died.

After that, I had no room in my heart for silks and trophies. From that moment forward, I fought for keeps.

I sipped my tea and focused my thoughts on Mia's Freddy.

I found him on page five beneath more articles about *Enter the Dragon*, reviews for the Freddy Krueger slasher movies, two obituaries, and a legal notice for a pedophile podiatrist.

Fredrick A. Weintraub worked as a planning supervisor for the LA County Metropolitan Transit Authority, known more simply as Metro.

"I'll be damned."

I glanced at the map pinned to my office wall and wondered if I could finagle a lifetime bus and rail pass out of Mia's secret lover.

Feeling more optimistic about my day, I went back to reading about Freddy. He graduated from UC Irvine and listed only one previous employment position, also at Metro. Aside from that, his profile was dismally bare. To his credit, he had included a photo. But since he had cropped it from a group of tall people, it made him look like a hobbit in the company of elves. The comparison was further exasperated by his plump face, round spectacles, squinty eyes, tiny teeth, and a muffler of dark hair that wrapped around a shiny dome.

The Siren Club waitress had said he was older and shorter than Mia with average buttoned-down looks. This had to be the guy.

Metro's website—with which I was exceedingly familiar—provided a wealth of information. Freddy served on the Planning and Programming Committee, which proposed new projects, and the Technical Advisory Committee, which evaluated those projects and made recommendations to the Metro Board of Directors. From what I could tell, the board concurred with just about everything TAC recommended, which wasn't surprising since the committee was composed predominantly by city mayors and council members.

Mia's secret lover ran with some political bigwigs. However, that didn't make Freddy powerful or sinister enough to know someone like Tran. I checked social media to gain insights on his personal life. Freddy wasn't on any of the platforms; however, I did find a person on Facebook who habitually mentioned his name and shared articles about L.A. mass transit—his wife.

Unlike her husband, Shannon Weintraub had a strong social media presence. She liked to share recipes, articles about parenting, photos of their children, cat videos—lots of cat videos—and news articles about Freddy. Shannon also posted anything to do with running. She had a gaunt face, softened by curly brown hair, and a possibly anorexic figure she covered in gypsy dresses and sweaters. Her photo gallery documented the growth of their nine-year-old daughter, Esther, whose name and age had been iced on a birthday cake, and their infant son, who, according to the caption, had been a "long-awaited blessing from God."

Obsessive tendencies, possible anorexia, and fertility issues—people shared the most astounding secrets through online photos.

How about the name of their synagogue, etched above the entrance? Or their home's proximity to The Grove—evidenced by stroller trips to nearby Pan Pacific Park? Or worst of all, their address? Yes, Shannon had actually posted a high resolution shot of her and Freddy standing in front of their house with the numbers 115 pinned to the wall.

I wished I could say it was unbelievable, but I corrected this type of security blunder all the time.

I had one client who had actually posed on the hood of her car with both her license plate and the name of her apartment building in the shot. And in case a potential stalker had missed the invitation, she had used the picture as her profile photo on every one of her social media accounts. It never occurred to her how a predator might use what he saw against her.

Hannibal Lecter was right: we covet what we see.

Chapter Twenty-Seven

I had seventy minutes to find Freddy's house, spy on him before he left for his Metro meeting, and get the car back to our restaurant in time for lunch deliveries. Since I had numbers but no street name, finding his house required a systematic approach.

There were several neighborhoods within jogging stroller distance of Pan Pacific Park. I concentrated on the thirty-two blocks to the east. Why? Because the street that bisected this neighborhood separated the northern addresses from the southern. This meant that each of the sixteen avenues running parallel to the park had two houses with the same address—doubling my chances for success.

Even so, it took me thirty precious minutes to find Freddy's house on the south side of Martel, just as it looked in Shannon's Facebook photo—brick path, white stucco, orange tile roof, the distinctive potted camellia by the door, and, of course, the numbers 115 pinned diagonally to the wall.

I parked a few houses down and hurried across the street toward the sound of a woman yelling. If morning arguments were a regular occurrence at the Weintraub household, I pitied their neighbors.

I jogged up their driveway to the back of the house where I could see into their bedroom window—yet another security blunder—and saw Shannon Weintraub in all her entitled glory.

"You couldn't be bothered to take Esther to school. So now I'm going to be late for my jogging date in the park, which will make me late for Jacob's play date at Susan's house, which will make me late to put him down for his nap, which means I'll be up all night. Again. So find your own shirt." She grabbed her running shoes and left the room, raising her voice as she went out of sight. "It's either in the hamper or hanging in your closet. My money is on the closet."

While Shannon had on layers of loose-fitting yoga clothes similar to those I had seen in her park photos, Freddy was still in the process of dressing for work. Not a pretty sight. His belt dangled from un-zipped trousers, displaying a muffin top layer of bulging white flab.

"Did you hear me?" Shannon called from the other room.

He'd heard her, all right—his shoulders had tensed to his ears—he just didn't want to answer.

Shannon appeared in the doorway, knuckles braced on hips, glaring as he rifled through the dresser. "Why would I put your shirt in a drawer? I told you to look in the closet."

Freddy ignored her and retrieved a folded shirt, still wrapped in plastic.

"You can't wear that, Fred. It's going to have creases all over it."

He wrestled with the package, flab quivering in the effort.

"Oh, for goodness sake." Shannon stormed to the closet and slid open the door, displaying a tidy row of shirts. "There. Now, if you can manage, I have to get Jacob ready for the park."

Freddy waited until she walked out of the room, then, with unexpected vehemence, ripped open the plastic. The shirt fell to the floor. "Shit."

He picked up the shirt and stuffed it back in the drawer. "Play dates and naps," he muttered. "I'm making a difference, dammit."

Shannon appeared in the doorway with their wiggling son in her arms. "Of course you are. Which is why you need a *pressed* shirt."

Freddy shoved in the drawer and trudged to the closet like a petulant child. "The Copper Line's going to cross social and economic borders from Chinatown all the way to Cerritos. It's a big deal."

I leaned in. The Copper Line? I knew about that. I had its proposed path marked on the Metro map hanging on my wall.

"I thought it was going to Huntington Park," Shannon said, more from rote than any real interest.

Freddy yanked a shirt from the closet. "That's just the first stage. Don't you realize how important this is? How important *I* am?"

"Of course I do. I brag about you all the time." Her tone sounded was lighter now that Jacob was strapped in his jogging stroller and ready to go.

Freddy looked unconvinced. "To your friends, maybe."

"Well, who else am I going to brag to, silly? Strangers?" She blew him a kiss. "Gotta go. See you tonight."

Freddy slumped on the bed. I turned away. If I saw his muffin top jiggle again, I'd be off my feed for a month. Besides, what else was there to learn? Freddy brought home the bacon. Shannon ran the house. Freddy was frustrated. Shannon treated him like a child. So what? Freddy might be a tad passive-aggressive, but enough to hire someone like J Tran?

Unlikely.

Although, he had made a nice life for himself—pretty wife, pretty home, pretty kids. What if Mia had threatened to ruin it? Would hiring an enforcer feel less confrontational than having it out with his wife or mistress? Maybe.

I headed for the street in time to see Shannon jogging around the corner toward Pan Pacific Park. If I didn't dawdle, I'd make it across town and back to our restaurant with ten minutes to spare. Instead, I ducked behind a bush.

Freddy had a visitor.

Mia Mikkelsen marched up the brick path with her breasts high, waist cinched, and lace swishing against her long, tanned legs. She had come ready for battle, and after ringing the doorbell, took great care to position both her weapons for maximum effect. Unfortunately for her, when Freddy opened the door, those weapons shot blanks.

"What are you doing here?" he said, rushing past her to check the street. He had finished dressing and looked buttoned down, zipped up, and belted for action. "Do you have any idea the trouble you could cause? What if someone sees you?" Questions tumbled out of his mouth while his eyes darted everywhere but at Mia. "You have to go." He tried to turn her around.

Mia was half a foot taller and probably weighed as much as he did. She wasn't going anywhere. "You didn't show up. I stood on that corner for an hour and you never showed up." Then she burst into tears.

Freddy sagged, head hanging, belly pushing against the buttons of his pressed pool-blue shirt. "I'm sorry. I meant to. But Shannon needed groceries and—wait a minute. How do you know where I live?"

Mia shrugged and looked suitably guilty.

"You followed me? You can't do this. We've talked about it. *I* come to *you*. Why do you think I help with your rent? This isn't right. It isn't safe. You have to go. Now."

He was so focused on Mia that he didn't see Shannon come

back around the corner. But Shannon sure saw him.

As Freddy continued to plead with Mia to go, I kept my eyes on his wife. I wanted to see how long it would take her to notice her husband arguing with a shapely blond and what she would do about it when she did. I didn't have to wait long.

Shannon stopped, took in the scene taking place in her driveway, then rolled the stroller into the street behind a parked car. Meanwhile, Mia's voice escalated with her tears.

"Promise me you'll come by this afternoon."

"I can't. I can't do this anymore."

"But I'm scared."

"Then move. Or find a man who can protect you. I have a family."

Without waiting to hear Mia's response, Freddy marched back into the house and slammed the door. Mia froze. Her affair had ended. The gravy train had left the station. The young blonde bombshell had gotten dumped by the middle-aged, balding civil servant.

Ouch.

While I felt bad for Mia, I hadn't signed on to mend her broken heart. I needed to know if this breakup made her safer or more vulnerable to physical attack. For that, I needed to know who, why, and even *if* someone had hired J Tran.

As I considered the possibilities, Shannon pushed the stroller out from behind the parked car. Even from this distance, I saw her smile.

Chapter Twenty-Eight

By the time I entered our restaurant kitchen, Baba's temper was as hot as his wok.

"Finally," he said, dumping the seared scallops onto a platter.

I checked the time: eight minutes late. But a glance at DeAndre packing the take-out box with fortune cookies, napkins, and chopsticks, told me my tardiness hadn't stalled any deliveries. Why was my ever-patient father damn near tapping his foot?

"The keys, Lily? We have a delivery for Sony."

Sony Pictures wasn't the big deal—we sent multiple orders to them every day. The big deal was that he had called me Lily instead of Dumpling. Baba had a typically Taurean disposition—even tempered and slow to burn—so if he was snapping at me now, it probably meant he had been worrying about something for a while.

"Sorry, Baba."

As soon as I dropped the keys in his outstretched hand, he tossed them to DeAndre, who looked far too pleased with himself. The eighteen-year-old lived with his mom in West Adams, a mostly Latino and African-American community adjacent to Culver City. DeAndre was a mixture of both. His dream was to one day own his own restaurant. Baba provided as many hours busing tables and delivering orders as the kid could handle and answered every one of his endless stream of questions.

"If Lily hadn't made it back in time, could I have borrowed her bike?" DeAndre asked.

I smacked his arm. "Not if you like living."

Baba ignored me and added a few extra fortune cookies to the box. "You would have borrowed my car, DeAndre. But you wouldn't have needed it. Lily's only late for family occasions."

I stole a cookie for myself and pondered this last statement.

If Baba was upset about last night, I wasn't about to ask.

I waved the cookie wrapper in DeAndre's direction. "If that's for Sidney's crew, you better get going. They get testy when they're kept waiting."

DeAndre nodded in Baba's direction. "They're not the only ones."

I glanced over at Baba in time to see him squirt a long stream of oil into the wok. It sizzled like a swarm of angry bees. Garlic-scented steam wafted up to the fan. My selfish stomach ignored the need for caution and growled.

"There's chow fun on the counter if you're hungry," said Baba as he dumped a metal tin full of chopped mushrooms into the hot pan, added a few more ingredients, and shoved them around the slopes of the wok with a wooden paddle. Black beans, scallions, and fish. My stomach responded even more loudly this time.

"You made it for me?"

He gave me a look that could have meant anything or nothing. Then he poured a generous amount of rice wine in the wok, followed by a touch of cornstarch, chili paste, and fish stock. The erupting steam hid his expression. He used the wooden paddle to point in the general direction of the prep counter.

"Table three thought they were ordering—what did they call it, Lee?"

Baba's sous-chef looked up from the roasted duck sprawled across his chopping block. "Skinny noodles," he said, then cleaved it in half with a kitchen axe. A server, timing his moment carefully, snatched the order of pork lo mein off the counter and whisked out to the dining room.

I motioned toward the bowl of my favorite fat noodles, dry-fried with strips of beef, bean sprouts, and soy. "I take it that was for them?"

Lee nodded and muttered in Mandarin, not Shanghainese, so I'd be sure to understand, "Yúchǔn de báirén."

I snorted. "Stupid white men, huh?"

He waved one of his hands. "Chow fun better. I know. I fix." He threw a pair of long cooking chopsticks straight at my face. I snatched them out of the air. Lee grinned and returned to chopping duck.

The sinewy chef had a suspicious habit of throwing things at me. After a particularly close call with a swinging pot, I asked him if he knew Sensei. He had grinned and cackled something about senility and carelessness, which I found amusing since Lee was neither old nor clumsy.

I couldn't imagine how a Chinese cook would know a Japanese ninja, but I wouldn't have put it passed my teacher to recruit someone at the restaurant just to spite me. As Sensei was fond of saying, every moment presented an opportunity to train.

Lee jabbed his kitchen axe toward the bowl of chow fun. "You eat. No waste."

"Yes, Uncle."

Lee Chang wasn't really my uncle, but he'd been with my father from the start, and since it was the Chinese way to call friends who became family—or any older person to whom you wanted to show respect—"Auntie" or "Uncle", that's what I had always called

156

him. In the early days, people had assumed Uncle was the Wong of Wong's Hong Kong Inn because he looked exactly the way the owner-chef of a Chinese restaurant should look—face weathered from heat and steam, burn scars on his arms, crotchety demeanor, and, above all, Chinese.

No one dreamed the restaurant belonged to Baba—let alone that a Caucasian could be responsible for authentic Hong Kong recipes. Even the Chinese community up in Arcadia had been fooled by Baba's cooking. How excited they had been to eat their precious Phoenix Talons Hong Kong style—deep fried, steamed, and then simmered with black fermented beans, star anise, and ginger. I thought their heads would explode when they'd found out a North Dakota Norwegian had prepared it. But they still sucked and chewed every last chicken foot until only the hardest bits of cartilage remained to spit back on the plate.

Baba eyed me suspiciously as he plated the black bean sole he had just sautéed. "Did you train yesterday?"

"Yeah. Why do you ask?"

He glanced at my wrists and shrugged. The bruises on my wrists had ripened. If I had crossed them together, the marks would have formed a purple rope around my wrists. "Never mind," he said. "Eat the noodles before they get cold. And take a moon-cake while you're at it. You'll need your strength for the day ahead."

What did that mean?

I started to ask then decided to heed Bestefar's favorite saying: Don't borrow trouble.

Besides, I had a love triangle to consider.

Had Mia's desperation turned her into a homewrecker? Had Freddy hired Tran to scare her away? And what about Shannon? What kind of woman reacted so calmly to catching her husband in front of her own house with a voluptuous young blond? Didn't she care? Or was she vindictive enough to terrorize her husband's mistress?

Before I could come to any conclusions, a car door slammed—inside the kitchen.

"What was that?" asked Baba, jabbing his wok spoon at the phone I had left on the counter. The screen had lit up with a map of Hollywood: Tran's GPS tracker had triggered an alarm.

Chapter Twenty-Nine

For the sake of speed, I called for a ride. My driver this afternoon was an athletic redhead named Kansas who worked as an intern for an architectural firm and had an uncanny resemblance to Joseph Gordon-Levitt, the star of one of my favorite box office bombs about a thrill-seeking bike messenger in New York.

"Have you seen *Premium Rush*?"

The randomness of my question threw her for all of two seconds before she smiled. "Were you the other one?"

I unstrapped the Merida from her car's bike rack and glanced at the entrance to the entertainment complex. The Hollywood and Highland's design drew from the Babylon set of DW Griffith's 1916 epic film, *Intolerance*, and had a grand staircase leading to a coliseum of trendy shops, mammoth slab archways etched with hieroglyphs and griffins, and stone pachyderms perched atop the towering pillars.

"You know, if they had set the story in Los Angeles," I said, "they could have raced across the Hollywood Walk of Fame, up those stairs, and skidded through the plaza's sidewalk fountain."

Kansas chuckled. "And straight to the casting couch."

The fiberglass daybed had sat at the end of The Road to Hollywood—a mosaic path with anonymous quotes from Hollywood celebrities about how they got their start in the business. The artist had ended the path with a sobering, poignant, and, at the time, amusing symbol.

"Yeah," I said. "The entertainment industry isn't quite as entertaining as it used to be."

"No shit."

We shared a laugh. I would have gladly hung out with Kansas, whose taste in movies, sense of humor, and social opinions clearly gelled with my own. However, since Tran had already been at the Hollywood and Highland for fifty minutes, I needed to hurry. Once I secured my bike and helmet, I bolted through the coliseum like a shopper on Christmas Eve.

I found Tran on the top level in a Japanese restaurant, sitting near the back of the sushi bar. I walked past him and rounded the corner, then took the last seat at the bar, kitty-corner from Tran, against the wall by the emergency exit. From there, I could watch him diagonally across the sushi station and escape quickly if things went south.

I ordered a yellowtail roll, huddled over my phone, and pretended to text while Tran ate a plate of octopus sushi and salmon roe. Exotic choices. Anyone who looked the way he did, ate tako and ikura, and knew how to write in Korean, must have some sort of Asian in the mix. Hopefully not from Hong Kong. Tran and I already shared a fondness for knives, sushi, and secrecy; Hong Kong kinship would put me over the edge.

"You should try this," he said, shaking me from my reverie and making me realize, much to my dismay, that I had been staring.

So much for ninja surveillance.

I forced a smile as he raised his seaweed-wrapped sushi and angled it to display the bright orange salmon eggs. "I've eaten ikura many times, thank you." I meant it to sound condescending, but he took it as acceptance and requested an order for me. "That wasn't necessary."

"Not for you, maybe. But I couldn't eat this in good conscience while watching you eat *that*."

I scoffed. "Really? Because you don't strike me as someone plagued by his conscience."

"What makes you say that?"

"Gosh, I don't know." I nodded toward the sushi chef preparing me food I had not requested. "Maybe because you do whatever you like?"

I picked up my phone and resumed typing. Maybe if I ignored him, he'd leave me alone.

"Who are you texting so furiously?"

I set down the phone and popped a segment of yellowtail roll in my mouth. Once again, he had disrupted my center. I needed a moment to calm my mind and keep from saying anything foolish. Instead, I swallowed the rice and fixed him with a withering glare. "If I told you, I'd have to kill you."

Tran raised a peaked brow. "That would be interesting."

My pulse raced. *Interesting?*

Sensei had warned me not to use obvious tactics against sophisticated opponents. What was I doing sparring with Tran? I didn't know what it was about this guy that scrambled my brain, but I needed to get over it quick. Because if I kept messing up, Tran would do a lot worse than slam me on a mat. So when the chef placed the ikura in front of me, I lifted the pretty package with my chopsticks, gave Tran an insincere grin of thanks, and popped the entire piece in my mouth.

I nearly choked; not from the taste—I loved ikura—but from the volume of rice, nori, and exploding fish eggs. One of these days, I was going to ask Sensei how women in Japan dealt with this issue. Smaller pieces? Secret chewing techniques? Whatever it was,

I wanted to know. Meanwhile, as I gagged behind a napkin, Tran pressed his advantage.

"My name's J. What's yours?"

"K."

The lie blurted from my lips, like a call and response. Tran had used honesty as a ploy to prompt the same from me, but I hadn't fallen for it. The kunoichi was back in control.

"You're not going to tell me, are you?" asked Tran.

"Already did."

Tran ignored the lie. "Then how about dinner?"

Excuse me?

Had I dropped into an alternate universe where killers shot dinner invitations instead of bullets?

"Look. I'm flattered and all, but I don't date guys like you."

His head tipped with interest. "And who are guys like me?"

"Muddled culture, narcissistic ideology, fluid sense of morality. How am I doing?"

He laughed—a deep throaty sound that invaded my body and vibrated my bones.

I reached for my tea as a business card sailed onto my plate.

"Give me a call if you change your mind."

I checked the card—gray on black, name and phone, no address.

When I looked up, Tran was halfway to the door.

The woman sitting next to me smiled. "You should call. He's *really* good looking."

"Yeah, I don't think I will. But it doesn't hurt to keep the card, right?"

I left her giggling and asked for my check, but Tran had already taken care of it. This had been a monumental mistake. I never should have come inside. I never should have sat at the sushi bar. *And I definitely should never have gotten into a pissing contest with a psychopath.*

Or was he?

After watching Tran dispatch the Koreans, I had assumed he didn't feel empathy or remorse. Based on his apartment's stark furnishings, I had also assumed he was anti-social. But not only had Tran drawn me into conversation when he could have easily ignored me, he had kept talking. Why go to the effort if he didn't, on some level, crave positive human interaction?

Unless it wasn't positive at all.

Psychopaths lived to mess with people's minds. Sparring with me could have been a way to work off the meal and clear his palate.

It reminded me of Bestefar's cat. The tabby loved to pin mice with one paw while clawing them with the other. Then she'd let them go to hunt again. With each catch and release, the mice became more frantic, more disabled. When I tried to stop her, Bestefar had stilled my hand.

"No, Lily. The cat has her way, and you need to let her have it."

"But it's mean," I had cried.

"Not to her."

"But—"

"Nope. The cat does us a service. It's not for us to tell her how to do it."

Was Tran like Bestefar's cat? If so, he was in for quite a surprise if he thought I was the mouse.

Chapter Thirty

I leaned on the railing and glowered at the kids below as they ran half naked through the plaza fountain. Their carefree joy darkened my already foul mood.

Served me right.

Tran had noticed me. There'd be no slipping under his radar now.

I pulled out my phone and gazed at all the pretty little icons. One, in particular, drew my attention—the floating circle with Daniel's smiling face.

I opened his texts.

Daniel: *I had a great time last night.*

Daniel: *There's another restaurant I think you'd love. Friday night?*

Daniel: *No pressure.*

Daniel: *PS: You're a terrific dancer!*

Four texts in forty minutes? Guess I was on someone's mind.

I thought of the sensual grace of Daniel's body and the surge of heat it had caused in me on that dance floor, and just like that, he was on my mind, as well.

Me: *Thanks. You're no slouch, either!*

Daniel: *Hey! Great to hear from you.*

Wow. Immediate response. Had he been holding his phone

waiting for my text?

Daniel: *And thanks. Dancing was fun. We should do it again sometime.*

It was. But did I want that kind of fun in my life? Look how easily Daniel had diverted my attention. I couldn't afford the distraction, not with so many women suffering and in need of protection. They had to take priority.

Daniel: *You still there?*

Me: *Yep.*

Daniel: *Friday? We don't have to dance.* (wink emoji)

Had we entered the emoji stage already?

Me: *Can I get back to you tomorrow?* I had no idea what I'd be doing in two minutes let alone in two nights.

Daniel: *Of course!*

Me: *Cool. TTYL*

Daniel: (thumbs up emoji)

I slid Daniel's smiling face off the edge of my screen. Dinner and a movie? It sounded unbelievably normal. Like something I would have done in another life.

Something I would have done before losing Rose.

A left swipe brought up boxes of top headlines in politics, entertainment, travel, international, and local news. The teaser in the local news box showed a photo of the Hollywood and Highland Metro Station. I clicked it to see what newsworthy event might have taken place during my disastrous lunch with Tran.

Two hours earlier, the vice mayor from Huntington Park had been interviewed in the subway station beneath me. She wanted a subway in her city and thought the Hollywood and Highland station, with its stylized red metal palm trees and film reel ceilings, did an exemplary job of conveying community culture.

"Huh."

Earlier this morning, Freddy had told Shannon that the first stage of the new Copper Line would go through Huntington Park. Was this the same Metro line the vice mayor wanted? I studied her overly-cheery face, as if it might answer my question, and noticed someone lurking behind her. It was a man, standing behind a pillar. All I could see of him was the sleeve of a black T-shirt stretched over a muscled shoulder and a well-defined bicep in the exact shade of Tran.

"Well, I'll be damned."

Tran had driven his car, so I knew he wasn't waiting for a train. Had he come to the Hollywood and Highland to spy on the vice mayor? But if so, why would he care?

I stashed my phone and headed for the escalator. While I didn't have an answer, I knew where I might find one.

Eleven stops on the Red Line took me downtown to Union Station, the largest railroad passenger terminal west of Chicago. Union Station serviced over one hundred thousand travelers a day, and yet, LA's traffic problems were second only to our nation's capital. Go figure.

I blamed Hollywood.

Almost every film or television program shot in Los Angeles glamorized cars and depicted our mass transit as rolling motels for the homeless—not that this wasn't true, especially on rainy nights. It just wasn't the whole story. There was a more legitimate reason why our mass transit scored low with public perception: it was a huge pain in the butt.

In a sprawling county like Los Angeles, a single commute could involve multiple transfers, on both trains and buses, and still leave the commuter miles from their destination. Unless they owned a bike. If a commuter were willing to sweat, they could bypass transfers and cut their time in half.

So why did the vice mayor want a new rail line through her city? Because most people did not bike, and like the song said, nobody walked in LA.

Such were my thoughts when a hand brushed against my thigh.

At first, I thought it was a mistake. After all, it was a crowded subway, and since I traveled with my bike, I was forced to stand in the open section opposite the door. Maybe the guy next to me had lost his balance and innocently brushed up against me. Except his palm had crept onto my butt, and the guy had a big ol' grin on his face.

I brushed off his hand, captured his fingers, and raised him onto his toes with a painful Take Ori wrist lock. With the sleazeball at the Siren Club, I had wrenched the fingers back, driving him to his knees. With this guy, I tucked them under and rose him toward the ceiling. Different direction, same result.

I captured his other hand for good measure and cocked my ear toward his mouth. "I didn't catch that. What did you say?"

"Let go of my fucking wrist, you bitch."

I tightened the lock ever so slightly, and asked again.

This time he answered. "I'm sorry, alright? Now let me go." He was having a hard time keeping his voice quiet and under control.

"You sure you're sorry? Because I'm not feeling it." I tightened the lock. "Are *you*?"

Sweat beaded on his forehead. "Yes. I'm feeling it."

"Good." I eased up on the lock but didn't release him. "Because I want you to remember this the next time you get the urge to cop a feel." I thought of the would-be rapist at the Siren Club, I thought of Harvey Weinstein, and I thought of every other sexual-harassing sleazebag in the city. Then I cranked his wrist to make sure he was listening. "Women were not put on this Earth for scum like you to paw."

When he grunted his understanding, I released the lock and watched as he backed away. Lesson in manners delivered.

TORI ELDRIDGE

Chapter Thirty-One

The flow of commuters led me up the stairs to a spacious terminal, where sunlight from above dappled the mosaic sunburst below. Glass doors led to an Aztec-inspired transit plaza, designed to resemble an oasis surrounded by a river of buses, taxis, and cars. I was headed to Metro headquarters, the tan tower at the end of the terracotta-paved road, but first I needed to adjust my appearance.

I always traveled with a change of clothes in my backpack. Today, I had the perfect dress. Its loose style fit easily over my tank top—so I didn't need somewhere to change—and its length fell well below my bike shorts. The dark eggplant color would have hidden any patterns and colors underneath as would the high neck with long sleeves if I had been wearing a thermal. Best of all, it rolled to the size of a cigar and fit into the pocket of my backpack. I should have worn it to dinner with Ma.

To complete the transformation, I exchanged my running shoes for a pair of flats, wound my hair into a bun, and pinned it with my trusty wooden spike. I wasn't expecting any trouble, but it didn't hurt to be prepared. As an added touch, I wrapped my forehead with a purple and black batik scarf and tied it behind my neck. This gave my outfit a more polished look and drew focus like a magnet.

Wear an uncommon article of clothing and everybody notices

it. Wear it well and they rarely remember anything else.

Once in the lobby, I smiled at the woman behind the reception desk and introduced myself cheerfully and professionally. "Hi. My name is Trisha. I'm doing a college report on—"

She held up a finger as she listened on the phone. "I'm sorry to hear that, ma'am, but there really isn't anything I can do about a late train." She shook her head as she spoke, and the braids that jutted from the top of her red and gold hair-wrap jiggled like a spray of wires. "Well, why don't you submit a complaint through our website. Yes, ma'am. It's on the same page as the train schedule. That's right. You have a nice day now."

The receptionist chuckled as she hung up the phone and smiled at me. "There isn't really a comment form on that page, but I'd bet you a dollar she's never looked at that schedule. Now, what can I do for you?"

"My name's Trisha, and I'm—"

"Writing a college report. Got it. And what do you need from me, honey? Because we have all sorts of information on our website."

"Oh, I've seen it. It's a beautiful site. I've even downloaded the app."

"Good for you."

I leaned closer. "But I was hoping to interview someone. You know, someone official? It would give my report more legitimacy." I gave her a big smile and waited to see if the good student routine would work. When she didn't respond, I stood up straight and tried a more professional approach. "I'm graduating this winter with a degree in urban planning, and I'd really like to work for Metro. Maybe start with an internship."

That got her attention.

"You know, honey, I wish more young people would understand the value of starting at the bottom and working their way up. A college degree isn't a fast pass at Disneyland. You can't just leapfrog over hardworking people just because you got yourself a neat little certificate with your name on it."

"So true. That's why I've read everything I can find online, even the meeting agendas. Especially the ones with Mr. Weintraub."

"You know Mr. Weintraub?"

"The planning supervisor? Anyone interested in a career with Metro should know about him."

She nodded so emphatically it sent her braids into a bobbing frenzy.

"You know something? You're a smart cookie. Let me see what I can do for you."

"Thank you." I stepped away to give her some privacy. People worked harder when they felt valued and respected—that's what Baba always told me—and that applied doubly to people who worked for the government.

In less than a minute, she waved me back to her desk with a grin and a wink. "Guess what I got for you."

Five minutes later, I was walking into Freddy Weintraub's office.

His pressed shirt had acquired some wrinkles and sweat stains since I had seen it this morning, but other than that, his appearance had improved considerably. In his own domain, Freddy sparkled with energy and confidence.

"So what can I do for you, Miss…?"

"Stevens. Trisha Stevens. I'm writing a paper on the future of LA's mass transit, and I read that Metro might be building a new line. Could you could explain a bit about that process?"

Freddy sat a little straighter and puffed out his chest. "I'd be happy to. In fact, you caught me at a good time. We discussed this very project in our PPC meeting this morning."

"That's the Planning and Programming Committee, right?"

"Yes. Good for you, young lady. Anyway, we're all very excited about the Copper Line since it will cross social, racial, and economic borders from Chinatown down and across through Cerritos."

I nodded approvingly. He had given a similar hype to Shannon.

"Of course, the line is too long to build all at once, almost forty-five miles, so we'll build it in sections. The first will go from Union Station to the southern border of Huntington Park, serving the needs of several lower income communities, then—"

"Wait. Doesn't the Blue Line already run near there?"

Freddy tightened his grin. "It does, but there's a great need for public transportation in the Gateway Cities." His voice sounded pinched. "Besides, it's already paid for through Measure R. Once the Technical Advisory Committee approves, we can acquire the necessary properties for subway stations and street-level staging areas. Then we'll start construction."

"You make it sound so simple. But what if the property owners don't want to sell?"

"Then the state would force the sale through eminent domain." He waved his hands to dispel any wrong impression he might have given. "The property owner still gets paid according to fair market value, you understand. It's all quite equitable. All the nearby properties will benefit. Greater accessibility means higher profits."

I kept my expression blank. Higher profits for whom? The old sellers or the new buyers? It seemed to me there were lots of opportunities for someone with inside information and a fluid sense of integrity to score some bucks. "Have you made the offers yet?" I asked.

He shook his head. "TAC still has to vote."

"The Technical Advisory Committee?"

"Yes. But I expect it to go through." He forced another grin.

"You don't seem pleased."

"Sure I am. It has to be done. It's the right thing to do."

"To cross social and economic borders?" I prompted, to which he sighed with relief.

"Exactly."

I backed off and let him ramble about how the proposed Copper Line would travel down Santa Fe Avenue then veer southeast through retail-oriented Cerritos—and all the other nuances he felt important to share. Then, when his enthusiasm had finally exhausted, I put away my pen and offered my hand. "Thank you, Mr. Weintraub. You've given me a much better understanding of what's really going on."

Chapter Thirty-Two

With my eggplant dress stored in my pack and my limbs free to move again, I tore through downtown gridlock. Traffic didn't get much worse than four o'clock on Spring Street, but eleven miles on a bike felt the same to me whether traffic flowed or clogged.

I weaved through honks and hip hop beats, spicy carnations wafting from the nearby flower district, and the mingled stench of urine and exhaust—a sensory overload I was glad to escape. Only when the streets had widened and the buildings lowered did I begin to chew over the day.

"Chew over" was another of Bestefar's sayings. It would please him to know I used it, although sexy, exotic killers and eminent domain weren't the cud he would have chosen for me to chew. He'd also liked to say that a farmer had to make do with the crops God granted him. Was it my fault God had given me a mixed bag of seeds? Yeah. It kinda was.

I stood on the pedals, legs churning with the added force of my weight, and cut through the intersection as yellow turned to red.

That mixed bag of seeds included two dead wannabe Korean gangsters. Wannabe anythings bugged the heck out of me. Not that I had an issue with deception. How could I? It was the unwillingness to pay the price that offended me. If people didn't like who they were, they should put in the work and change. Without a cost, status meant nothing.

I sped through another yellow light.

What was so special about this Copper Line, and why did everyone I met seem connected to the thing? What was there to hide that would make Planning Supervisor Freddy Weintraub brag, justify, then defend himself to an insignificant college student like Trisha Stevens? And did Freddy really believe the Copper Line was "the right thing to do"?

I braked to avoid a collision then squeezed between bumpers to ride along the curb.

My gut told me if I figured out the Metro mystery, I'd know why Mia had been attacked.

It seemed likely that some corrupt entity had hired Tran to terrorize Mia, but I had a hard time believing that entity could be Freddy. While a planning supervisor had inside information, from what I had seen, Freddy didn't have the money or the viciousness to capitalize on what he knew. No. It was far more likely that Freddy was a victim.

But why would anyone care enough about him to threaten his mistress?

As Metro's planning supervisor, he probably could have pushed the Copper Line through the Planning and Programming Committee but not through TAC. The Technical Advisory Committee had thirty voting members. Swaying Freddy, no matter how influential he might be, wouldn't have made enough of a difference.

Unless he was just one among several key people getting pressured to push the Copper Line forward.

My phone played a ringtone I never ignored. I tapped my Bluetooth. "What's up, Aleisha?"

"Are you anywhere near Leimert Park?"

"I could be. Why?"

"Yolanda Burch just called. Benny's acting up again, and she's scared."

"Did you tell her to get out of there?"

"Of course I did. But you know how she is. I don't think she'll leave."

"Yeah, probably not. What's the address, again?"

"On Exposition, where it forks into Rodeo Road."

"Oh yeah, the gray building on the right."

"That's the one."

"Okay, I'll swing by and check on her."

"Thanks, Lily. And you be careful now."

I ended the call, ducked low on my handlebars, and swerved to the wrong side of Jefferson so I could jump the curb onto Trousdale Parkway—the main pedestrian/bike thoroughfare through USC campus. Then I followed the yellowish brick road to Exposition Boulevard and raced to the Rodeo Road fork. A couple blocks away, I heard a gunshot.

I sped to the short, gray apartment building, rode up the sidewalk, and braked to a stop. Benny was on the garage-roof patio of the complex, waving a gun and yelling at someone I couldn't see.

"Please be Yolanda," I said as I stashed my bike behind a hedge. If Benny was still yelling at her, it might mean she was still alive. Then again, it wouldn't be the first time a violent man had yelled at his dead wife; I had witnessed some grim situations working for Aleisha.

I called 911 then pocketed my phone and vaulted onto the wall. A short leap from there to the garage had me clinging to a drainage pipe and peeking over the top through a wooden patio railing.

I had met Benjamin Burch the year before when Aleisha had

asked me to escort Yolanda home after a short stay in the refuge. Benny had promised to reform and had groomed himself to make a good impression. Not so today. Clad only in a sleeveless tee and boxers, Benny looked like the wife-beating thug he was: broad back, hairy legs, and fists the size of my knees. One of those fists hung low at his hip. The other gripped a semi-automatic pistol, which he waved in the air as he shouted accusations of infidelity, nonsensical comments about Six Flags Magic Mountain, and declarations of love.

Not only was Yolanda still alive, she was armed with a kitchen knife and madder than a cornered cat. This could definitely get ugly. And not just for them. The last time I had interceded in a domestic violence crisis, the woman I had been trying to save had broken a chair over my head.

I had learned three valuable lessons that day: Never assume a person wanted help. The weakest one in a fight was often the most dangerous. And no one was truly unarmed until they were lying in a morgue.

I climbed over the railing and landed softly on the deck, positioning myself behind Benny so his bulk would block me from Yolanda's view. I didn't want her to see me until I had taken him down. I couldn't afford a fair fight with an angry man twice my size. If I wanted to come out of this alive, I had to be smart, quick, and silent.

When Benny began his next tirade, I ran and leapt up behind him, coiled for attack. In one clean move, I struck the toes of my shoes into the backs of his knees and arched my fingers over the top of his head to rake his eyes. The dual assault bucked his legs and yanked back his head, causing his hands—and the gun—to raise in the air. Then I landed behind him, my fingers still lodged in his eye sockets, and slammed his head onto the deck.

I removed the pistol from his weakened grip and stepped back to a safer distance.

Benny moaned and rolled onto his side, head lolling, as he tried to push himself from the deck.

"Stay put. Unless you want a hole through that hairy thigh of yours."

"What the fuck?" he said, seeing me for the first time.

I got that a lot. Bad enough to get brought down by a woman, but one as small as me was downright emasculating.

Yolanda screamed and rushed to his aid.

I adjusted my position so I could cover them both. She still had the knife, and not only did I not want to get stabbed, I didn't want her bringing a weapon within reach of Benny.

"Take it easy. Calm down and no one will get hurt." I glared at her husband. "Isn't that right, Benny?"

He stared at the muzzle, still pointing at his thigh, and nodded.

"Aleisha sent me. She said you needed help. That's what you told her, right? Benny was acting up?"

Yolanda looked from me to Benny to the city. Police sirens could be heard. I was running out of time. I needed Yolanda firmly on my side before they arrived.

"That's why I'm here, to help you. This is Benny's gun, remember? He fired it once, and I stopped him from firing it again."

Sirens stopped. Car doors slammed. Yolanda nodded and sniffed back her tears, but she still had the knife. Bad enough the cops would see me holding a gun, I didn't want them worried about her as well.

"Put the knife down, okay? I got this."

It was too late.

The police barged through the apartment door. Yolanda screamed and dropped the kitchen knife. Benny shouted for help.

I held up my hands and dangled the pistol upside down from the trigger guard and prayed to God that I didn't get shot.

Chapter Thirty-Three

I wasn't arrested, but I sure didn't get thanked either. Law enforcement took a dim view on civilian intervention, especially when the altercation involved a firearm. Although I understood their position, I also knew this situation could have ended in a body bag. One smiling word of thanks didn't seem like too much to ask.

So far, this day was proving to be as hazardous as Baba had predicted.

Thinking of him reminded me of food, which made my stomach clench—but not from hunger, from worry. I hadn't seen Mia since that morning when she confronted Freddy at his house. Had she recovered from the ordeal? Or would I find her at the bottom of a bag of beignets? More importantly, was she still safe?

Tran's tracker alert would have sounded if he had entered Mia's neighborhood. I checked it anyway and found him in the valley, a safe distance from her apartment. If I pedaled hard, I could make it to her place in thirty minutes. The six-mile detour would double my distance home, but I didn't care. I couldn't rest until I'd seen her.

Mia was standing on her balcony drinking a beer when I rolled up to the curb. She looked down at me and shook her head, as if I was the last person she wanted to see. "What are you doing here? I thought you'd ditched me."

"Why would you think that?"

"Because I haven't heard from you since yesterday. How can you protect me if you're not around?"

Mia didn't know I'd seen Freddy reject her this morning, and I didn't think she'd appreciate my telling her.

"I may not be with you twenty-four seven," I said. "But I *am* keeping tabs—on you and everyone involved. How are you holding up?"

She shrugged. "I don't know. I'm alive. How's that?"

"All things considered, I'd say pretty damn good." My attempt at levity failed. "Hang in there, Mia. Things will change. I promise. This is just temporary."

Mia scoffed and stared into the distance. The setting sun bathed her face in golden light that enhanced both her beauty and her sadness. Then, without another word, she walked back into her apartment.

Although safe and physically sound, Mia's emotional state bothered me. Depressed people did foolish things, especially when they didn't think they had options. I'd need to check in on her more often.

Which reminded of Kateryna. I sighed. Apparently my work wasn't done for the night.

I flipped my bike in the other direction and bolted down the avenue. By now, Kateryna would have brought Ilya home from kindergarten, fixed him a snack, and helped him with whatever projects he'd brought home. His routine with Mommy made him happy. His time with Daddy not so much.

Dmitry's schedule varied, although by dusk most weekdays he was planted in front of the wide-screen television in their downstairs family room. On good nights, Ilya would color at his daddy's feet. On bad nights, he would hide in his room while Mommy turned on every light in the house.

Despite my prayers for gentle lighting, the Romanko house blazed as brightly as the Staples Center on Lakers game night: Dmitry was in a dangerous mood.

I shrugged off my backpack and took out my favorite spying jacket. The dark gray blended better with dusky shadows than black would have and the stretchy material allowed me to pass through tight or thorny spots without snagging. I muted my phone and zipped it in a pocket. I'd hate to have the screen light up while I was skulking in the night. Lastly, I retrieved the karambit.

I held it with a forward grip so I could keep the talon-shaped blade folded and ready for quick release. This grip also allowed me to use the knife's handle as a kubotan to dig into pressure points, stun nerves, and incapacitate muscles. As a bonus, the metal security ring could act as a brass knuckle for my pinky finger.

I loved this knife almost as much as I loved food.

Properly armed and camouflaged, I snuck into the backyard. As before, glass doors were open for ventilation and the screen doors shut against the bugs. Ilya sat on the left side of a U-shaped granite counter, swiveling on a high kitchen stool and engrossed in writing or drawing. Kateryna stood in the center of the U, facing the garden, chopping vegetables for dinner. Dmitry stood at the freezer in the back, filling his tumbler at the ice dispenser, which clattered in the silence.

Of the three, only Dmitry went about his task with confidence. Kateryna and Ilya concealed their movements behind rolled shoulders and hunched spines. Both flinched when Dmitry smacked his ice-filled glass onto the counter.

"They still treat me like a fucking kid." He poured several jiggers of vodka. "How many deals do I have to make before they show me some respect?"

Kateryna raised her shoulders reflexively.

"What? You agree with them?"

She held still, and I knew from experience that she was straining not to shake her head. Not to engage.

"Of course you do. Your tiny brain cannot fathom what all I do."

He came up behind her, set his tumbler of vodka on the counter, and trapped her between his arms. Kateryna stared ahead, knife clutched in her hand, as Dmitry pressed against her back. Her eyes widened with fear as he rubbed the side of his face against her temple.

"I don't hear anything." He pulled away. "I think your tiny brain has gone to sleep. What do you think?"

Kateryna twitched.

"Yes. I think that's exactly what it's doing. Let's not wake it up." He grabbed the tumbler, gulped some vodka, then sloshed his glass toward Ilya. "I bet your brain is wide awake, though. Isn't it, Ilya? Keep studying and you won't have to attend some shit college like your mother and I did in Ukraine. You can go straight into any American university you want. You won't even need anyone to pull strings or pay your way if you want to go to American law school."

He slapped Kateryna's arm, nearly causing her to chop her fingers. "Isn't that right? Our son can have anything he wants if he works hard."

Kateryna put the knife down, then picked it back up.

Good girl. I'd want the knife in my hand, too. I'd seen similar scenarios before and knew how quickly the situation could escalate. It made me want to barge into the house. But Kateryna had made her decision, and unless she changed her mind and asked for my help, it wasn't my place to fight her battles.

Unless he turned on Ilya. Then God help him.

Kateryna returned to cutting vegetables—sawing rather than chopping in case he knocked her arm. I approved. Dmitry would not catch her unaware again. Ilya, on the other hand, did not even notice his father's approach.

I tensed for action, eager to bust through the screen door and bash the karambit's hilt onto the bridge of Dmitry's ugly snubbed nose. Sensei's voice whispered in my mind and calmed me down. *Patience, Lily-chan. Your moment will come.*

I was counting on it.

Dmitry peered over Ilya's shoulder and scoffed. "What is this? How are you going to make the grades if you waste your time drawing pictures?" He crumpled the paper and tossed it at Kateryna. "Where are those books you're always buying him? The chubby ones made of cardboard that are supposed to teach children how to read. Shouldn't he be studying those?"

She didn't answer.

"Well?"

She mouthed something too quiet for me to hear. Whatever it was, Dmitry didn't like it.

"See. That's what I mean. You're stupid." He flicked Ilya's shoulder hard enough to make him flinch. "Go study your books until dinner. Go on."

Ilya jumped off the stool and hurried out of the room.

Dmitry poured more vodka. "I'm going to watch the game. Call me when the food is ready."

When he left the kitchen, I stepped into the backyard light and waved until I caught Kateryna's attention. She froze. I mimed holding a phone to my ear and faded back into the shadows before Dmitry entered the family room. Kateryna would either call or she wouldn't. At least I had let her know I would be there for her if she changed her mind.

Chapter Thirty-Four

Like most restaurants in downtown Culver City, Wong's Hong Kong Inn catered to the business crowd. So by the time I wheeled my bike through the back door, the kitchen was deserted except for Uncle and DeAndre. The two of them were always the first to arrive and the last to leave: Uncle because he thought he owned the place. DeAndre because one day he hoped he would.

I stopped in the shadows of the entryway nook, where my bike and I could blend in with the mops and buckets, and watched the men put the kitchen to bed.

"Anything else?" DeAndre asked as he hung the last of the pots on the wall.

"Go home already. What more I need from you?"

DeAndre smiled as if he had received a compliment, which might have been the case. With Uncle it was hard to tell. "Okay, then. See you tomorrow."

Uncle grunted and flicked his wrist to shoo DeAndre out of his kitchen, and in the process, launched a handful of dried beans straight at me. They bounced off my helmet as I swung it up to deflect the predicted attack—it paid to remain vigilant in Uncle's company.

DeAndre, on the other hand, stumbled in surprise as the beans pattered onto the floor. "Damn, girl. I didn't hear you come in."

He bent to pick up a garbage bag and saw the beans. "Oh man, I didn't see these, either."

"Leave it," said Uncle.

"You sure?"

"What, you live here now? Go already."

I nodded. "Go home, DeAndre. Lee will clean up the mess." I glanced over my shoulder. "Won't you, Uncle?"

He snorted in response. "You late," he said, disregarding my comment so completely that I checked the floor just to make sure I hadn't imagined the beans.

"I love you too, Uncle."

"Bah! Too much talk of love. Not enough talk about respect." He nodded at a plastic wrapped plate sitting on the prep counter. "Eat your food."

I chuckled. Uncle or Baba always made me a plate of extras. Sometimes, they left it on the counter. Other times, I found it in the fridge. Regardless, it was always there.

"I'll take it upstairs and pop it in the microwave."

"No need. Tastes good as is. I know. I fix it."

I laughed. Everything Uncle fixed was good. The moment Baba had tasted Uncle's sizzling shrimp in that hole-in-the-ground restaurant in Shanghai, he knew he wanted the man cooking in his kitchen. And since working as a secondary chef in a low-level restaurant had barely kept Uncle above poverty, he had jumped at the chance to move to America. Twenty-four years later, Lee Chang had a small house, US citizenship, and a wife.

I smiled. "No microwave. Got it."

He huffed his assent and collected his jacket to leave. "And turn off light. All the time you waste."

He walked out the door grumbling in Mandarin about how young people in Shanghai were so much smarter and more respectful than their Los Angeles counterparts. He didn't mean it. Needling me was an indirect way of showing he cared. The only Chinese person I knew who gave me direct compliments was Gung-Gung. And since he only did that when Ma was close enough to hear, it always felt more like a dig at her than praise for me.

I shook the ill thoughts from my mind. This was not the night to unravel cultural mysteries. Time to put heavy thinking away, mount my bike on the wall, and carry my dinner up the stairs—preferably without alerting Baba, whose sedan was still parked outside.

I tiptoed along the edges of the steps to keep them from creaking. As expected, Baba had left his office door open. If this had been a luckier day, I might have made it to my apartment without him noticing. But today was not a lucky day.

"Bring your dinner in here, why dontcha."

He hadn't looked up, so I couldn't just wave. And after Uncle's comment about disrespectful youths, I didn't feel good about fabricating a reason why I couldn't join him.

"You're here late," I said, pausing in the hallway, uncertain whether to accept or decline his invitation.

"Just finishing up some orders." He glanced at me over the wire rims of his glasses. "And waiting for you."

Great.

I stared into the shadows behind him as he typed away at his computer. Better to say nothing than to dig myself deeper into trouble. Besides, the sinister backdrop fit my mood.

Baba's office doubled as storage for the restaurant. Stacked tables and upended chairs. Scrapers and knives protruding from crates. Oddly-shaped equipment hiding in the dark like monsters in a cave. The rumble-tumble from the washer and dryer added to the effect.

I was projecting my darkness onto him. There wasn't anything sinister about Baba's tattered brown couch, or his chipped wooden desk, or his creaking leather office chair, and there certainly wasn't anything sinister about my bear of a father. In fact, the only sinister element in the entire building was me.

And the silence.

He still hadn't told me why he was waiting, and if I knew my baba, he wouldn't. He'd simply wait for me to digest the information and make a decision. If I left, I'd prove Uncle right, and would spend the rest of the evening berating myself for my lack of respect. If I stayed, I'd find myself in a conversation I didn't want to have.

Lose-lose. An apropos end to an unlucky day.

The cushions of Baba's couch were so worn-down from use they were difficult to sit on without sinking. I perched myself on the edge and set my mixed-plate dinner on the coffee table. When Baba still didn't turn around, I picked up my chopsticks and ate. The eggplant was soft and yummy and the chili paste cleared my head. It tasted so good I didn't care if he never turned around. But wouldn't you know, the moment I stuffed my mouth with a big chunk of deep fried tofu, he swiveled his chair to face me.

I chewed.

He creaked back in his chair and laced his fingers over his belly.

I pinched a floret of broccoli and nibbled at the edges as if I had buckets of time and not an ounce of stress.

A noise escaped Baba's tightly sealed lips that sounded suspiciously like "Uh-huh," which could have meant a variety of things, but tonight I was pretty sure meant, "You can't fool me."

I put down the sticks. "Okay, spit it out."

He shrugged. "Just waiting to hear what's in the way."

"Of what?"

"You."

"Why does anything have to be 'in the way'?" Most of the time I found Baba's North Dakota idioms charming. Tonight was not one of those times.

"It doesn't," he said. "But it is." He frowned as I gnawed at another piece of broccoli. "You know, you used to be more forthcoming."

"Oh, right."

"It's true. Even when you were hiding your ninja lessons in the park."

I put down the broccoli. "Wait. What? You knew about that?"

"We both did."

"Ma knew about that, too? Why didn't you say something? Why didn't she make me quit?"

He sighed. "Why do you always think she's against you?"

I shook my head. I had no answer.

"Well, if you guys knew I was keeping secrets, how can you say I used to be more forthcoming?"

"With your feelings. With your fears. You always came to me, Dumpling. You always let me help." He took off his glasses and rubbed the weary from his eyes. "Ever since your sister—"

"Was murdered," I interrupted. "Rose was murdered."

He flinched. My words had struck him deeper than my karambit ever could.

"I'm sorry. I shouldn't have said that."

"We all have our own ways of handling grief. Your mother delved deeper into her work, and in many ways, you did the same. But here's the thing." He leaned in, rested his elbows on his knees, and peered into my eyes. "I don't know what your work is."

We sat that way for an impossibly long time: him in his chair imploring me to answer, me on the couch wishing I could be anywhere else but in that office. But I wasn't. And if I didn't want to destroy the dearest relationship I had in the world, I had to speak. I took a breath, gathered my courage, and prayed I wasn't making an irrevocable mistake.

"What do you want to know?"

Chapter Thirty-Five

Baba knew me well enough to know that too broad of a question would invite an equally broad response, so he took his time formulating his words. When he felt satisfied, he looked me straight in the eyes and said: "Are you endangering your life to protect others?"

Dang, he was good.

I could have hedged on whether or not scaling buildings, spying on assassins, or even disarming guns from wife abusers constituted life-threatening risk, but I couldn't deny that protecting Kateryna Romanko had almost gotten me killed. There wasn't anything subjective about a Ukrainian thug trying to cleave my skull with a hatchet. Baba had found the perfect words.

"Yes."

He exhaled long and slow. "Thank you." His whisper sounded so much like a prayer that I couldn't tell if he was speaking to me or to God. "And this began after your sister was killed?"

"Nine months later, but yes."

During those nine months, I had stopped competing for the UCLA Wushu team, dropped out of college, and dedicated all of my time to training with Sensei. My mission had been to find Rose's killer, turn him over to the cops, and make him pay—not necessarily in that order. Sensei understood and trained me accordingly. It was a grueling and dangerous process.

"And when you came home with that gash on your head," Baba said. "It wasn't from training, was it?"

"No."

Both my parents had gotten used to my martial arts injuries, but aside from the time I cut my leg twirling Wushu broadswords or the time I miscalculated my Ninjutsu defense against Sensei's live katana, none of my training injuries bled anywhere near as profusely as that gash. It had taken nine stitches to repair the damage from that criminal's crowbar.

Baba nodded. "And how do you decide who to help?"

I sighed. "That time, it was a woman getting mugged in front of her house. I just happened to be passing by at the right time."

I didn't mention that the woman had been Aleisha Reiner or that I later discovered the house was a refuge for battered women. I didn't want Baba to track her down.

"These days, I work for a non-profit organization that helps women suffering from domestic violence." When he peered at me over his glasses I added, "And sometimes I just…help."

Baba formed a steeple with his fingers and pressed it to his lips. As he hummed, I thought of the women I had rescued from their abusive husbands. I thought of all the good work Aleisha and Stan did at the refuge. And I thought of Rose's rapist and killer roaming free all those years before I finally found him. How many women had he hurt? How many lives had he destroyed before he preyed on me? Even though I thought I had put an end to him, I couldn't be sure because his death was never reported. So yeah. There was a strong possibility he was still out there hunting.

"What I do is important, Baba."

"I don't doubt it. But we have law enforcement for that."

I shrugged. "They can't help everyone."

It wasn't that the police didn't care—they did, fiercely—or that they weren't competent—LAPD had one of the most skilled departments in the country. But it also had one of the worst personnel-to-population ratios. There was a limit to how much they could do with the inadequate funding they were provided. So while new officers went unhired and existing officers had their salaries frozen, crimes went unsolved, perpetrators slipped into shadows, and deals were made for the greater good. Even when the criminals were caught, it didn't mean the legal system would—or could—ensure justice.

"I have the skill, grit, and determination to save lives. How can you ask me not to do what I can?"

Whether he wanted to acknowledge it or not, Baba had raised me with this work ethic. Never half measures. Never leave a job for someone else to do when you can do it yourself.

Now it was his turn to sigh. "Okay, then. What can I do to help?"

I smiled. Typical Baba.

His support meant more to me than I could put into words, but when he leaned forward and squeezed my hand, I knew he understood.

"You'll keep yourself safe, then?"

I nodded while he chewed over a thought or two.

"And if there's anything I can do to help, you'll ask? You can promise me that much, can't you?"

I don't think I ever loved my father as much as I did in that instant. Even terrified for my safety, with the barest amount of information, he trusted me and had my back.

"I will."

He exhaled his relief. "Alrighty, then. I guess that's that."

We shared an awkward moment of unshed tears with neither of us knowing quite what to do.

193

"Well," he said clearing his throat. "I've got more work to do before I head on home."

I smiled without comment, picked up my plate, and walked around the coffee table to kiss his head. The vanilla-blond hair felt silky against my lips.

"I love you, Baba."

He wrapped an arm around my hips and squeezed me into a hug. "I love you too, Dumpling. Don't you ever doubt it."

Chapter Thirty-Six

The next morning, I awoke feeling more at peace than I had in years. Although there wasn't anything Baba could do to help, and while there were bound to be unforeseen consequences from sharing the truth, at least I could stop keeping this secret from my father. I wouldn't tell him everything—no one deserved to suffer the burdens I had chosen for myself—but from this day forward, I would feel less alone.

I held my ceramic tea mug in my palms, enjoying the warmth. It would be another hot August day, but until the sun crossed overhead enough to shine down on my balcony garden, my apartment remained chilly. I took a sip of the Dragonwell and scrolled through the information on my computer screen.

I had learned quite a bit during yesterday's meeting with Freddy Weintraub in his office, including the segmented way the Copper Line would be built: first through Huntington Park beneath Santa Fe Avenue, then diagonally through Cerritos, the home of the massive shopping center and industrial park. The project would create new jobs and boost the economy—providing the Technical Advisory Committee voted to proceed.

I pulled up the Metro website to see who, besides Freddy, was on that committee. The thirty voting members were comprised of government officials representing a wide range of public interests.

Eight of these were members of the League of California Cities, three were council members, two were mayors, and one was the vice mayor of Huntington Park who had been interviewed at the Hollywood and Highland Metro station just before my infamous lunch with Tran.

Interesting.

The vice mayor had seemed awfully gung-ho about having a Metro line run through her city. Had Tran inspired her enthusiasm? Was that why he was watching her during the interview? Or was he there because he worked for her?

A quick investigation showed nothing suspicious, tragic, or even noteworthy about the woman. The vice mayor was new to her office and, from what I could tell, had very little influence. She seemed to be exactly as she appeared: second in charge for a small city that could use the economic boom a new Metro line would provide.

I returned to the list of committee members, and this time, breezed past low-level officials representing bicyclists, pedestrians, and other ancillary public concerns, and focused on the big guns. I found two who piqued my interest. Both were top-level elected officials who represented communities in the path of the proposed Copper Line. And both had enough power to sway numerous votes.

Evelyn Young was a Chinese-American serving her second term as mayor of Cerritos—the Copper Line's destination and a city with a significant Asian population, known for its retail and industrial centers. Mayor Young also served as the president of the League of California Cities. And since all eight of those city representatives were on the Technical Advisory Committee, Mayor Young had some serious clout. Nine votes out of thirty. That kind of influence could make Mayor Young a prime target.

Or a prime suspect.

I snorted at the thought: Evelyn Young looked more like one of my socialite aunties than a criminal mastermind. I couldn't imagine her taking an extra tea cake let alone hiring someone like J Tran to swindle people out of their money—and it always came down to money. No. It was far more likely that she was a victim.

I dug further and discovered that the mayor's goddaughter, Julie Stanton, had recently died in a hiking accident in the Santa Monica Mountains. According to the reports, Julie had ventured off the Mishe Mokwa Trail, the ground had given way, and the twenty-year-old woman had fallen fifty feet into a ravine.

If I hadn't known about Mia, Tran, Freddy, and Metro, I would have written it off as an unfortunate accident, just as the detectives had done. After all, Julie wasn't actually a relative, and there had been no cause to think the mayor was being blackmailed or pressured.

However, once I added Julie's accident to Mia's attack, it seemed a little fishy: Evelyn Young and Freddy Weintraub both held key voting positions on Metro's Technical Advisory Committee, both had spouses and children to protect, both had bad things happen to non-family members who were close to them.

Was this the link?

Had Tran killed Julie Stanton and terrorized Mia Mikkelsen as a warning?

After witnessing the brutal efficiency with which Tran had executed those Korean punks, the theory seemed plausible.

But two incidents of possible coercion did not constitute a pattern. So I checked into the other influential voting member who had caught my attention: Henrique Vasquez, council member for District 14.

Henrique Vasquez had served on the LA city council for the

last seven years. He was a native of East LA, had married his high school sweetheart, and had three young sons. Rumor had it that the charismatic politician planned to run for mayor with a distant eye on the governorship, which, unbelievable as it seemed to me, would make him the first Mexican-American California governor since Romualdo Pacheco in 1875. But, of course, his political trajectory wouldn't stop there. Vasquez for president!

As a viable Latin-American presidential candidate, the campaign money would pile up so quick Henrique would need one of Bestefar's tractors to shovel it to the bank.

And if power and ambition weren't enough, Vasquez was also a strong supporter of rail expansion. I knew this because he mentioned it in every interview I found. Union Station sat smack-dab in the middle of his downtown district; The Copper Line would be a major win.

The councilman had a motive and possible means. But that didn't prove he had hired Tran to sway the votes that would get the Copper Line approved. In fact, his influence and ambition would have also made him the perfect target. I searched the Internet for recent tragedies or trouble involving someone Vasquez might have cared about—someone close enough to matter yet distant enough to avoid causing suspicion—like Mayor Young's goddaughter or Freddy Weintraub's mistress.

Nothing.

I sipped my tea. Cold. Just like this trail. The only thing I felt certain of was that Metro was key and Shannon Weintraub had nothing to do with the attack on Mia Mikkelsen. Other than that, I was as blind as a cow in a blizzard.

How was I going to find my way when answers kept getting buried beneath more questions? Chief among them: if Evelyn and Henrique all had something significant to gain from the Copper

Line, why would Tran need to pressure them? Wouldn't they vote the way he wanted anyway?

And what about Freddy? Why had he sounded so conflicted about building what he supposedly wanted to build? Were there better uses for the remainder of the Measure R funds? Were there better plans on the table?

And what about the Korean punks I had watched Tran assassinate? What—if anything—did they have anything to do with this Metro business?

I downed the rest of my cold tea and shut off the computer.

I needed to step away from the problem, clear my mind, and sweat out my frustrations. Time for a hike to Sandstone Peak: maybe Evelyn Young's goddaughter had left me a clue.

Chapter Thirty-Seven

The trailhead to Sandstone Peak offered two choices: the vertical climb to the summit or the more scenic six-and-a-half-mile loop via the Mishe Mokwa Trail. Julie Stanton had apparently opted for the scenic route, which, according to her obituary, had been her favorite local hike. I had taken it over a dozen times and understood the attraction.

The Mishe Mokwa Trail passed through every terrain California could offer—meandering desert paths, cozy wooded canopies, red rock cliffs, lush valleys—with stunning views of the Malibu Lake and the Pacific Ocean as it culminated at the tallest peak in the Santa Monica Mountains. If I had to pick the last hike of my life, I might have chosen this one.

But Julie Stanton hadn't been offered a choice. According to the news article, she had ventured too close to the edge and either slipped or had fallen when the rocks gave way.

I didn't buy it.

Julie didn't strike me as a careless person. Her Instagram account recorded a life of moderate but sensible adventure without a single Darwin Award selfie—no handstands on a rooftop for this gal—just an outdoorsy young woman who should have lived long enough to take her grandkids on hikes through the hills she loved.

Should have, but hadn't.

And I wanted—no, I *needed*—to know why.

From the landmarks I had spotted in the news article's photo, Julie had fallen closer to the summit end of the looping trail. I'd get there faster if I took the steep shortcut to the top and worked my way down and around.

I scrambled up the giant railroad ties, embedded to form steps in the eroding sandstone, and up the rocky grooves of the mountainside. Near the top, where the trail forked, I descended the back of the peak via the looping Mishe Mokwa Trail. A mile later, I spotted the landmark.

I had stopped at this lookout point the last time I hiked the trail and could easily understand why Julie had done the same. The sheer drop into the ravine made the distant peaks and valleys all the more dramatic. If I hadn't been so preoccupied, I would have taken the time to properly enjoy it. Instead, I scanned the ground for clues.

Too many weeks had passed to find shoe prints marking the dirt in an elaborate dance of death—as Westley and Inigo Montoya had done in one of my favorite movies, *The Princess Bride*—but I did hope to find something the police had missed embedded in the soil or caught in the cracks of a rock. Maybe even Julie's missing cellphone.

No such luck. I moved closer to the edge.

The bluff angled slightly up then cut almost straight down. It looked scary but stable: no crumbling rocks, no changes in geologic color or striation that might suggest a recent break, not even exposed roots or rocks on which to trip. Everything about the lookout appeared to be secure.

So how had she fallen?

I peered into the ravine. There was a ledge about fifteen feet below where Julie could have hit before she smashed onto the rocks at the bottom. Although it didn't have the width to stop her fall, the scrub brush might have snagged her clothes, or her phone.

Only one way to find out.

If anyone had seen me scoot backwards on my belly and slide over the edge of the cliff, they would have called for Search and Rescue. And by the time I had climbed down to the scruff-covered ledge, I almost wished they had.

This was nuts.

While the ledge felt secure and the ragweed and chaparral appeared to be lodged deep into the cracks, I was still suspended over a fifty-foot drop with barely enough room to park my butt. If I slipped, I might be able to slow my descent by grabbing at plants and rocks, but ultimately, I would tumble down the rocky face and onto the crags below—stranded, broken, or dead.

I was starting to feel like one of those Darwin Award candidates I had so recently maligned. But hey, I had come this far, might as well make the most of it.

I searched the brush and crevasses for some vestige of Julie's passing, anything to suggest she might have hit the ledge on her way down. Nothing. I crawled out and peered over the edge. If I found something out of reach, I could at least photograph it.

That's when I saw the glint of metal in a nest of purple sage—three feet down and a foot away from my ledge.

I crawled back to safety and thumped my forehead on my knees. "Don't do it, Lily. Don't be stupid." But no matter how emphatically I grumbled, I knew I wouldn't listen. There was no way I could leave what appeared to be Julie Stanton's missing cellphone lying in a bush when there was a possibility, albeit suicidal, that I could reach it.

I lifted my face and searched for signs of hikers. "Anyone up there?" I yelled. "Get your video ready. You're going to want to capture this." I shook my head and muttered, "It might go viral." Then I took off my hiking shoes and socks and proceeded to do something ridiculously stupid.

Ever since I was a child, I liked to pick things up with my toes—tissues, pencils, paperback books. I became so adept at it, Baba used to claim I was part chimpanzee. Then, after watching a video of an armless girl who used her feet as hands, I became obsessed with writing the way she did. It drove Ma crazy to watch me pick up pens and scrawl my name, but I didn't care. I stuck with it until my signature looked good enough to fool my teachers. Then I lost interest.

Hopefully, I hadn't lost the skill.

With my feet bare and my toes wriggling free, I rolled onto my stomach and scooted backwards across the rocky, scruffy ledge. Thorns snagged my clothes and scratched my thighs. I let them. If I stopped now, I wouldn't start again. So I kept scooting and scratching until my legs extended over the ravine like flagpoles off a building. When I reached the tipping point of my balance, I grabbed hold of what I hoped was a deeply rooted plant and gave myself one last chance to abandon this foolishness and do something sensible like ride down the mountain into cell range where I could call the sheriff's department.

I thumped my forehead in the dirt and blew dust in my face as I exhaled. Realizing that the case was closed and no one would care but me, I stopped talking to the ants, shook the dirt off my forehead, and inched backwards.

"Please, God, don't let me fall. Ma will kill me."

A sharp rock dug under the base of my rib cage, making it hard to breathe. Too bad. I had already aligned my body with the cellphone. If I shifted my ribs to a more comfortable spot, I might not be able to find the phone. Or worse. I might kick it out of the sage brush.

"Come on, monkey toes," I grunted. "Mama needs a new phone."

When I touched something unnaturally smooth, I knew I had found it. I braced the phone with the top of one foot and grabbed it with the toes of the other, and after a few tense moments and one serious cramp, had it secured.

I flexed my arms and pulled, scraping my chest and stomach across the rocks as I dragged the dead weight of my legs behind me. And when the manzanita ripped from the crack, I jammed my elbows into the gravel to keep from sliding. If I had been able to separate my legs, I could have brought up a knee and levered my way over the top with ease. However, since I needed both feet to hold the phone, I had to inchworm my way onto the ledge with core strength and grit.

I flopped onto my back, muscles drained of strength, phone safe between my toes, and stared at the clouds.

When I had caught my breath again, I put on my socks and shoes and pocketed the phone, taking care to face the screen safely against my thigh. It had a protective case, but after everything I'd risked to retrieve the thing, I didn't want to take the chance of it getting scraped. I had a cliff to climb.

The distance should have seemed shorter with me standing on the ledge—it didn't. It looked impossibly far, and from this angle, as smooth as glass.

And woefully familiar.

I had been here before. My dream about Tran—this ledge, this cliff—wondering what to do next. But this wasn't a dream; nor would Tran be waiting at the summit to tell me why he had invaded my thoughts and tormented me with doubt. I wasn't lying in my bed, struggling with my subconscious; I was standing on a rock in the Santa Monica Mountains over a fifty-foot drop. If I fell, Farmor's quilt wouldn't be there to catch me. There would be pain and injury or death.

It didn't get more real than that.

I shoved my dream-memory away and climbed. As I did, finger and toe holds appeared as if by magic, accompanied by images: Ma opening the front door to a pair of somber policemen, Baba crying at his wok, Uncle leaving a plate of chow fun on my grave. I couldn't break their hearts. Pinch by pinch, I made my way up the unforgiving face until I sprawled, heaving and twitching, on the summit.

I crawled away from the edge and planted myself on a boulder to take in the view. Back at my apartment when I had fried my brain on the Copper Line puzzle, I had hoped physical exertion would clear my mind. It damn near cleared it for good.

Once again, I thought of Tran.

He was in my life for a reason—I was fairly certain of that—but why? Why would my higher-self intentionally attract someone who shattered my calm, disrupted my center, and caused me to question whether or not I was inherently good?

Scary question.

In my dream, when I had reached the top of the cliff, Tran had been gone. At the time, I had interpreted the symbolism as struggle, frustration, or futility. Now, Tran's absence symbolized something more profound.

Perhaps there was no Tran *and* me.

Perhaps there was—and always had been—only me.

Chapter Thirty-Eight

I sped down the steep, winding road with only occasional touches to the handbrakes. Leaning into the curves, I quickly outpaced the car behind me and would probably overtake any vehicles in front of me before I made it to Pacific Coast Highway—provided I didn't skid on gravel or smash into an oncoming truck. If every second presented an opportunity to train, then riding a bike down Yerba Buena Road offered twelve hundred of them.

All I had to do was stay alive long enough to reap the benefits.

One might think I had taken enough risks this morning to last me the week, but then, that person wouldn't have known me. High-speed biking attuned my mind and body to the moment in an active meditation that calmed my emotions and alleviated my stress. Like training with Sensei or practicing Parkour in the city, it required my full attention. At these speeds, if an approaching vehicle hogged my side of the road, I wouldn't have time to think, I'd only have time to act.

Which is exactly what happened when the FedEx van appeared.

At the first glimpse of white and green, I held to the cliff-side of the road for a second longer than I normally would have before cutting across the apex of the turn. The slight delay allowed me to pass alongside the stunned FedEx driver's window—instead of splatting on his windshield—and continue on my way with hardly a flutter to my heart.

I slowed my speed by half as I neared the bottom of the mountain and turned into the parking lot of Neptune's Net. The Malibu fish fry was a popular stop among bikers, surfers, and anyone traveling up this rural stretch of highway on their way to Santa Barbara. Technically, the property sat on the Ventura side of the county line, but since it occupied one of the last few buildable lots before the mountains met the sea, it scored a Malibu address and area code. It just didn't fit what most people thought of as the Malibu vibe.

The general misconception was that Malibu was Beverly Hills with surf—ritzy shops, gated mansions, expensive cars. Although the exclusive beach town had all of those things, it also had mobile homes parked on vacant lots, farmers selling fresh produce out of vans, and motorcycle clubs vrooming up the highway. And while there were tons of expansive horse properties and obscenely expensive celebrity compounds closer to Los Angeles, this far up the coast where the distance between mountain and sea gradually reduced to the width of a two-lane highway, life was a bit more laid back. Folks who lived out here valued star-filled night skies, raccoons staring at them through windows, and hiking trails that began at their front doors. They didn't care about easy commutes or the social life that accompanied it.

If my life had gone a different way, I would have enjoyed living out here.

I locked my Merida next to a pristine Harley Davidson Fat Boy and found an empty picnic table on the front patio. Then I took out my phone and checked the bars. Cell reception was notoriously spotty out here, so I wasn't surprised to find only two bars. Hopefully, it would be enough to text for a rideshare. Seconds later, and much to my surprise, I had confirmation from Kansas—the same woman who had driven me to the Hollywood and Highland Entertainment. She would pick me up in five minutes.

I put my phone aside and brought out the one I had risked my life to retrieve. Did it belong to Julie Stanton? I sure as heck hoped so. Unfortunately, I'd have to wait to find out. Although the hard case and clear plastic screen had protected the phone from impact, fog, and dew, none of these things could keep it charged. In the meantime, I used my own phone to check on Tran.

His tracer dot showed him traveling east on the 101 toward Downtown LA. Was he off to Metro headquarters or city hall to pressure another TAC member? If so, maybe I could get there in time to record him in action.

I looked at the highway, hoping to see Kansas's familiar olive-green SUV driving up from town, and instead, saw it pull a U-turn from the beach across the street. No wonder she could get to the boonies so fast: she was already here.

She hopped out of her car and grinned at me with that same brow-arching smirk I remembered. "Hey, Lily. What's up?" Beach humidity and wind had turned her red hair into a wild mess.

"Didn't expect to get you again."

She nodded to the beach across the street. "Surfing."

"I figured. Especially when I saw the Malibu U."

Kansas laughed. "Caught that, huh? Anyway, there aren't many women drivers with bike racks, so the odds of getting me again aren't as slim as you might think."

She had a point. Less than fourteen percent of rideshare drivers in Los Angeles were women. I patronized this app because they attracted a higher percentage. They also provided profile photos and allowed passengers to customize ride requests. Since I promoted safe and empowering opportunities for women, and since I was rarely without the Merida, I normally requested female drivers with bike racks. Although if I was in a hurry, I'd take a space alien on a hovercraft if it could reach me the fastest.

"What's so funny?" Kansas asked as we settled into the car.

"Nothing. Just thinking about some of the crazy people I've met through rideshares—presently company not included, of course."

"I should hope not." Every time she laughed, her mouth opened wide and her eyes disappeared, like a laughing emoji. While Kansas might not be crazy, she was easily becoming the most fascinating driver I had met.

"So what's the story behind your name?"

"My college roommate gave it to me because I'm from Wichita. And since my real name's Petunia—yeah, go ahead and snicker—I decided to keep it. I mean, who wants to go through life with a name like that? Not that there's anything wrong with being named after a flower," she added before I could take offense. "But Petunia? Come on."

I waved it away. "Hey, I don't blame you. Names are important. They have to resonate."

"Right? Although, you don't really strike me as a Lily."

I held out my dirt-caked arms and scraped hands. "What? I don't look like a delicate flower?"

"Not even close."

I chuckled. "All the women on my mom's side of the family are named after flowers, but my dad calls me Dumpling."

She burst out laughing. I joined her. Dumplings were plump and soft. I was lean and hard. Taken out of context, the name didn't seem any more appropriate than Lily. However, what the doughy packages and I had in common were the secrets we hid.

Chapter Thirty-Nine

Not only did I enjoy Kansas' company, her cellphone charger worked perfectly with Julie Stanton's phone.

As I wandered through Julie's apps, I found icons for all the major social media sites, including two for dating. The last was particularly illuminating. From her profile, I learned that Julie had just landed an assistant manager position at a trendy discount clothing store, had recently cut her long blond hair into a bouncing bob, was thrilled to announce that she was halfway to her goal of losing thirty pounds by the end of the year. Also, she enjoyed long walks on the beach, ocean sunsets, and mango margaritas. No joke. The only thing missing was a cutesy photo of her cuddling a puppy.

Why would a young, attractive, intelligent woman like Julie Stanton feel she had to peddle herself online for a date? It boggled my mind. To make matters worse, she only got one response: a guy who went by the name T-Rex and used the Jurassic dinosaur as a profile photo.

T-Rex: *Are we still on for Saturday?*

Julie: *Absolutely!* (Smiley face.)

T-Rex: *Excellent. Meet me at the Yerba Buena trailhead. 9 a.m.*

Julie: *OKAY!* (Laughing face. Smiling sun. Thumbs up.) *I can't wait to meet you!* (Blushing smiley face.)

T-Rex: *See you tomorrow.*

I looked over at Kansas. "Ever used one of those online dating sites?"

She gave me an incredulous look. "Uh, no. Why? Are you thinking of giving it a try?"

"Nope. Just reading a text from a friend who's about to go on a blind date."

"With a guy she met online? Kind of risky, don't you think?"

"You have no idea."

Kansas grunted. "Well, I hope she's gonna meet the guy somewhere with lots of people."

I stared at Julie's blushing smiling face emoji and sighed. "If only."

As Kansas negotiated traffic, I opened Julie's photo gallery in the hopes of finding a picture of T-Rex, who I assumed to be J Tran. While he wouldn't have allowed her to photograph him, she might have snapped a shot of him on the sly.

If I could prove that Tran had been with Julie on the Mishe Mokwa Trail the day she had died, I'd be on my way to making the connection between Julie Stanton's murder and the TAC vote for Metro's Copper Line. On the other hand, if I found a photo of Julie happily hiking with some guy wearing a T-Rex T-shirt, I could let go of this theory and explore another direction. Either way, I hoped Julie's gallery would lead me closer to the truth.

Appearing from most recent to oldest, the first image I saw was of twigs and leaves. The second was a useless blur of rocks. The third showed a botched attempt at a selfie. The fourth was taken in motion—probably while Julie was switching her camera from the front to rear lens. And the final picture in the collection—which actually was the first one taken—showed a perfectly framed shot of the view.

Looking at the series again in chronologic order, I saw a mini-story of a girl taking a shot of the view, switching the viewpoint of her camera lens to take a selfie, getting it set up, and dropping her camera over the edge. If this had been the case, Julie could have fallen while trying to catch her phone.

But if T-Rex was with her, why take a selfie at all?

Unless Julie had invited him to join her for a selfie and gotten pushed off the cliff. The phone could have slipped from her hand, hit the ledge, snapped the blurry photo of the rocks, then landed with another photo-snapping thump in the sage.

Although both scenarios seemed plausible, the question remained: had Julie Stanton been alone on that mountain or had someone else been with her?

When I scrolled back to the blurry shot of the trail, something dark and out of place caught my eye. I zoomed in. The corner of the frame had captured the outer edge of a black boot. Not a hiking boot. A soft-soled boot. The kind purchased from expensive European stores aimed at athletes with deep pockets and discerning tastes. The kind used for treading quietly through a Koreatown parking lot.

I smiled and turned off the phone: I had found my connection.

Chapter Forty

Come on, Mia, pick up.

My imagination flitted from one tragedy to the next with every unanswered ring. Mia sprawled on the floor, mouth foaming from an overdose. Mia scraped off the sidewalk, her lifeless body zipped into a bag. Mia—

"What's wrong?" Kansas asked. "You look kinda tense."

"Nothing," I said, and called again.

Mia answered on the fifth ring. "Hello?"

"Why didn't you answer?"

"I was taking a shower. Is that okay with you?"

I sighed with relief. Snark and hygiene—Mia had improved.

"Of course."

"I'm dripping on the floor. What do you want?"

"To give you an update. I've connected Tran to a possible conspiracy. I think he might have attacked you to send a message to someone involved."

"Who?"

"I'd rather not say at the moment, but if I'm right, Tran won't be coming back for you."

I didn't mention Freddy. Knowing Mia, she'd barge into his office, make a scene, and put them both in danger. Besides, Freddy had a family; the less she thought of him the better.

"What if you're wrong?" she asked.

"Then I'll deal with him. In the meantime, stay vigilant. I'll call you when I know more."

"Sure, take your time. It's not like I have anything else to do."

I ended the call before Mia's sarcasm made me regret she was safe.

"Feel better?" Kansas asked.

"Getting there."

I chose the next contact in my recent call list and closed my eyes as I pressed the green button.

"Hey," Daniel answered. "I was hoping to hear from you. Are we on for tomorrow night?"

"Still not sure."

"About the night or the date?"

Truthful answer? Both. But since a kunoichi faces her fears I said, "The night. I've got some things going on, and I'm not sure they'll be done by then."

"Would they be done by Saturday night?"

I laughed. "They might."

"All right then. I'll pencil you in for Saturday."

I smiled. "I'll do the same." We hung up with a promise to touch base the next day.

Kansas smirked. "Now I know you're feeling better."

"Mind your own business."

"My car. My business."

"Good to be queen."

"Damn right."

Queen Kansas turned up the tunes.

It took her two hours to drive forty-five miles. If we had left Malibu an hour later, it would have taken three. Thursdays weren't as miserable as Fridays, when everyone cut their workday short, but rush hour in LA was never fun. Downtown was the worst.

We had been heading to the last place Tran's GPS tracker had stopped: three blocks from a familiar address.

"Can you drop me at city hall?"

Kansas smiled. "Do we have another cheating politician?"

"Probably, but I don't think that's what I'm after."

She nodded toward the tracker app on my phone. "You a PI?"

I shrugged. "Something like that." I liked this woman. She paid attention, had common sense, and a good sense of humor. "Mind if I request you the next time I call for a ride?"

"Go for it. Just give me some notice so I can get in your area. If I'm free, I'll accept. If not…" She shrugged. "You know how it is."

"I do, and I will."

"Cool. And call if you ever want a hiking or biking buddy. I'm always up for a new adventure."

We exchanged cellphone numbers, promised to keep in touch, and headed in our separate directions.

The garage under the city hall building was reserved for elected officials, government employees, and savvy bicyclists. Tran's locator placed his car in the visitor's lot several long blocks away. Even if he knew where he was going, thirty minutes would not have been enough time to travel from the parking lot to city hall and through the mausoleum-inspired building to find whomever he needed to see. So if my assumptions were correct, Tran was still here. But he might not be for long.

I sped to the rear of the first parking level, chained my bike behind a pillar, then bolted for the elevator and stairs that connected the three parking levels below me to the twenty-eight floors of government offices above. The fourth floor of City Hall housed all of the district offices, including those for Councilman Henrique

THE NINJA DAUGHTER

Vasquez. If Tran had come to pressure a vote, I figured that's where he'd go.

I bypassed the elevator and took the stairs. I'd have some explaining to do if I ran into Tran, but what the heck? Compared to the risks I had already taken this day, a chance meeting in a stairwell barely registered as a blip on my danger radar. Besides, I would likely hear his approach and have ample time to race down the stairs or bolt out the nearest door.

As it turned out, the acoustics worked better than I had expected.

The moment I stepped into the cement stairwell, I heard a man's angry voice echoing up from one of the parking levels below. It didn't sound like Tran, but that didn't mean the man's anger wasn't directed at him. Besides, the angry man sounded Hispanic, arrogant, and professional. Councilman Henrique Vasquez?

"I don't know what you expected, but I'm not someone you can dick around. I have the ear of the highest levels of government. Do you understand what I'm telling you?" He literally wheezed with anger. "When I call, they pick up the fucking phone, take what I fucking give, and do whatever the fuck I want." With every sentence, he sounded less like a political power broker and more like an East LA thug.

I crept down the next landing and crouched low before peeking around the corner. If anyone glanced up the stairs, I didn't want my face at the expected height.

The man doing the yelling was standing near the stairway exit. The recipient of his tirade was hidden around the bend. Could it be Tran? Possibly. But the angry, wheezing politician was, without a doubt, Vasquez.

I backed out of sight and took out my cellphone. If something violent was about to occur or something incriminating about to be said, I wanted it captured on video. I pressed record and snuck the phone around the corner while Vasquez continued his diatribe.

"You don't get to tell me what to do. I tell you what to do. Are you listening to me? Because I know a dozen guys like you, and every one of them would chew you up and spit you out."

The recipient didn't respond, but if it was Tran, the councilman could be wheezing his last breath. When the silence continued, I started to worry. What if Tran had slit the councilman's throat? What if Vasquez was bleeding out on the stairs? I leaned forward to see, but stopped when I heard the garage door clank against a wall and Vasquez deliver his parting words. "Don't ever come here again. You got that? I'm done with this bullshit. And I'm done with you."

I listened as the councilman's dress shoes clacked on the cement. Then the stairwell door slammed shut. Had Tran followed? If so, I hadn't heard his steps. But with those soft-soled boots, Tran could be walking up the stairs toward me, and I wouldn't hear him.

Time to go.

I pocketed the phone and hurried up the stairs. This time, my floating feet sounded dreadfully loud. If Tran was listening for sounds of a witness, he'd certainly hear me.

I fell back into the Futae Ibuki breathing pattern. In-out-out. In-out. In-in-out. The pattern focused my mind and kept my breaths even and quiet, allowing me to move more efficiently. When I arrived at the next landing, where the stairs made their turn, I paused to peek around the wall.

Tran.

I yanked back before he could see me and considered my options. If I sprinted up the stairs, he would hear it and pick up the pace. If I continued to move quietly, he would maintain his present speed. Either way, he would catch up with me before I reached the next landing. Either way, I'd have to fight on precarious footing against someone who had more reach, more muscle, and possibly more skill. Either way, my chances of survival were slim.

And this was assuming Tran didn't just pull me down the stairs and let the cement do the work.

But if going up was not a good plan, neither was going down. Whether I charged, jumped, or attacked with more deliberation, my lighter weight would work against me. The best I could hope for was both of us falling down the stairs together—and I was pretty sure his body would fare better than mine.

All of this flashed through my mind in seconds. Unless I wanted to have a conversation with Tran on the landing of a deserted stairwell—and I most certainly did not—I needed to act.

I listened carefully to the soft pad of his boots then sank into an Ichimonji stance with my weight loaded on the back leg. Then, when he was just steps away, I launched a fully committed Zenpo Keri stomp kick to the spot where his footfalls told me he would appear. My force against his upward momentum stopped us both, and for a moment, I couldn't tell who had won. Both of us struggled for balance—me on one foot and Tran with his arms out like a tightrope walker. Then our eyes met, and he gasped in surprise. The inhalation rocked him beyond the tipping point, and he tumbled down the stairs.

I grabbed the edge of the wall to keep from falling after him, so I didn't see if his spine cracked on the edges of the steps or if his arms broke beneath his weight. But I did hear the awful thump when he landed at the bottom.

Should I check on him? Call an ambulance? Leave before someone saw me? Every option pulled me in a different direction, and in so doing, rooted me into place. Then I heard him moan and my decision was made: Tran could take care of himself.

I ran up the stairs and shoved open the metal door, not caring when it crashed against the wall. The time for stealth had passed. As far as I knew, Tran had regained his strength and was following close behind. And when the door crashed open a second time, I feared the worst.

I sprinted across the garage, weaving between cars—parked and moving—until I reached the pillar that hid my bike. While I hadn't seen a gun, it didn't mean Tran didn't have one holstered under his jacket. I had to get out of this garage before he turned it into a shooting gallery.

I grabbed my bicycle chain and helmet, not bothering to fasten either, and ran the Merida into the flow of traffic, hopped on while it was in motion, and sped for the exit ramp. I didn't stop until city hall was out of sight and I had found a safe haven for me to stop and make sense of what I had witnessed.

I leaned the bike against a wall and waited for my heart to stop racing.

Tran had done something to make Henrique Vasquez very angry, but apparently not scared. So either the councilman was a foolishly arrogant victim or a dissatisfied employer.

I played the video and listened carefully to his choice of words: *"You don't get to tell me what to do. I tell you what to do. Are you listening to me? Because I know a dozen guys like you, and every one of them would chew you up and spit you out."*

Did Vasquez intend to hire one of those "dozen guys" to do what Tran had failed to do? Or was there more to this picture than I could see? Because at this point, the wheezing councilman sounded an awful lot like Cigarette Smoking Man.

I shook my head. This wasn't a television show. It might not even be a conspiracy. All I knew for certain was that a new Metro line passing through the councilman's district would make a powerful talking point in his bid for Mayor of Los Angeles.

Henrique Vasquez had a motive for hiring Tran. If he could get the most influential TAC members to vote his way, he'd get a shiny new Copper Line he could ride all the way to the governorship.

But did he have the means?

LA city council members received the highest annual salary of any city council in the nation. However, $178,000 didn't count for much in Los Angeles, not after taxes, and not when supporting a family. Even with all the perks of the office, Vasquez would need to make a whole lot more than that in order to maintain his big shot image and still have enough left to hire an assassin.

Unless someone else was paying the tab.

I put away the phone and dug my fists into my aching hips. This case had turned into a royal pain in my ass, and I didn't just mean figuratively—my glutes were killing me. After biking up and down Yerba Buena, clinging for my life on that godforsaken cliff, and my narrow escape from Tran, I didn't have energy left to puzzle out this Metro business.

I needed more information. I need to talk with someone who understood the world of finance and the ways in which it could flow undetected. I needed my mother.

Chapter Forty-One

"Lily. You look lovely," Ma said, her tone tinged with surprise.

I tried not to feel offended and consoled myself with the success. Ma was pleased. Score one for the home team.

I had changed out of my grimy hiking clothes into the same outfit I had worn to meet Freddy Weintraub, minus the headscarf. Although the rayon dress had felt a bit breezy during my bike ride from the Arcadia Metro station to my parents' home, I had made it work. Practicality didn't matter. For this encounter, I needed to look feminine and respectable—the perfect Asian daughter.

"Thanks, Ma. You look lovely, too." No surprise. She looked as classic as ever in her ivory silk blouse and pencil skirt, a striking backdrop for the imperial jade Sì Xiàng bracelet she always wore on her wrist.

We exchanged cheek-kisses. While I could have used my house key and gone straight to her office, I always rang the bell. I think Ma appreciated the opportunity to school her emotions. I know I did. Besides, this house stopped feeling like a home to me when Rose died. It held too much sorrow, anger, and painful memories of sweeter times. Ringing the doorbell helped me feel like a visitor, which, in turn, kept the emotions at a distance.

Ma closed the door, breaking my train of thought and sealing in the cool air. "Would you like some tea?"

"Sure. That'd be great." My voice echoed off the walls and balconies. The two-story entry was long and wide enough for two nine-year-old girls to do six consecutive front walkovers. I knew, because my friend and I had tried the tumbling trick after Wushu practice and caught holy hell in the process.

"Is something funny?"

I shrugged. "Just remembering those walkovers."

"Aiya. You're not planning to do that again. Are you?"

"You kidding? And risk your wrath? I don't think so."

Ma chuckled and walked ahead. I could have sworn I heard her say, "Good."

Our house was shaped like a horseshoe, with an office and family room on the left, a dining room and formal parlor on the right, and an enormous chef's kitchen across the back. A sweeping staircase led upstairs to five bedrooms tucked behind a long balcony sitting area.

Back in the early nineties, when California real estate crashed, Ma had arranged for Gung-Gung to buy the seven-thousand-square-foot house at fifty cents on the dollar. Since then, the value had octupled, elevating the property value to well over three million dollars. Supposedly, Gung-Gung had given the house to Ma as a wedding present, except that he neglected to sign over the deed. So in actuality, the house belonged to Hong Kong International Finance. As long as my mother represented the interests of HKIF and its clients, both in Hong Kong and the United States, her home was secure. I had no idea what would happen if she ever quit. Gung-Gung had a fickle disposition.

When we reached the kitchen, Ma turned on the electric water kettle and brought out a canister of tea. "Jin Xuan okay?"

I nodded. Jin Xuan meant Golden Daylily. It was one of my favorite teas. I pulled out a stool and took a seat at the counter. "How could I not like an oolong named after me?"

"Ha! You just like it because it tastes like milk."

I laughed. She had a point. When Rose and I were little, Jīn Xuān—also known as milk oolong—was the only tea we would drink. I remember us climbing onto these high bone-colored stools and leaning across the pearly granite counter to watch Ma pour. We'd press our tiny hands around the ceramic cups and let the sweetly scented steam warm our faces. Even now, drinking milk oolong felt like a warm hug.

"Do you ever have this when I'm not around?"

"Not really. I keep it for you because I know you like it."

As I watched her spoon tea leaves into the mesh basket of a cast-iron pot, I wondered how many other acts of kindness my mother did on my behalf that I never had taken time to notice. Maybe Baba was right, I had created an antagonist where none existed. I shrugged the thought away. The answer was bound to be uncomfortably layered. I'd have better luck deciphering it during meditation than while sitting in her kitchen.

Ma raised her perfectly plucked brows. "So? To what do I owe this visit?"

She poured the heated water into the teapot and placed two matching ceramic cups beside it. The tiger motifs were not lost on me—Ma was fortifying herself for hard negotiations.

"I need some information about political campaign financing and real estate investment."

She laughed, relief mixed with incredulity. No doubt she had expected one of our infamous mother-daughter quarrels, not a discussion about business. When her posture relaxed, I realized how tense she had been and how at ease she now felt. Once again, I wondered how much of our problems were caused by me.

"Why the sudden interest?"

I shrugged. "Daniel was talking about things I didn't understand, and I don't like feeling ignorant."

It wasn't a lie, but it wasn't exactly the truth. My mind had glazed over more than a few times during dinner at République as Daniel had rambled about his and his father's real estate deals. But I hadn't felt ignorant. I just hadn't cared. If the conversation had come on the heels of today's discovery, I would have paid more attention.

Ma turned the teacups until the Tigers aligned perfectly. "Then the date went well." She tossed out the comment as though it meant nothing and she wasn't secretly jumping for joy. "Well enough to have another?"

"I'm considering it."

Ma smiled and poured the tea.

"Well, I don't know much about campaign financing in this country except that the government requires all contributions to be made accessible to the public and that there are limits. I'm sure the information is easy to find. I've just never had the need to know. None of our US clients contribute to politicians, or if they do, they don't do it through us. And as for our Hong Kong clients..." She chuckled softly. "Well, Hong Kong politics are too complicated to discuss in one afternoon."

I nodded, remembering some of her past phone conversations with Gung-Gung. "What about real estate investment?"

"Aiya. You have to narrow down the question. What exactly do you want to know?"

I sipped my tea. I hardly knew where to begin. So I decided to start with the basics. "How long would it take for a commercial property to go up in value?"

She pursed her red lips. "Are we talking about natural inflation or an event of some kind?"

"An event. Like a new Metro line in the neighborhood. How long after the announcement would property values escalate? How quickly could you sell and make a profit?"

She hummed and tapped her red lacquered nails on the granite. "The real question isn't how much you could get by selling the property but how much you could get a bank to loan you based on the upcoming value of the property. For something like a Metro line, which would bring in new commerce, the perceived value would spike with the announcement."

"Even before it was built?"

"Sure. Government agencies don't make announcements like that until the various stages have been approved and the project has been funded. Otherwise, the announcements would be about meetings and propositions. But you're talking about a green light announcement, correct?"

"I guess. I'm just trying to figure out how an investor could make some quick money."

Ma frowned. "Is Daniel investing in something like this?"

"Uh, no. At least, I don't think so. He was just talking about some of the ways investors capitalize on major changes in infrastructure. To tell you the truth, I didn't understand half of what he was saying."

"I'm not surprised. It's complicated." She leaned in. "It's like this. An investor would have to see the trend well in advance and acquire the property before anyone realized its potential. And for that, he'd want a long escrow."

I nodded. I had heard Ma speak of this many times. "That's a holding account, right? Where the buyer puts down a deposit to secure the property while he does his due diligence?"

"Very good, Lily. And yes, there are always contingencies."

"Like making sure there are no liens on the property or that the building isn't going to slide into a sink hole the moment he takes possession."

"Well, maybe not so dramatic as that, but yes. There are many things to check. With commercial real estate, due diligence could take anywhere from a week to three years, depending on the complexity of the deal."

I smiled. Now we were getting somewhere.

"And while the funds are in this holding account, the seller is committed to the sale, right?"

Ma nodded. "Until the contingency removal date. Then the buyer either releases his contingencies and goes through with the sale, or he backs out of the deal and the seller can put his property back on the market."

"But what if the buyer needs more time but still wants the property?"

"Ah." Her dark eyes twinkled and a mischievous grin bloomed on her face. "In that case, he would need to release the contingencies and hope he can raise the balance before the final sale date. If he can, good for him. If he can't, he not only loses the property, he forfeits the escrow money."

I laughed. Not at her words, but at the delight she took in saying them. "Sounds kind of risky."

"Not if he knows he can close the deal. But if he has to borrow the funds?" She held out her hands and jiggled her head, reminding me of those bobble-headed cats in Little Tokyo. "Very risky."

I couldn't believe how much fun she was having talking about escrows and theoretical investments, as if we were gossiping about the latest Hong Kong movie stars. Who knew? Maybe next visit I'd ask her about retirement funds.

"But that's not the only risk, right? I mean, if the buyer bets on Metro and Metro decides not to build the new subway—"

"Not necessarily," she said. "It depends on the timing." Ma steeped more tea as she cheerfully explained about asset-based lending and speculation. "The potential is huge. But investing borrowed money against risky ventures is like hiding from a typhoon in a house made of sticks." She snorted her opinion of that. "The investor could lose everything."

This sounded like a motive.

"For what?" she asked.

I looked up in surprise. I must have spoken my thoughts out loud. But having made the mistake, I couldn't just ignore it. Ma would expect an answer.

"For murder," I said, and when her brows arched in surprise, I added, "You know, like in a TV show?"

She chuckled at what she assumed was a joke. "Well, needless to say, Gung-Gung and I don't promote that kind of behavior with our clients."

"I'm sure you don't."

We exchanged a wink and a giggle. Then Ma brought out a bag of gourmet potato chips and poured the whole thing into a giant bowl. Had we entered another dimension where my elegant mother ate greasy potato chips? We must have, because otherwise this could not be happening.

"Close your mouth, Lily. It's unbecoming to gape." She pinched a chip with her red lacquered nails and pushed the bowl in my direction. "Do you want some or not?"

Chapter Forty-Two

I woke up the next morning sprawled on the couch with the television on, a young William Shatner calling for Scotty to beam him up from a barren planet. His communicator looked hilariously like Uncle's ancient flip phone. I aimed the remote and clicked. Captain Kirk dissolved into particles. I relished the power. It was a good way to begin the day.

After a long, hot shower to ease my aches, I dressed in an outfit for all occasions—a Lycra blend polo, pants, jacket, and a pair of black soft-soled boots not unlike Tran's. Regardless of where I went or what I needed to do once I got there, this kunoichi would be prepared.

Kunoichi. Who would have thought I'd become a female ninja?

I snorted. Apparently, my parents.

I still couldn't believe they had known—that *Ma* had known. And all this time I had been so certain she would have forbidden it. Boy, was I wrong. Not only had she allowed me to train in the park, unsupervised, with a man, she had allowed her Chinese daughter to study a *Japanese* art. I could hardly wrap my brain around that notion. Even at twelve years old, I had felt the underlying mistrust Ma and her relatives in Hong Kong had for the Japanese. They didn't share the kinship most Americans assumed they would feel. Heck, Hong Kongers didn't even like being identified as Chinese, let alone grouped together with other Asian ethnicities.

I fixed myself a cup of tea and sat down at my desk, taking care to place the teacup a couple inches away from my pen. *Peas can't touch the carrots, Mama. They don't get along.* What a silly girl I had been. Although, didn't I still do the same thing now? No one in my life knew anyone else. Knew *of*, perhaps, but not knew. Not really. *They won't get along, Mama.* Or would they? Now that Baba knew about my secret life, maybe should I introduce him to Aleisha and Stan. Invite them over for Sunday dinner in Arcadia....

Yeah—maybe I'd wait on that one.

I deleted a bunch of emails and bypassed the SMG notices alerting me of new trials and arrests. I had enough to deal with on Mia's case, I didn't need to borrow trouble. What I needed was information on Henrique Vasquez. Whoever was funding the councilman's mayoral campaign sat at the top of my suspect list. I closed my email and opened up a search to follow the money.

At least, that was the plan.

The councilman hadn't officially declared his candidacy. And since he hadn't declared, any contributions he might have accumulated hadn't yet appeared on the Ethics Commission website. Which also meant there was no money trail for me to follow.

I typed in "dirty politics" plus "Henrique Vasquez Metro".

I found a crop of articles and videos. It took a while to sort through the chaff, but I finally found a kernel of something interesting—glowing praise from Hardington, the CEO of a major discount retail chain. Why was this interesting? Because the retail chain had four stores in District 14, one in Huntington Park, and two in Cerritos.

Sure enough, when I checked the city council website, I found all sorts of generous contributions from Hardington to Vasquez for past elections and current projects—more than enough to hire someone like Tran.

I shook my head. I needed more than dirty politics and conspiracy theories if I was going to take this to the district attorney. She and I had a history. If I didn't bring her solid evidence, she'd toss me and my creative theories to the curb. And since I didn't have the time, skill, or resources to check for embezzlement, I'd have to find my evidence down another track.

Chapter Forty-Three

I found the glorified boxcar that housed Magnum Realtors—a one-story building with reddish-brown paint and metal window frames—across the street from a four-track railway junction. It was perfect. Any realtor who worked in this rundown firm would be hungry for business and unlikely to question my story or ask for credentials.

I opened the door. A string of sleigh bells chimed. A man in his forties with an '80s Wham vibe glanced up from his burrito. He wiped his mouth with hairy knuckles and stood to offer his hand.

"Welcome to Magnum Realtors." Plural, as if his wasn't the only desk in the office. "The name's Ed Baker. What can I do for you today?"

Desperation dripped from him like sweat, which might have explained the armpit stains on his periwinkle shirt. Someone should tell this guy to stick to dark colors. I glanced at his hand. At the burrito. And back to his hand.

"Breakfast," he said by way of explanation, then crumpled the foil and shoved the decimated mess to the side of his desk. "You know how it is. Busy, busy. Gotta eat when I can." He wiped his hand on his pink trousers and offered it again.

This time I accepted, freezing my face into a grin to hide my disgust. "Trisha Stevens. It's nice to meet you Mr. Baker."

"Trisha Stevens," he said, repeating the same alias I had given Freddy while crushing my hand in his grip. What was it with men who felt so insecure they needed to lord their strength over women? Did they think it impressed us? News flash: it did not. Two seconds later, without realizing how close he had come to an emergency room visit, Ed Baker released my hand and smiled. "Please, have a seat."

The maroon chair he offered matched his own and clashed horrendously with the seafoam leisure jacket he had draped across its back. I sat on its edge so as not to touch any more than necessary.

Baker, on the other hand, plopped into his seat and leaned back until the hinges creaked in protest. "So, are you looking to buy or sell?" He held out his stubby fingers as he said this then laced them together on his belly. Apparently, having displayed his enthusiasm and manliness, it was now time to demonstrate an exaggerated sense of ease, as if he didn't need my business to pay this month's electricity bill.

I gave him another cheek-hurting grin. "Buy. I represent an international financing firm based in Hong Kong, and I'm looking for property in Huntington Park—commercial, under-valued, potential for growth, that sort of thing."

His eyes grew wide. "Well then, you've come to the right place."

I smiled. "That's what I hoped."

"Do you have anything particular in mind? Strip malls, car washes, apartments?"

"Actually, I was hoping you could give me a feel for what's been selling."

"Recent sales? Hold on a sec." He typed a few commands on his keyboard and turned the monitor around for me to see. The screen showed a map of the city's grid, sprinkled with red location bubbles. Each one had a dollar symbol and the first few digits of an amount that would likely expand into more detailed information when clicked.

The city of Huntington Park had an odd shape that reminded me of an old-fashioned steam engine, with the body on the left and a cow catcher dangling in the front on the right. According to Freddy Weintraub, the Copper Line would be built beneath Santa Fe Avenue, one of the five main roads that ran down the city. So naturally, that was where I expected to see most of the sales. I was wrong. The majority of red markers ran down Pacific Boulevard, eight blocks to the east.

"What's so popular about this street?" I asked, turning the computer display halfway between us so he could see.

Baker cocked his head. "It's our main commercial thorough-fare. You didn't know that? All the big stores are on Pacific. Although it might also have something to do with the Metro hoopla a while back."

"Really. What hoopla was that?"

The realtor shrugged and glanced at his unfinished breakfast. "Oh, it didn't last long. Just enough to cause a fuss and get some investors excited about a new subway. But then Metro changed their plans. No sense paying attention until they nail it down. Who knows where they're going to build the damn thing. Or when. Or if. You know how it is with government-funded projects."

I nodded. I knew a lot more than that, including why Ed Baker should have been paying more attention.

He gestured to the screen. "Several of those Pacific properties are back on the market. I can get you a good price if you think your clients would be interested."

I examined the grid of streets. While Santa Fe Avenue ran due south from Union Station, an existing Metro line already ran through Watts just half a mile to the west. The Copper Line would have serviced more people if they had stuck with the original on Pacific Boulevard.

I leaned toward Baker. "Do you have a map of the properties for sale now?"

He perked up like a pup at dinnertime. "In Huntington Park? Sure thing." He typed some more and hit enter. A new map appeared.

I pointed to the three red dots on Santa Fe Avenue. Each were cheaper than the properties on Pacific Boulevard, and each occupied a corner lot on one of the three major intersections: Slauson, Gage, and Florence. I could almost hear the conductor's voice announcing the stations: *Slauson Street, Huntington Park. Next stop, Gage.*

"What's the status of these three properties?"

Baker checked the first dot and frowned. "Sorry. It looks like the Slauson property is off the market. Let me try the one on Gage." He clicked the next red bubble. "Hmm. That's strange. Hold on a sec." He tried the one on Florence. "Well, I'll be damned. Something must be wrong with my service. Either that or all of these properties went off the market in the last couple of days."

Now it was my turn to perk up. "Does that mean they're in escrow?"

He shrugged. "Could be."

"Well, is there any way to tell?"

"Only if Magnum Realtors had made the deal. And even then, it wouldn't be ethical for me to divulge any information."

"Oh sure, I know that. I only asked in case the owners pulled it off the market or it fell out of escrow, in which case a savvy realtor might be able to get me a good deal." I waited for him to catch on. When he didn't, I gave him a conspiratorial wink.

"Oh," he said, finally catching my meaning. "You know, I could call the owners and find out if the properties are still available."

I pointed my finger at him as if he were the smartest man I had ever met. Then I let him get on with his calls while I pondered the implications of the red dots.

What if the mysterious entity who had hired J Tran wasn't trying to pressure TAC members to vote in favor of the Copper Line? What if that entity wanted the subway built under Santa Fe Avenue, where the properties were cheaper? According to Freddy, The Copper Line would eventually travel through thirty miles of real estate. There could be dozens of properties in escrow along that route whose value would spike with the announcement.

"The properties on Slauson and Florence are in escrow, and the owner of the Gage property is Korean and didn't speak English. Or at least, he forgot how when I asked if he still wanted to sell."

"Korean?" I thought about the young punks Tran had murdered.

Baker shrugged. "Something like that. Not Chinese, though." He held out his hands so I wouldn't be offended. "I can tell the difference."

I scrunched my nose and forced a smile. "I'm sure you can. Were the other owners willing to talk?"

"They were when I told them I had an interested buyer. Neither of them seemed to trust the attorney who poached them from their original brokers. Slimy bastard—"

"Wait a minute. Same attorney for both deals?"

"Uh-huh. Son of a bitch approached them directly, lured them with buyers, and snagged them from the broker the day his listing ran out."

"So the same person is buying both properties?"

He sighed as if I had missed the point of his indignation. "Not necessarily. The attorney could have lots of clients."

"But why did the owners even mention him? Weren't they afraid you'd mess up their deals?"

He grunted. "I think they were more concerned the deal might be bogus. They both wanted to know if I had heard of him, which I hadn't, and I know every agent from Huntington to South Gate." He slapped the table for emphasis then tapped his computer screen. "So, you want me to pursue it?"

I stood. "Not at the moment. Sounds kind of messy. But if I change my mind, I know where to find you."

He spread his arms to encompass his office. "Magnum Realtors." Then he flexed one of his arms. "The big guns of real estate."

I smiled and wagged my finger, pretending, once again, to be impressed with his cleverness.

He pointed to the stack of business cards. "Give me a call if you want to buy." Then he unwrapped his burrito. Now that I was no longer a serious prospect, he wanted me out of his office so he could eat in peace. I couldn't blame him. I wanted me out of there as well.

"By the way," I said, taking a card. "Who's the attorney? He sounds like someone I want to avoid."

The realtor paused mid-bite. "Good idea. Slimy bastard. Name's Dmitry Romanko."

Chapter Forty-Four

Dmitry Romanko.

That was a name I had not expected to hear. Although, when I thought back to the newspaper article about Mia that I had seen in Kateryna's bedroom, the connection made sense. Of course Dmitry would have a vested interest in what happened with Tran's preliminary trial. I just hadn't known it at the time, which was why—when I had seen the SMG notice about that same prelim—I had taken it as a celestial sign for me to get involved. It had never occurred to me that Dmitry Romanko might have something to do with the attack on Mia Mikkelsen.

Which reminded me—time to check in.

Me: *How's it going?*

Mia: *Nowhere. My ass hasn't left the couch.*

I laughed and sent Mia a thumbs up.

I pocketed my phone and considered the Mexican food shack in front of me: Paco's Tacos, the likely origin of Ed Baker's captivating breakfast burrito. I hadn't eaten anything since the char siu bao I had snuck out of Baba's steamer; and that was hours ago. I needed brain food.

The taco shack was a cheery place with orange plastic table cloths, bright yellow and turquoise chairs, and the requisite paintings of Jesus and Mother Mary. It had a small, well-organized kitchen and a diminutive chef wearing a neat white apron and a yellow tee. Baba would have approved.

"Hola, señorita. What can I get for you?"

Paco, or so I assumed, continued dicing as I examined the menu board above his head. My stomach growled. It all looked good, but I settled on the carne asada platter, a tamale—I couldn't get enough of those—and a horchata. Then I sat down at the window table to consider the new development.

What was Kateryna's husband doing in Mia Mikkelsen's mystery?

If Dmitry Romanko was brokering a deal to buy property on Santa Fe Boulevard, did that mean he was working for the same person who had hired J Tran to threaten the TAC voters? Could that person be Councilman Vasquez or the CEO who was pouring money into the councilman's mayoral campaign? Or was the councilman just another victim like Freddy Weintraub and Mayor Young?

I took out my phone. I had done a cursory Internet search for tragedies connected to Vasquez, but I hadn't delved deeper because of the way he had spoken to Tran in the garage stairwell. His arrogant fury had made him seem more like a political thug than a vulnerable family man. This time, I looked more closely and found mention of a murder.

Magdalena Chavira, a forty-year-old elementary school teacher, had driven to Downey to buy an antique coffee table and never made it home. A cyclist found her body two days later in an alley. The reporter called it "A Craigslist Purchase Gone Bad", and at the bottom of the article, buried in the last paragraph where no one would notice, had added that "Magdalena Chavira was the college sweetheart of Councilman Henrique Vasquez."

I sat back in the chair. This wasn't a political conspiracy to groom a future Mexican-American governor or perhaps even a distant POTUS. This was a real estate scheme.

I thought back to the way Vasquez had yelled at Tran in the stairwell: *"I know a dozen guys like you, and every one of them would chew you up and spit you out."* I had assumed Vasquez was threatening to replace Tran with another enforcer. Now it seemed as if he had been threatening to hire thugs to keep Tran away from him. *"Don't ever come here again. You got that? I'm done with this bullshit. And I'm done with you."*

It made sense. Vasquez had a wife and three sons, just as Mayor Evelyn Young had a husband and a daughter, and Freddy Weintraub had a wife, a daughter, and a baby. All three of these key TAC voting members had suffered a tragedy—or in Freddy's case, an attempted tragedy—that was close enough to send a message but not so close that it would raise suspicions with law enforcement. I shook my head. Vasquez had not been angry with Tran for botching the job, he had been angry with him for threatening his family.

Paco interrupted my theorizing with a tray of succulent steak, a tamale, extra tortillas rolled in foil, and a golden-tinted glass brimming with sweetened rice milk. "Anything else?"

"No, gracias. This will do."

"Bien. I'll be in the kitchen if you want some dessert. I'm frying up some churros."

I laughed. No matter the restaurant, all good chefs were the same—they loved to feed people who loved to eat. I took a bite of the steak and sighed. Maybe Paco would adopt me.

The door opened as a couple of new customers arrived. Paco hurried to greet them, wiping his hands on his spotless apron before gesturing to his signboard menu. "Hola, amigos, what can I get for you?"

I left him to his business and dug into the tamale. The sweet corncake tasted so good I almost didn't hear the response.

"A dozen tacos and all the cash you've got in that register. Me comprendes, papi?"

The instructions were delivered casually and quietly, as if the robber expected them to be obeyed without a fuss. From the acquiescing tone of Paco's assurance, I assumed they would.

I pretended to eat, searching the window for a reflection that would show me what was happening behind and to the right of my chair. There were two men, one black, the other Latino, and neither much taller than Paco—which put the robbers between five foot five and five foot eight. Both looked under thirty years old and in athletic condition, wore baggy jeans, wife-beater tanks, and open bowling shirts. Neither had facial hair. Both wore their dark hair cropped close to the scalp. I had seen enough to chase them through the streets, but if they changed clothes or stood separately, I couldn't have identified them in a lineup. More importantly, I couldn't see if they were armed.

And then I did.

The Latino robber on the right raised the gun and angled it down at Paco. "You want me to pop you in the head? Hurry up with that money."

"And the tacos," said his buddy. "Don't forget the tacos, man. I'm hungry."

"Right. And throw in some churros, too."

He lowered the gun and leaned on the counter. Only one of them was armed. Neither of them paid attention to me as I pondered what, if anything, to do. If I stayed out of it and let the robbery run its course, Paco would lose his money. If I interfered and things went wrong, Paco could lose his life. Then again, Paco could do something—either on purpose or accidentally—that escalated the situation. Or the gunman could squeeze too hard and shoot him by accident. There were too many variables, and most of them deadly.

Two robbers, one gun, one me—I needed a weapon.

I found it perched in the corner by the door.

Keeping my knees bent and my head at the same level, I eased out of the chair. The robbers still had their backs to me, seemingly unconcerned. Once again, my diminutive size and fairer sex had played to my advantage. I just needed my luck to hold out long enough to take six very careful steps.

I lunged into the last step and reached for the broom. If the robbers turned now, I'd either have to start sweeping and hoped they believed it or attack. Fortunately for me, they were far too interested in bullying Paco.

I moved closer. As I transferred my weight toward the robbers, I slid the handle of the staff behind me into Gedan no Kamae. Poised in this fighting stance, with the bristles of the broom in front of me and the wooden handle trailing behind, I now had the ability to strike them both in quick succession from a surprising distance.

When the robber on the right raised his pistol and aimed it at Paco's forehead, I knew the moment had arrived.

"Ándale, papi, we don't have all day."

I took him at his word.

I lunged forward and snapped the handle of the broom up along my leg and struck the gunman's wrist. The pistol flew out of his hand, sailed over his head, and landed safely on the far side of the room. Then, as the disarmed robber yelped and clutched his wrist, I snapped the handle across the other robber's face.

Two strikes in two seconds.

Now to finish the job.

As the disarmed robber turned to attack me, I circled the

broom and wedged the bristle end of the staff under his armpit, and hurled him into his buddy with a Ganseki Nage throw. If I had done this technique on Sensei, he would have rolled effortlessly to his feet. Not so with these bozos. They crashed into each other and landed in a tangled heap.

I dug the wooden tip of the broom into the spine of one guy and pinned him on top of his buddy while Paco raced around the counter, raining insults. At least, that's what I thought he was doing. The little man was speaking so fast, I couldn't decipher a word of his Spanish until he said policía.

"Did you call them already?" I asked, jamming the wooden tip harder onto the robber's spine to stop his squirming.

"Sí, naturalmente. I called them as soon as you knocked that cholo on his trasero." Paco's excitement had him mixing languages, but the message was clear: I had to go.

"Do you have a rope, cord, zip ties?"

"Sí, zip ties."

"Good. Get them."

The robbers struggled to break free, so I rapped them both on the head. Hard. Then Paco and I trussed them, wrists to ankles, on their bellies like twin presents for the LAPD.

"Look, Paco, I gotta go. These guys shouldn't give you any trouble. But if they do, just whack them with a skillet."

"Don't listen to her, papi. We'll come back and mess you up."

"Oh really?" I dropped my knee onto the big-talker's spine and yanked his head as far back as it would go. "Take a good look at my face, because if you ever come here again, it will be the last one you see." I slid my knee off his spine and ground it into his kidney. "Comprendes?"

I shoved his face into the tile, not caring whether or not he answered. He had gotten the message, but just in case, I took his wallet, pulled out his license, and dropped it on the floor next to his nose. "Family neighborhood, huh? Don't make me visit."

I stood up and shook off my anger like a wet dog. People like Paco, who made an honest living by feeding and caring for others, represented the heart and soul of my city. He didn't deserve to be robbed and threatened by a couple of thugs.

I turned to Paco. "You going to be okay if I go?"

He nodded then disappeared around the counter. I went to collect my backpack, pinched a strip of carne asada off my plate, but left the rest. While it pained me to leave good food uneaten, I didn't want to talk to the cops.

I had just opened the door when Paco tapped me on the shoulder. "Señorita." He handed me a paper bag filled with a several foil-wrapped bundles. "Tamales for life. Anytime you come, I will feed you. Whatever you want."

I took the bag and hugged it to my chest. The corncakes felt as warm as his heart. "Muchas gracias."

He followed me outside. "What is your name, señorita?"

I shrugged. "My friends call me Dumpling."

He laughed. "It's a good name. Hasta luego, Dumpling. See you soon, I hope."

"Count on it. Oh, and, Paco, those guys won't be telling anyone they got hogtied by a girl, so just blame it on a good Samaritan. Okay?"

"Claro que sí." He winked and went back inside to guard his captives.

The cops arrived five minutes later. I watched their squad car speed by as I finished my third tamale against the wall of a vacant lot. My new friend had a gift for cooking, and I had meant what I said about returning soon.

In the meantime, I had a puzzle to solve that now included a new piece—Dmitry Romanko. And if Romanko was involved, so was the LA Ukrainian mob.

I dropped the tamale in the bag. This new revelation had stolen my appetite. Not only did the mob employ Romanko, I knew they had paid for him to come to California and attend law school. Where? Irvine University, College of Law, Cerritos, California.

I was starting to hate that city.

The Copper Line, Mayor Young, Dmitry Romanko—everything came back to Cerritos. And if I wasn't mistaken, even Romanko's law office sat on its border. It all fit except for Tran.

Why would the Ukrainians hire an outsider when they had enforcers of their own?

I thought of Mr. Disco, who had strung me up and beaten me with that knotted rope. He wouldn't have had the skill or finesse to pressure high-profile officials without botching up the job. Could the same be true for the rest of the mob enforcers?

I tossed the bag in a Dumpster and hopped on my bike. Time to find out.

Chapter Forty-Five

The fifteen-mile bike ride from Paco's Tacos to the law office of Dmitry Romanko took me through some serious ugly, misrepresented by charming names like Fruitland, Maywood, and the Mid San Gabriel River Trail. The "trail" part was especially deceptive.

A few years back, I had ridden the full twenty-eight-mile route from mountain to ocean through lush parks and wilderness. This three-mile stretch down the edge of Norwalk to Cerritos consisted of a cement aqueduct, mounds of dirt, transmission towers, and an asphalt bike path. And that wasn't the worst of it. After leaving the southbound trail, I had to cut due east through Asian, Filipino, and Mexican gang territories, plus an underworld of transnational crime syndicates. It was a miracle I made it from one side of the U-shaped Cerritos to the other without getting caught in a drive-by shooting.

Of course, this part of LA County wasn't all bad. Cerritos had much to praise: art, industry, beauty. And sprinkled into the crime and ugliness were homes, schools, and legitimate businesses of people from all cultures who raised kids and led good lives.

Typical Los Angeles.

Angelenos didn't melt together into a pot; we sparkled with individuality—sometimes dangerously, sometimes ridiculously, but always proudly—as if that quality alone defined our collective identity. We weren't an exotic stew; we were dot art. When you stood back and took in the whole, you could see a cohesive picture. But when you stepped in close, all you saw were millions of isolated bits. A tiny fraction of those bits belonged to the Ukrainian crime family, and one of those was Dmitry Romanko.

His office address led me to an industrial park with nondescript gray buildings set on a communal asphalt lot. I found his building in the back with ample parking and a loading dock for delivery trucks.

Why would a lawyer need a loading dock?

He wouldn't. But the mob might.

I locked my bike and gear behind the wall of Romanko's plumbing company neighbor, pocketed my phone, and clipped the karambit to my waistband. To my knowledge, Romanko had never seen me, so I could always claim I was lost and looking for the plumber. If that didn't work, I'd do what ninja did best: I'd improvise.

The interior of Romanko's building was stark and white, not what I expected from a law office. The entry hall went straight back about twenty-five feet and culminated in a heavy steel door with a small security window. Both were latched shut. Based on the modest square footage of the entry and the massive size of the building, I figured the real purpose of this business lay beyond the steel door. All they wanted me to see was Romanko's opulent law office, showcased behind a wall of glass.

Instead of modern furniture that would have matched the sterile entry hall, Romanko's office had been decorated like a gentleman's den with heavy leather chairs, a brass-studded couch, plush rugs, and polished hardwood floors. His giant L-shaped desk, cabinets, and the coffee table in the sitting area were all made from rosewood with accent items in brass and ceramic. The office décor was so perfect it could have been a showroom display. Or perhaps it was simply for show.

With no one in sight, I decided to find out.

I proceeded into the office, using the Shinobi-Ashi method of walking to keep my steps quiet enough to hear any movement from the steel door in the back of the building or the glass door in the front. Touching first with my pinkie toe and rolling inward and down through the rest of my foot, I was able to lessen the creaks.

It also kept my mind alert.

Intense focus on movement and breath amplified all of my senses and allowed me to take in more information than I might not normally have noticed—like the way Romanko's real estate license and law school diploma hung on the left wall, perfectly centered between a photo of him in a UC Irvine cap in gown and a business portrait of him in a suit and tie. The rest of the walls featured land and seascapes in perfectly coordinated colors. In fact, the only item out of alignment and of a discordant color was the yellow legal pad on his desk. Naturally, I went to look.

The front page was filled with addresses, phone numbers, and brief descriptions about properties in various communities. The five addresses at the top, in neighboring Bellflower and Artesia, had black check marks next to them. The dozen below had question marks. Each of those had addresses in South Gate and Paramount, communities between Huntington Park and Cerritos through which the proposed Copper Line would travel. None of them matched the addresses I had seen on the Magnum Realtors' computer screen.

I paused and listened to my surroundings. A car door slammed, an engine turned over, but I didn't hear anything from behind the steel door.

If Romanko had brokered those two Huntington Park properties, as Ed Baker had claimed, he would have legal documents and other information somewhere in this office. I found them in the file cabinet between metal dividers marked *Copper Line*. And they weren't the only documents. The Copper Line section had over twenty other folders, each for a different property and each under a different LLC. Six of them had been stamped *Contingency Waved*.

Ma had told me that waving the contingency locked in the seller but put the buyer at risk of losing his escrow deposit if he couldn't close the deal. The escrow deposits I saw in the files tallied to just over two million dollars.

I exhaled quietly. That much money at risk could easily have motivated disreputable people to perform lethal acts.

I reached for my phone, intending to snap some photos, but stopped when I heard the faint sound of voices and footsteps and the clank of the steel door.

I closed the drawer and considered my options. While I could stick with my original plan and wander into the entryway as if searching for assistance, the risk felt greater now that I had discovered the files. If Romanko was buying investments on behalf of the Ukrainian mob, he or they might not take kindly to an interloper. And what if the thug who had strung me up on that scaffold had snapped a few photos before I had regained consciousness? And what if he had shown those photos to Romanko? And what if Romanko had shown them to the mob? Were Eurasian sex slaves popular in Ukraine? I couldn't take the chance.

I hurried around the desk and had just crawled underneath the side wing where Romanko kept his computer. I hugged my knees and prayed he wouldn't get the urge to fire off some emails.

I listened to the voices and footsteps for clues. The prime talker had a heavy Ukrainian accent and the low raspy voice of a lifetime smoker. He was going on about a car or a jar, I couldn't tell which. Whoever accompanied him remained silent except for occasional grunts of agreement. Mostly, I heard the sounds of three different types of shoes as they moved across the entryway tile: heavy boots, hard heels, and rubber-soled loafers.

The wearer of the boots stopped near the entrance of the office and planted his feet so decisively I could feel the vibration in my sit bones. The man in the loafers padded toward my hiding spot with a softer step, then leaned against the front of the desk and made it tremble.

The third man—the one wearing the hard-heeled shoes—took his time. I listened to the click of his shoes on the hardwood floors and imagined him examining the certificates on the wall or perhaps stroking the bronze war horse on the bookcase. Then the clicking changed to padded thuds as he stepped onto the plush rug of the sitting area. Leather cushions exhaled beneath his weight and creaked as he shifted into a comfortable position. Then he spoke in the same low and raspy voice I had heard before. "Kostya, put the box on table. I want Dmitry to see what I bring him."

"Yes, Mr. Zherdev." Kostya's voice came from the doorway where the heavy boots had landed. I heard rustling, as if he might have adjusted his hold on something cumbersome, followed by plodding steps and one decisive thud. Then he retreated back to his post.

The third man, who I assumed to be Romanko, tapped his soft-heeled shoe nervously against the desk. If I had been hiding under that portion, the sound might have kept me from hearing what Zherdev said next. However, since I had ducked under the side wing of the desk, not only could I hear his words, I could hear the danger in his tone.

"You will like it, I think. But not yet. First, we have things to discuss. Many things. Like our little problem. Did you solve it, Dmitry?"

The tapping stopped. "Yes. The man I hired is very good. Very discreet. And he's from outside the family, so there's no connection to your organization."

It was Romanko. No doubt.

He shifted against the desk and continued. "The Santa Fe route will be approved next week. You have nothing to worry about. The property values will soar, and your investments will be secure."

Zherdev grunted, but whether with doubt or approval, I couldn't tell. "You spread?"

"Of course. Different LLCs for every purchase."

Zherdev cleared his throat, and the sound reminded me of a lion I had seen on the Discovery Channel coughing up pieces of bone and fur from its latest kill. He continued this process for several seconds until I thought he might actually be choking. Then he inhaled a great raspy breath and snorted into what I hoped was a handkerchief. When he was done, he proceeded with his interrogation. "And the money?"

"Clean. Everything's been refinanced two or three times. I took a second on this warehouse to raise funds to purchase the other properties. I'll pay it off after the announcement is made and the appraisals double."

"And what about you and me, Dmitry? You say you hire some good guy, better than my men, to get me what I want. You say you push my money here and there so I can afford to pay for it. But how does it go between you and me?"

Romanko shifted again, shaking the desk. "Soon. I promise. I'll have your money with interest as we discussed."

"What we discussed was a short-term loan. Six days, maximum, you said. Guaranteed, you said. What day is this, Kostya?"

"Friday, Mr. Zherdev."

"See? This is Friday. You made these promises on Saturday. How many days is that, Kostya?"

There was a long pause as Kostya did the math. "Six days, Mr. Zherdev."

"See? Six days. Guaranteed."

"I know," said Romanko. "And I'm sorry about that. I just ran into a slight obstacle. Koreans—never mind. It's not important. What matters is that the obstacle has been removed, and that I will repay the loan. I just need one more day, until the end of banking tomorrow, then I'll have your money in full. I promise."

Zherdev sniffed and snorted, the sound alternating between clear and muffled the way it might if he were wiping his nose with a handkerchief. The leather creaked beneath his weight, and I imagined him stuffing a dirty rag into the pocket of his pants. All the while, Romanko's heel tapped nervously against the desk.

Then it stopped. "The Mykola!"

"What about it?"

"The painting has increased in value since my wedding. It must be worth ten thousand dollars."

"So?"

"It's yours, Mr. Zherdev. A gift for being so patient."

As Romanko hurried around the desk, I hugged my knees tighter and willed him not to look down. Instead, he rolled his chair out of the way, hit the speaker button on his phone, and planted his hands on the desktop to wait. A dial tone sounded followed by the eleven-note tune of a phone number. After five rings, a woman answered.

"Hello?"

It was Kateryna. She sounded mildly put out, the way she usually did when someone interrupted her from whatever she was doing. At two in the afternoon, she would probably have been fixing Ilya an after-school snack.

Romanko retrieved his chair and sat. "It's me. I need you to do something. Right now."

Kateryna sighed. "What do you want me to do?" She sounded resigned, as if she already knew she wouldn't like whatever he had to say.

"I need you to take the Mykola off the wall, wrap it in a blanket, and put it in the rear entrance. Make sure the door is unlocked."

"What? Why?"

"Just do as I tell you."

"But it's mine. You bought it for me for our wedding."

"Yes. And now it's time to sell it. We need that money for Ilya's college fund. Don't you think that's more important than a pretty painting for you to look at?" He waited for her to agree. She didn't. "Now, Kateryna. Someone is coming to pick it up."

Romanko slammed his hand on the speakerphone and killed the connection.

"The painting is yours, Mr. Zherdev. You can send someone to pick it up right now if you like. I just need until five o'clock tomorrow to finalize my banking, and I will have your money."

Zherdev took his time, making Romanko shift nervously beside me, heel quivering against the floor. "Okay, Dmitry. I take your gift. Now, you open mine."

Romanko froze. He didn't seem too eager about opening his present. I didn't blame him. Zherdev's tone sounded ominous.

Finally, he spoke. "Of course."

He walked around the desk and I heard him tread from hardwood onto soft rug. The rip of tape. The thud of cardboard. The rustle of paper. And silence.

Zherdev chuckled. "It's a good photo, I think. Don't you agree?

With a strong frame to match your impressive desk." Zherdev's voice dripped with disdain. "Not like your parents. They are not so strong. See how your mother droops? What would she do if your father was not there to support of her?" He let the implications hang. "Ukraine winters are harsh. But maybe you've been here so long you forget. Go ahead, Dmitry, put the photo on your desk where you can see your parents every day and remember the hardship they endure."

Romanko did as he was told.

The cushion inhaled as Zherdev rose from the couch. "Come, Kostya. Let's leave Dmitry to think of the sacrifices parents make for their sons."

Chapter Forty-Six

Romanko waited until the steel door had opened and shut before coming back around the desk. Once again, he sat in his chair and rolled forward.

I hugged my legs and pinched the cramps from my hamstrings. The muscles were still tight from my adventures on the cliff. I'd give Romanko one minute to vacate his office and then I was coming out. But when I heard the dial tone on the speakerphone, I decided to give him a little longer.

Kateryna answered in a soft, defeated voice. "Hello."

"It's me."

"What do you want now?"

"To explain."

"What is there to explain? You want my painting, and so you take it."

Romanko shifted in his seat. "You don't understand. You don't realize the risks I take so we can live like we do."

Kateryna waited. When he didn't continue, she prompted him cautiously. "What have you done, Dmitry?"

"I got us a piece of our own," he said, more to himself than to her. "It should have gone to Zherdev, of course, but he had so much I didn't think he'd miss it. And that property..." He laughed. "It would have set us up for big things. So I took a second on our house and used the money to put it into escrow. But everything took so damn long. The bills piled up and still no Metro announcement. No jump in value to show the banks. No collateral to get a loan and close the deal. Just God shitting on me!"

He leaned back in his chair and stared at the ceiling, muttering to himself, his wife forgotten.

"I had to let the escrow dissolve. I had to use the money to pay our bills. But that fucking shopkeeper wouldn't let me back in the deal. Changed his mind. Wanted to leave his sorry strip mall to his good-for-nothing sons."

He kicked his desk and sent his chair rolling.

"Fucking Tran. If he had offed those punk kids just one week earlier, the Korean would have gotten the message—dead nephew today, dead sons tomorrow—and let me back in the fucking deal!"

Kateryna's whisper cut through the silence. "What did you do, Dmitry?"

"Huh?" He stared at the speakerphone as if just remembering it, then rolled his chair back to the desk. He leaned forward and rested his head on the box, his mouth inches from the speaker.

"I did what I had to do. I borrowed from Zherdev."

She gasped. "No. You would not do that. Tell me you did not do that."

When he didn't answer, she sobbed. Each gulp of breath wrenched my heart and made me want to leap from my hiding spot and smack Romanko's face.

Then the sounds coming from the speakerphone changed. I heard pounding in the background, a crack, and a slam.

Romanko stood. "Kateryna? What's going on?"

Something crashed. Men barked orders in Ukrainian. Kateryna begged and wailed for them to stop.

"Kateryna. Answer me. What's going on? Who's there?"

Ilya screamed in the distance, followed by another crash and the shatter of glass. It sounded as if someone were pulling him down the stairs because his cries for his mommy grew louder and louder.

Romanko shoved something heavy off his desk and bellowed. "What is happening?"

Neither Kateryna nor Ilya answered. They were too busy screaming for each other and at the men who seemed to be forcing them out the door. The scuffling noises grew fainter. An engine revved. Car doors opened and slammed. Tires screeched.

Romanko ran out of the room. I crawled out from under the desk and raced after him. He had gone to the steel door and was trying, in vain, to turn the handle. He pounded on the steel. "I need to speak to Zherdev. Can you hear me? Open up."

No one answered, and no one opened the door.

Romanko ran back toward his office and straight toward me. I stepped back, slipped my right arm under his left, and threw him into a cartwheeling fall onto the marble floor. He scrambled to his knees, and his eyes grew wide in recognition. I guess he had seen a photo of me after all.

"What's going on, Dmitry?" I asked as I advanced.

He hurried to his feet and barged into his office. "I don't have time for you."

I let him go and watched as he punched in numbers on his speakerphone.

Zherdev's raspy voice filled the room. "Think carefully before you speak."

Romanko pulled his hands away from the desk and spun, clenching and unclenching his fists in an attempt to regain control. He saw me standing a few feet away, a target on which to focus his rage, and expelled a warning blast of air. But he didn't charge. Instead, he took a calming breath and returned to the speakerphone. "What have they done with them? Where are your men taking my wife and son?"

"A debt must be paid, Dmitry, on time and in full. You know this. And yet, you beg like a child and bargain with paintings. Am I your father, that I should care about such things? No. But you should think of your father. And of your mother. A son should always care for his parents above all others."

Romanko looked to the ceiling for guidance and found none. "Please, don't hurt them. Any of them. I'll get you the money. I promise. Don't worry."

Zherdev snorted. "Why should I worry? I will get a good price for Kateryna and Ilya. And they will bring much money for their new owners. Until they lose their looks. But then, that won't be my problem."

"Give me until tonight. Please."

"Don't bother yourself, Dmitry. You can always get another wife and make another son." He chuckled "Oh. And I almost forgot: thank you for the painting."

The line disconnected. I waited to see if Romanko would smash the phone or sweep it off his desk. He did neither. He just straightened his spine, ran his hands down his shirt, and turned to glare at me. "What do you want?"

Loaded question.

I thought about the twisted path from Mia and Tran to Freddy and Metro. I thought about the gangster wannabes in the Koreatown garage and Evelyn Young's goddaughter and Henrique Vasquez' college sweetheart and anyone else who might have been killed to leverage the Copper Line vote. I thought about Kateryna's bruised face and broken ribs and terrified son. And I tried, very hard, not to think about the terrors facing them.

Dmitry Romanko had caused so much pain to so many people; he didn't deserve to live. But I couldn't afford for him to die. Not yet.

"The same thing I've always wanted," I said. "To keep Kateryna and Ilya safe."

He grunted. "And how do you propose to do that? I don't know where Zherdev's goons have taken them. Do you?"

"No. But I'll find out. And I'll get them back."

"No, you won't. Didn't you hear what Zherdev said? He controls everything in my life. He could end me in an instant if he wanted to. No. The only way to make things right is to get him that money."

"Fine. When's the deadline?"

"Thirty minutes ago."

"Then it's too late for money." I was so angry I had started to sweat. "Where would he take them? Would he bring them here? Lock them in the back?"

"No."

I grabbed him by his shirt. "Then *where*?"

"It doesn't matter. I have to get the money. Now go away. You're slowing me down."

He went to shove me aside, but I had known it was coming. Bullies like Romanko were predictable. He hit the ground fast as I locked his arm and prepared to break it. "Where are they?"

"I don't know," he cried. "I don't. Why do you think I need the money? Let me go, so I can get it."

He was telling the truth, but I didn't like it. I released his arm and stepped back. I needed to think.

Romanko stood up and brushed me off. "This is my problem; I will solve it." He rubbed his elbow and glared. "And if I don't, Zherdev's right: I can always find another wife and make another son."

Anything else he might have said after that was swallowed in anguish along with his testicles.

I snapped open the karambit and jabbed the talon claw blade against his crotch. "Get the money, Romanko. Because if anything happens to Kateryna or Ilya, you won't have the necessary parts to get another wife or make another anything."

Chapter Forty-Seven

Still seething, I marched back to my bike and gear. If not for the danger to Kateryna and Ilya, Romanko would be bleeding out on his office floor. If I didn't get to them in time, I'd go back and finish the job.

I growled with frustration. For all I knew, it was already too late to save them. They could be locked in the back of a car on their way to the border, or in a boxcar on a freight train, or in the cargo hold of a ship. Unspeakable things could be happening to them right now.

Stop it, Lily.

I couldn't let myself go there. I had to stay optimistic. I had to believe I could save them.

But this time, conviction wasn't enough. I needed help.

I retrieved my backpack from behind the plumbing company's wall and dug into the outside pocket.

Tran's business card looked as elegant as it had when it landed on my sushi plate: gray on black, name and phone, no address. I thought of his smirking face as he had watched my reaction from his seat across the chef's station. "Give me a call if you change your mind," he had said. Of course, that was before I had stomp-kicked him down the cement stairs of the city hall garage. Hopefully, he didn't hold a grudge.

He answered after two rings. "Speak."

I paused, taken aback by the terse command. Who answered their phone like they were training a dog? Then again, who would be calling someone like Tran except a mongrel like Romanko? And apparently, me.

"It's K," I said, using the name I had given him, the one that had burst from my mouth like a call response to his own single initial name—J and K, good and evil. I shivered and switched the last pair around to evil and good. My superstitious nature couldn't let the misalignment stand. Tran was the evil one, not me. I had to get this straight in my head. I was the one who fought on the side of good. Me, not Tran.

I hovered my thumb over the end call icon. This was a terrible mistake. But before I could decide whether or not to press it, Tran spoke in a quiet, amused, and infuriatingly sexy voice. "It's been two days since our lunch. I had given up hope."

I could feel the smirk through the phone and would have given a hundred bucks to slap it off his face. But Kateryna and Ilya were in jeopardy, and as much as I hated it, the smug assassin was the only lead I had.

I took a deep breath and did what had to be done. "I know what you are. I know who you're working for. And I need your help."

He chuckled. "Well, that was unexpected."

"Knock it off, Tran. Dmitry Romanko reneged on a deal, and Zherdev—I assume you know who he is—took Romanko's wife and son in payment. Romanko won't tell me where they are. He's too afraid Zherdev will kill his parents or fire him from the mob. I'm not sure which he thinks is worse."

"Zherdev took the child?"

"Keep up. I don't have time to repeat myself. He took Kateryna and Ilya. I need to know where they are."

When Tran didn't respond, I shook my head. This was a stupid idea. What made me think an assassin would ever—

"Why do you care?" he asked.

"What?"

"Keep up, K." His tone reeked of menace.

Truth was a dangerous and valuable commodity. I didn't want to waste it. But what choice did I have? Tran's tone had made it clear: If I wanted his help, I'd have to cough up the truth.

"Romanko beats his wife and possibly his son. I'm trying to protect them."

"Ah," he said, as though a piece of the puzzle had just fallen into place. "Not doing a very good job of it, are you?"

I ignored the dig. "Zherdev's goons have taken them, and I think you know where. Am I right?" His silence made me want to scream. I needed him to say yes, and I hated myself for that. "Are you going to help me or not?"

"I think not."

I raised the phone away from my mouth so he wouldn't hear my grunts of frustration. What did I think he would say? *Sure, K, I'll be right over. Just let me saddle up my white stallion, and I'll come to save the day.* What a fool. Did I really think he was so fascinated with me that he would risk his reputation and snitch on his employers? Ma was right: I was born vain. Although, according to Farmor, I was more stubborn than Baba and Bestefar put together.

J Tran didn't know it yet, but he was going to help me whether he wanted to or not.

"I videotaped you. In the Koreatown garage. When you assassinated those kids."

Tran paused. "I see."

"Good. Then you'll tell me where they've taken Kateryna and

Ilya."

"No." He chuckled. "I don't think I will."

"You want me to send the footage to the cops? Because I will. I'll hand deliver the video to the freaking D.A. Don't you think I won't."

"Relax, K. I'm not going to tell you where they are."

I slumped against my bike. I was all out of cards to play. I didn't even *have* a video. I only said it because I thought it sounded more incriminating than photos—as if Tran wiping a stiletto over the body of dying man wasn't enough to convict. It didn't matter: I'd tried truth and lies, and neither had worked. I'd have to find Kateryna and Ilya on my own.

Tran interrupted my thoughts. "I won't tell you where they are. I'll take you there."

Chapter Forty-Eight

The bike ride to the Alondra Library where Tran wanted to meet took five minutes, which left me ample time to pace the lot, battle with my conscience, and consider the very likely possibility that Tran would simply drive up and shoot me in the head.

What the hell was I thinking? I had blackmailed an assassin. How could he *not* get rid of me?

As I asked this question for the dozenth time, Tran's black BMW drove into the lot. Too late to run. I flexed my legs, preparing to pull a *Matrix* at the first sign of a gun's muzzle—as if that would do any good—but none appeared. Instead of rolling down the window, Tran cut off the engine and stepped out, setting the car alarm with a chirp as if it was a normal day and he was meeting a girl for a date. He even had on nice clothes. Although to be fair, that's what he always wore: tight black tee, black jeans, the familiar soft-soled boots, and a dark gray jacket loose enough to hide myriad weapons.

All I had was the karambit under my black polo, clipped to the waistband of my black pants.

He approached with the graceful swagger I had admired in the sushi bar rather than the stalking gait I had witnessed in the Koreatown garage. Although the sexier walk promised a better outcome, I would have been more comfortable with the stalk: at least then I would have understood his intention.

He stopped a sword's length away and nodded in greeting. "K."

I nodded back. "J."

"So…" he said, letting the word hang and the implications free for me to fill.

"Yep," I said, not really sure to what I was referring: we had more crap flowing between us than the LA River after a storm.

Tran bridged the gap. "I was surprised to hear from you."

"Understandable. How's your head?"

He pursed his lips as though reliving the pain of cracking it on cement then smiled. "I'll live." Then he headed for the sidewalk at an infuriatingly slow pace.

I matched it but said nothing. Words had become a form of currency, and like any negotiation, the first one to speak lost.

After half a block, he chuckled. "This is interesting. You. Me. Working together."

"Who said we're working together?"

He raised a brow. "You did."

"No. I said I needed to know where Zherdev had taken Kateryna and Ilya. You're the one who insisted on tagging along."

He held out his hands in mock innocence. "Well, you've shown yourself to be a violent person. I have a reputation to protect. Can you blame me for wanting to safeguard it?"

"Oh, give me a break. What are you going to do? Lead me to the kidnappers then stop me from bashing in their heads?"

"I didn't say that."

"Then what? Why are you even bothering to help? And don't tell me you're worried about the video, because I don't believe it. You could have shut me up with a drive-by shooting and no one would have been the wiser. But you didn't. Why?"

Tran grinned. "I'm here because I want to see what you'll do."

"Not good enough. I need to know why."

He stopped and placed his hands on his hips, exposing the butt of a pistol holstered under his arm. "Why I want to see what you'll do? Or why you're not already dead?"

I held his gaze and tried not to flinch. "Why are you so interested in me?"

He smiled—a truly happy smile. "Because we're the same. I felt it at the sushi bar. And I saw it again at the train station."

"You followed me."

"Only so far. I had other things to do, after all. But long enough to recognize violence."

"I didn't do anything."

He chuckled. "You didn't have to. Violence recognizes its own."

He started walking again, and not knowing what else to do, I joined him.

"Where are we going?" I asked, choosing the least dangerous question in my mind. "I need to know what I'm walking into."

"Fair enough. On occasion, the Ukrainian mob does business with the Varrio Norwalk 66. If Zherdev has sold Romanko's wife and son, it would most likely be to them."

I felt ill. Although not the largest or most notorious street gang in Los Angeles, the Varrio Norwalk 66 had a nasty reputation. "Human trafficking?"

He nodded. "Unrestricted. Anything goes."

I closed my eyes and walked blind for several yards—something I often did on fire roads where the surface was smooth and the traffic scarce. It calmed my mind and raised my awareness. Right now, my mind needed a whole lot of calming. When I felt more under control, I opened my eyes.

"I do that," said Tran.

"What?"

"Walk with my eyes closed."

"Great."

He grinned. "Yes. It is."

I sighed. The last thing I needed was another point in common with Tran.

"Does Romanko know where they've taken Kateryna and Ilya?"

He shook his head. "I doubt it."

"Yeah, I don't think so either. Zherdev would want his money before he told him. And by then, they'd be—"

I couldn't say it. The devil didn't need my help to do his work. If I was going to speak any words of power, they'd be positive.

"They're alive," I said, infusing the statement with absolute conviction. "And I'm going to save them."

Tran laughed. "You see? This is why you fascinate me— determined, unpredictable, ferocious."

I turned away, not wanting to encourage this line of conversation. I didn't know what kind of game Tran was playing, and I didn't care. I just wanted to find Kateryna and Ilya before the Varrio Norwalk 66 sold them, killed them—or worse.

"So where are we headed?" I asked. "All I see are houses."

"Why not houses? They have rooms and privacy. What else would the Varrios need to sell their goods?"

I thought of Ilya tied up and tortured in a cutesy home with plastic slides in the front yard. It made me want to kill. "They're not *goods*."

Tran shrugged. "They are to the Varrios."

"Why do you call them that? A varrio is a neighborhood, not a person."

"What do you want me to call them? Gangsters?" He snorted. "I don't think so."

"Whatever. Call them anything you like as long as you kill

them." I didn't mean to say it. I just wanted Tran to knock off the smart remarks. Instead, he stopped walking.

"There's something you need to understand, K. This gang is repulsive, no question, but they serve a purpose. Like carrion birds, they dispose of things. And sooner or later, everyone has something or someone they want gone. So you can't just go in there maiming and killing whoever you like, or the rest of the criminal community will get testy."

"Testy?" I didn't appreciate the lecture. "And what if I kill *you*?"

I meant it to sound clever, but when Tran's brow peak again, I knew I had made a dangerous mistake. My fascination index had jumped another level. If I didn't put an end to his attraction, I'd find myself digging my own grave. Nothing good could come from being a killer's crush.

"You don't get to tell me what I can and can't do. Not after what you've done. Not after you murdered those Korean punks, and Vasquez's college girlfriend, and Evelyn Chang's goddaughter. She was twenty years old. Don't you have a conscience?"

I shut my mouth. I had crossed the line of civility and broken whatever truce we might have established. Worse, I had listed four specific kills. If he had doubted my video before, he now had to assume I had the evidence to put him on death row.

"Well?" I said, daring him to answer and careless of the consequences.

The smirk fell from his mouth. He wasn't amused anymore. He wasn't anything. His face had become an expressionless mask. I braced myself for the knife or bullet that must surely be on its way. Instead, he whispered, "Whatever conscience I might have had, I buried in Vietnam."

He stared at me, as if he could communicate his meaning through force of will. What horrible thing had happened to him there? He was too young to have fought in the war—at least, not our war. Was Tran Vietnamese? Had he suffered through things unknown or disregarded by Americans?

I started to ask, but the tension broke, and his amusement returned as if none of this had happened. As if I hadn't accused him of murdering four people. As if he hadn't shared some deeply personal secret.

He stepped closer, and the corners of his mouth twitched into a sad smile. "But that's not really what you want to know, is it?" His warm breath caressed my face. "No. What you really want to know is…are you like me?"

Chapter Forty-Nine

Everyone who had ever traveled east of LA's notorious South Central knew the One Ways were bad news. The twenty-eight-block neighborhood north of Alondra Boulevard, where Tran and I had left his car and my bike, was a grid of one-way streets. It was a rare teen who didn't get pressured into joining one of the many Latino gangs, especially when he or she had an uncle, father, brother, or sister leading the way. Turf scuffles erupted over the slightest infractions. Shakespearean romances incited drive-by shootings. At the same time, innocent children played in their yards and devoted parents did their best to provide.

All of this represented typical life in the One Ways.

Simple dwellings, surrounded by chain-link. Cement walls implanted with metal spikes. Bars on the windows—not the graceful kind that bulged on the bottom and arched up at the top as one might find south of Beverly Hills, but bars straight from county jail. And yet, there were no winos or crack addicts sprawled on the sidewalks or hookers shouting their wares from doorways. Young toughs hung around parked cars, smoking joints and talking shit, but they weren't brandishing weapons.

So how could I have known what the third house on the left concealed?

It was painted the same bland color as the ones on either side, a cross between curdled cream and dirt. A cracked cement path led to the front door, and a tricked-out copper-pearl Mitsubishi sat in the driveway. A plastic lawn chair peeked beneath a hillock of weeds so large it could have hidden a couple children and a rusted tricycle. I tried to imagine what the inside of the house might look like—strewn toys, dirty dishes, an exhausted mother asleep in front of a television.

Tran nodded across the street toward the driveway that ran along the far end of the property. "See it?"

I did. In the backyard, shielded from view, stood a small structure with blacked out windows and burnt skin for paint.

"Is that where they are?" I asked, hoping he would say no. The thought of little Ilya in that dark den, subject to unspeakable deeds, made me want to vomit. Or kill.

Tran nodded.

I unclipped my knife. "We can't wait. We have to go in."

"Not yet. Look."

Two hefty thugs emerged from the back house and strolled up the driveway. Both were Mexican-American, bald, and broad. One wore an oversized purple and gold Lakers jersey. The other had on a brown and black striped crew. Both wore shorts that hung from their butts and stopped mid-calf over white socks and designer kicks. They passed a Mitsubishi and entered the side door of the front house. A blast of Mexican rap faded as the door closed.

I looked back at Tran. "Now?"

He nodded. "But remember our agreement: if even one of them sees us, they all have to die."

My mouth flinched into a hard grin. Tran had explained the situation during our walk. This street gang was connected to the Mexican drug cartels. If we were seen, we could be identified, and if we were found, we wouldn't be the only ones who suffered: the cartel would kill everyone dear to us. I nodded my agreement. There was no way I was going to endanger my parents. But I also wasn't going to leave Kateryna and Ilya to this gruesome fate.

We crossed the street and edged up the driveway to the car. When no one came out of the side door of the house, we continued up the driveway and stopped at the end. Tran nodded toward the back of the main house and spread his hands to signal that the curtains were open. Anyone looking out would see us running across the backyard.

I shrugged. We didn't have time for stealth. The Varrio gangsters could come back at any moment. We needed to break into that ugly back house, free Kateryna and Ilya, and get out—preferably without being seen.

We ran for the door. Tran had a bump key ready, and with practiced efficiency, inserted it partway into the lock and bumped it with the handle of his knife. Then he repeated the action with the dead bolt and we were in.

The place stank of sweat and semen, which caused my stomach to heave. I swallowed down the bile and closed the door behind me, sealing us inside. Tran went ahead to the left and checked around an accordion screen similar to the one I used to separate my bedroom from my dojo, but larger and crudely built. This one divided the main room into sections—a shabby parlor in front and only Tran-knew-what behind.

Off to the right was a kitchen with dirty windows and an easy-to-clean rubber floor. Up ahead, a hallway with a bathroom and two closed doors.

I followed Tran, past the frayed couch, and checked behind the screen. Then wished I hadn't.

A double bed dominated the space. Handcuffs dangled from four metal posts. Graduated shades of blood stained the mattress pad—some dark from age, others bright and fresh. A wooden table ran along the left wall. Desk lamps sat on either end, the kind with bendable stems that aimed directly at the bed. If turned on, the white bulbs would shine like spotlights illuminating…what, I didn't want to consider, especially when I saw the implements available for use.

"Come on," Tran said, motioning me toward the kitchen.

He was right. Whoever had suffered here was beyond our help.

Please, God, let it not have been Kateryna or Ilya.

In the middle of the tiny kitchen, we found a butcher block table with an axe in the center. Blood and gashes marred the wood. I turned away. The bathroom came next—filthy but not villainous—which left two more rooms behind closed doors.

I nodded to the one on the right. Tran the one on the left. Neither of us were holding firearms—me because I didn't own one and Tran because we couldn't afford the noise—but we both had nasty blades in hand and a grim determination to use them. If we could rescue Kateryna and Ilya quietly, no one had to die.

We exchanged a glance and opened our respective doors simultaneously.

I didn't know what Tran saw in his room, but what I saw in mine made me want to cry.

I rushed over to Ilya, lying on his side against the wall, and ripped off his blindfold. He stared blankly in fear until he recognized me, then his eyes flooded with tears. I put a finger to my lips and untied the gag, checking behind me to make sure the hallway remained clear.

I didn't hear any noise coming from the room Tran had entered, but was confident whatever he found, he could deal with it on his own.

I turned back to Ilya and examined his bindings. The bastards had zip-tied his ankles and wrists behind him and secured them to a pipe that ran along the entire side of the room. I cut through the plastic. Ilya struggled to his knees and threw his arms around my neck and sobbed.

I rocked him gently and murmured soothing words. "I got you. It's going to be fine. But right now, you have to be quiet. Okay?"

When I felt his head nod, I peeled him off my neck. He still wore the navy polo and khaki pants of his Catholic kindergarten uniform. He looked tiny and helpless but otherwise unharmed.

I helped him to his feet. He wanted to be lifted, but I shook my head and grabbed his hand instead, holding it against my back so he would follow. I still hadn't heard any noises from the other room. Whatever was going on, I wanted Ilya behind me where he wouldn't get hurt and wouldn't be able to see.

Tran had his back to me, mostly shielding the body on the bed. I recognized Kateryna's blonde ringlets, but couldn't see anything else except bare feet and one bare arm draped off the edge. Ilya hugged my thigh and buried his face against the small of my back. Although it would be hard for me to fight with him plastered against me, I couldn't bring myself to push him away. Not yet.

"How is she?" I whispered, fearing the worst. Tran stepped aside so I could see. Whatever else had been done to her, Kateryna was alive and awake. Her pink sundress showed no sign of blood and had not been ripped.

I turned back to Ilya. "She's okay." When he looked up at me with those big half-moon eyes, I almost dropped to my knees to hug him. *Almost.* We weren't out of danger yet. I pried his fingers off of my thigh and held him back with my hand. I needed room to move.

It was a good thing I did because, at that moment, the front door rattled.

I shoved Ilya into the bedroom with Kateryna and Tran and darted across the hallway into the bathroom.

If trouble was coming for Ilya, it would have to go through me first.

Chapter Fifty

Tran waited just inside the doorway of the back bedroom, where I had left him to guard Kateryna and Ilya. He glanced at me and nodded. I nodded back then peeked out my doorway to see what was happening. I caught a flash of a purple jersey disappearing into the front room as his buddy in the brown and black striped crew marched through the front door.

"You always blaming me," Striped Crew said. "Maybe you left it open."

"No way."

I swallowed a curse. I had intended to re-lock the door on our way out. Clearly, I should have locked it on the way in.

I heard a loud thump and muffled curses, it sounded like he had knocked over the accordion screen and was trying, unsuccessfully, to set it right. He groaned and hissed and cursed the same word over and over in escalating volume until the screen—or so I assumed—crashed onto something solid and triggered a domino effect of clatter, thuds, and shattering glass.

Striped Crew followed him into the room and out of my sight. "What the fuck? That shit came from Carlos's mama's house. Hijo de puta! Why'd you break it?"

The house shook as something hard pounded into the wall. "Will you shut the fuck up?"

"*You* shut the fuck up. You the one making all the noise."

"Go check on the kid."

"Why?"

"Because the fucking door was unlocked."

"I told you, I locked—"

"Just check on the fucking kid."

"All right, already."

"Wait," Purple Jersey said, then dropped his volume too low to hear.

I glanced at Tran. He shrugged, then held up his throwing knives. I nodded my understanding and crouched low. Tran did the same. Both of us were ready to launch a silent attack, but neither of us wanted our heads and chests at the expected level in case the Varrios led their charge with bullets.

When an arm holding a pistol came into view, I slashed up his wrist and down his belly.

It was Striped Crew.

The pistol fell. Striped Crew grabbed his bleeding gut. I sliced back across his thigh, hoping to sever his femoral artery, but the blade caught in his baggy shorts. As I yanked the karambit free, Striped Crew hammered his fist into the side of my neck and pounded me to the floor like a sledgehammer.

He had struck the vagus nerve—one of twelve cranial nerves that sent messages throughout the body. I had experienced this strike many times at the hands of my teacher. When targeted perfectly, the body shut down and crumpled to the ground, giving the attacker precious seconds of vulnerability on which to capitalize. Although I doubted Striped Crew had hit this nerve intentionally, the results were the same.

My vision blurred. My head throbbed. Striped Crew loomed over me—arms bulging, fingers splayed, blood dripping from his gut— ready to tear me apart. I needed to get up, but my legs wouldn't obey.

My arms, on the other hand, worked fine. The security ring on the handle had kept the knife in my hand, so I slashed the thug's calf, right below the hem of his shorts and above the rim of his fancy kicks. He shrieked, teetering dangerously above me. Legs working once again, I crab-crawled back to avoid getting crushed or smothered.

Behind him, Purple Jersey shifted from one side to the other, looking for a clean shot. "Get out of the way!"

Striped Crew crumpled to his knees. Purple Jersey took aim. I rocked to the side, hoping to take my head and heart out of the path of the bullet, but there was nowhere to go. I was trapped in a four-foot hallway, less than ten feet from the gun. Purple Jersey would have to be the worst gangbanger in all of Los Angeles to miss this shot.

In a last-ditch effort, I swooped forward, flattened my body on the rubber floor, and waited for the bullets to tear through my back.

No searing pain. No coughing blood. No silence of death.

I pushed up onto my knees and looked beyond the hulking body of Striped Crew, still gripping his bleeding gut, to see Purple Jersey waver on his feet. He gurgled the noises I had expected my own throat to make and pressed his hands around the blade that protruded from his throat.

Tran's throwing knife had hit its mark.

Blood spurted through Purple Jersey's fingers. Try as he might, he couldn't seal the wound. But one of his hands still held the gun. If he fired it, whoever was in the main house would come running.

Tran shoved me aside. He had seen the same threat as I had and was on his way to disarm Purple Jersey before the weapon discharged. Unfortunately, that also meant he had to get past Striped Crew.

The beefy Varrio swung a backhanded fist at Tran and turned to follow it with a hooking punch. Tran could have stopped him easily, but it would have used up precious time. Instead, he slipped underneath the Varrio's attack and ran for the greater threat—the man with the knife in his throat and the gun in his hand. With nothing to stop the force of his hook, Striped Crew fell against the wall, giving me a clear view of his dying buddy—eyes crazed with fury and blood spurting from his throat—as he aimed his pistol at Tran's face.

Tran leapt. The gun fired. I gasped.

I couldn't tell if Tran had been shot, but I knew the alarm had been sounded.

I dove forward and used the momentum of my shoulder roll to launch a double kick into Striped Crew's gaping belly wound. I leapt to my feet. Before I could even react, Tran slit his throat.

He sheathed his knife and drew the SIG Sauer from his holster. "Let's go. We don't have much time."

I clipped the karambit onto my waistband and grabbed the gun from Purple Jersey's lifeless hand. Although I didn't own a gun, Sensei had made sure I knew how to use them. Not surprisingly, this one was an FN-57, a popular choice among Mexican drug cartels who also favored AK-47s and grenade launchers. Lucky us.

Tran went to clear the yard. I ran for the bedroom and found Kateryna and Ilya huddled behind the bed. I grabbed Ilya's hand and yanked him to his feet. "Come on!"

Kateryna screamed at me to let him go. I didn't listen. At this point, all I cared about was Ilya. She could follow or not. I didn't have time to protect them both.

We had just exited the front door when a gun fired. I hunched over Ilya and raised my weapon, scanning for the threat. In the center of the yard, a Varrio gangster crumpled to the dirt, his forehead marred by a bloody hole. Two more ran up the driveway from the main house.

I shoved Ilya behind me. "Get back in the house!" Then I ran for the tree. With Tran on the left and me on the right, the gang members had two targets to shoot and two sets of bullets to dodge. Equally important, neither of us were in firing line of the people we were trying to protect.

Bark sprayed off the tree a foot above my head. I leaned out the opposite side and fired back. Although I didn't expect to hit anyone, I hoped that if I kept up the pressure, Tran would. He took advantage of the cover and fired one shot, and one body thumped against the car. Another Varrio cursed in Spanish and yelled for backup.

We didn't have much time.

I ran back to the little house for Ilya and Katerina as Tran darted across the yard to the driveway, firing in quick succession. Another Varrio died, chest jerking and arms flailing with every impact. When I reached the driveway, Kateryna yanked Ilya away from me. The message was clear: *Don't take my son from me again.*

I nodded my understanding and led them behind the car. "Stay low."

As Tran crept along the wall of the main house toward the side door, I covered him over the car's roof. The coast was clear. I wanted to get out while we still had the chance. "Let's go," I whispered to Tran, then motioned to Ilya and Kateryna.

Stupid move.

Two more guys charged out the door, this time armed with AK-47s. They caught me standing directly in front of them with my head perched over the car's roof like a pumpkin on a fence. Someone was going to die.

Although guns were far from my weapon of choice, I had gained enough skill to be able to hit a two-hundred-pound man in center mass at ten feet. Unfortunately, my bullet only made this man angrier.

I shot him again, this time in the face.

The act so unnerved me that I paused, just for a second, but long enough for the other man to turn his sights on me. I didn't have time to aim. I pulled the trigger and prayed for luck.

The window beside him shattered. The Varrio shot up in a wide arc, chipping tiles off the neighbor's roof. When he fell, I saw Tran standing on the driveway, pointing a gun where the man's head used to be. I nodded my thanks as Kateryna screamed, Ilya cried, and neighbors yelled for loved ones to get down or for someone to call the cops.

Time to go.

I shoved Kateryna and Ilya toward the street and was just about to follow when a woman exited the house, wrapped in a bath towel. A lush tattooed vine of orange and blue flowers flowed over her naked shoulders and down her bare arms. Her hands were empty. Her mouth hung open in horror as she looked from her dead friends to us.

I glanced at Tran and shook my head.

If even one of them sees us, they all have to die.

I knew what I had promised, but Tran had to understand the difference between the Varrio Norwalk 66 and some clueless gang groupie. Didn't he?

I raised my weapon—not at the unarmed woman but at Tran.

His mouth tightened into a sad smile as he stared at me with those beautiful cruel eyes. He never looked away from me, not for a moment, as he raised his arm to the side where he knew the woman would be, and shot her in the chest.

She crumpled to the driveway. Blood seeped through her towel and mingled with the orange and green ink of her tattoo.

Tran lowered the SIG and holstered it under his jacket. He knew I could have killed him at that moment.

But I didn't.

And he knew that, too.

Chapter Fifty-One

I wiped the handle of the FN-57 with my shirt and tossed it under the car. If we ran into the cops, I didn't want to get caught with a firearm. Better to leave it with the owners. Maybe the ATF would trace the weapon back to their Fast and Furious scandal. I'd like that. Regardless, another gun on the scene made it look more like a gang-related hit.

I checked to see what Tran was doing and couldn't find him, so I gathered Kateryna and Ilya. "Time to go."

I led them on a frantic serpentine route away from the house and into the gathering crowd, ducking and dodging as though fearing to be hit by stray bullets. Sirens blared as squad cars sped to the scene. Neighbors gathered in clumps to exchange information and express their horror. No one cared about two frightened women and a crying child—until a man yanked Ilya from my grip.

"Let go of that boy," he yelled, shoving Ilya behind him.

Kateryna screeched. I tried my best to sound calm and reasonable as a large black woman blocked her path to Ilya.

"That's her son," I said.

"Maybe he is, and maybe he ain't," she said, keeping Kateryna corralled as she spoke to me. "Why you running from that hell hole of a house? You part of that gang? You sure as hell ain't no relation to this here boy."

As the sirens grew louder, the neighbors closed around Ilya to protect him from us. I scanned the area for surviving members of the Varrio Norwalk 66. Depending on who spotted us first—cops or Varrios—the good intentions of these people were going to get Kateryna and me detained or killed.

I held out my hands to show the woman they were empty and glanced at Kateryna and Ilya. "Bullets shot through their kitchen. They were scared. You know how that is. I'm trying to help—just like you." I gestured to the neighbors behind her. "We're all just trying to help, right?" I put my hands on Kateryna's arms and rubbed them up and down to comfort her. "Can't you see how you're scaring her?" I looked at Ilya. "How you're scaring him?"

The woman turned around and bent in front of Ilya. "Is that your mama?"

Ilya nodded and sniffed while tears rolled down his adorable cheeks.

The big woman's shoulders rose and fell as she sighed. "Let him go, Kenny."

When she stepped out of the way, her neighbors did the same, making room for Ilya to run into Kateryna's arms. It was a sweet moment that we didn't have time to savor.

I steered them away from the commotion as the patrol cars arrived. When we rounded the corner, I took out my phone and made a call. "It's Lily. I need a ride."

Since I couldn't afford to have a record of this trip logged in a ride-share system, and since I didn't want to use public transportation this close to a crime scene, I had called Kansas directly.

Please be my friend.

After a very long two seconds, Kansas responded. "Sure thing. Where are you?"

I sighed with relief. "The Alondra Library in Norwalk."

"Be there in twenty."

I pocketed the phone and examined my clothes. The black polo and pants hid the blood that had splattered on me when I had cut open Striped Crew. At a distance, it could easily be mistaken for water or coffee. Up close, under the scrutiny of law enforcement? It looked exactly like what it was.

When we got to the parking lot, I checked Kateryna and Ilya for injuries. Although neither were bleeding, both had bruises and dried-up cuts on their faces and arms. Kateryna's golden ringlets had tangled into a ratted mess and her mascara had smudged from her tears. Whatever shoes she had been wearing with her pink sundress had fallen off long before Tran and I had found her tied to that bed.

I knelt down to Ilya. "Are you okay?" When he didn't answer immediately, I felt his ribs and back. No broken bones. And from his comfort at my touch, probably no emotional breaks, either. Tran and I had gotten to him in time.

I left Kateryna to cuddle her son and walked my bike to the curb to wait for Kansas.

Tran's BMW was gone, just like him, but the image of him murdering that woman remained. He hadn't felt remorse for taking her life. He hadn't even looked at her. He had been looking at me as he raised his arm, pointed his gun, and shot her in the chest. I could still see her blood as it stained the white towel and pooled on the gray cement.

I could have stopped him.

I could have pulled the trigger and ended his miserable life.

But I hadn't. And now, that foolish girl was dead.

And part of me was relieved.

As much as I hated to admit it, Tran had been right. Even if we *had* been able to get her away from the gang in the confusion—which was doubtful—the remaining members of the Varrio Norwalk 66 would have found her. Then, having tortured every detail from her conscious and sub-conscious mind, they would have come for Tran and me and everyone I loved.

Had Tran thought of this as he raised his gun? Had his sad look of regret been for the girl who he knew had to die? Or had it been for the loss of whatever existed between us?

He had to have known that I couldn't forgive him, no matter how necessary or inevitable the girl's death might have been.

Chapter Fifty-Two

Kansas and I kept our voices low in the front seat while Ilya slept in Kateryna's arms in the back.

"So, all those sirens for you?" Kansas asked.

"Afraid so—or rather, for the commotion we caused. Hopefully, they weren't searching for us specifically."

"But the witnesses. It's broad daylight. How could they not have noticed?"

I shrugged. "Everyone was so worried about getting shot, no one looked to see who was doing the shooting. And by the time we ran away, we weren't the only ones: the neighborhood was swarming like an angry hive. No one took note of us except for that man and woman."

"Won't they say anything?"

"I doubt it. They were feeling pretty guilty about traumatizing Ilya, and didn't realize we were coming from that house."

Kansas nodded but kept her eyes on the road. It was a lot to process. I let her do it in silence until we arrived.

"Thanks for the ride. You're a lifesaver."

She smiled. "I'm just driving the getaway car."

"No small thing."

"Look, how 'bout I wait out here and give you a ride when you're ready to go."

"You sure?"

"Yeah."

I led Kateryna and Ilya up the path to Aleisha's Refuge.

The cheery yellow house looked just as it had five days ago when I had hobbled up this walkway, bruised and bloody, expecting to find them safely inside. If they had stayed, would everything have gone as planned? Would Ilya be attending an Argentinian school and living with Kateryna in her cousin's home? Or would Romanko's thugs have found them and sent Ilya to Ukraine as he had threatened to do?

Stan opened the door before I reached the stoop. He must have heard the car and seen who I had brought with me because his expression was already fraught with concern. I watched him struggle to stay put and not pull me into a hug. He knew I wouldn't appreciate the gesture. Not today. Instead, he motioned us inside.

Seconds later, Aleisha bounded into the room. "You okay?" She took one look at Kateryna and Ilya and went into overdrive. Within a minute, we were all seated in her living room with iced tea, milk, cookies, and a first aid kit.

"Same plan as before?" she asked, watching Ilya devour one of her homemade chocolate chip cookies.

I turned to Kateryna. Despite all the bloodshed and horror, it wasn't my decision to make. This was her life and her son and her cousin in Argentina. If Kateryna wasn't willing to make the move, I couldn't force her to do it. I could, however, call social services, because there was no way in hell I'd let Dmitry Romanko get near his son ever again.

Much to my relief, Kateryna nodded her assent. I squeezed her. "Yes. Same plan as before. But this time, they can't use their own passports."

Stan grunted his approval.

I leaned toward Kateryna. "You're sure you never told Dmitry about this place?"

She shook her head. "Never."

"Okay, then. We're set. I'll get the passports, you call your cousin, and Aleisha and Stan will get you and Ilya on a plane. What do you want your new names to be? My thought is to use your cousin's last name. That way she can tell everyone you're relatives from her father's side of the family. Any preference for first names?"

"Alex," Ilya said, spitting crumbs in his haste to speak. "Please, Mommy. Can I be Alex?"

She kissed his head. "Of course you can. And I'll be Anya. Anya and Alex Vovek. It sounds nice." She glanced at me as she wrapped Ilya in a hug.

I smiled. It sounded more than nice; it sounded like freedom.

Chapter Fifty-Three

Kansas stopped at the entrance to the alley behind our restaurant. "Are you sure this is where you want to be left off? Because I'm happy to drive you to the door."

"Nope. This is fine." I took five twenties from my backpack and handed them to her.

She pushed it back. "Are you kidding? I play superhero for free."

I laughed. "Me, too. Sometimes."

I lived rent free with unlimited food, no car expenses, and a standard of living I could support with what I earned from Aleisha and Stan. The tips and bits I got from waiting tables in Baba's restaurant and helping his community friends with their website and social media needs kept me in pocket change. Any splurges were paid for with red envelope money gifted to me from Ma or Gung-Gung for Chinese New Year, Christmas, or my birthday. I could afford to help women like Mia. I just never had a pro-bono case collide so spectacularly with one I had been hired to do.

I unstrapped the Merida and rolled it to the sidewalk then hunched so I could see Kansas through her open window. "I don't know how to thank you."

She waved it away. "Don't worry about it. If you want a ride in town, use the app. But if you're ever in trouble, call my cell. I'll come get you—no matter what."

I nodded, swallowing the rising emotion. I had lost most of my friends after Rose's death. It was nice to make another.

As the olive SUV vanished into dusk, the weariness kicked in. The ultralight pack on my shoulders weighed me down, and the alley to our restaurant elongated with every trudging step. I yearned for sleep, but it was only six-thirty and sunset was still over an hour away. It had been a very long day.

The sun cast deep shadows that played tricks with my vision and made me see things that shouldn't be there—like the man standing beside the black BMW.

I leaned my bike against the wall and walked toward Tran. "You followed me from the library?"

"I did."

"So you know where I've been."

"I do."

"And where I'm going?"

He glanced at the back door of our restaurant beneath a sign for Wong's Hong Kong Inn.

"Peachy."

He smiled, and the corners of his eyes crinkled with amusement. He had brushed his hair into smooth, dark waves and changed into a new jacket and pants that were free of blood. Once again, I thought he looked ready for a date. Then his amusement vanished and the inscrutable killer returned.

"What now?"

His pointed brow raised. "We have unfinished business."

I unclipped the karambit, slid it behind my thigh, and flicked open the blade. No matter what business Tran thought we had between us, it wasn't going down without a fight.

He raised his empty hands. "Not that kind of business."

I relaxed my arm and let the karambit hang into view, blade open and ready. "I'm listening."

Tran glanced from the blade to my face and nodded with approval. "Things ended abruptly today. Things that should have been said were not."

I relaxed my stance. I finally understood what he wanted, but the words I needed to say wouldn't come. I kept seeing the unarmed woman lying dead on the driveway. How could I thank the man who had done that to her?

Still...

Without Tran, I never would have found Kateryna and Ilya. And if by some miracle I had, I never would have gotten them out on my own. They wouldn't be safe with Aleisha and Stan, and I'd probably be dead. I knew this, and yet I couldn't bring myself to thank him. Because none of his heroics would have been necessary if he hadn't first killed for the Ukrainian mob.

I sighed. None of that mattered: Tran had saved lives today.

I folded the karambit, clipped it to my waistband, and spoke the words that needed to be said.

"Thank you." And was surprised to find they weren't as painful as I had expected.

"You're welcome. But that's not what I meant."

"Oh my God," I whispered. "You're here to clean up." We were standing in the alley outside the restaurant where Baba, Uncle, DeAndre, and all the other good people of our staff worked.

"Easy, K. Or should I call you Lily? I'm not going to hurt your family or you." He glanced at my hand, now poised over my knife. "Unless you give me reason."

I crossed my arms. "Fair enough. What do you want?"

"To say goodbye."

"For the day or for good?"

Time suspended as everything we had never said and never would say flew back and forth between us. A gamut of emotions welled inside of me: mistrust, admiration, respect, hate, and other emotions I would never—ever—admit.

"For good," he said, then turned and headed for his car.

"Wait. That's it? You ambush me in a dark alley so you can say goodbye? Not buying it. What's going on, Tran? Why did you really help me? And don't give me that crap about wanting to see what I'd do. You risked your life and pissed off a lot of people today. Why?"

His shoulders slumped as he turned. "They shouldn't have taken the boy."

I thought about our conversation in the library parking lot before we had gone to rescue Kateryna and Ilya, when I had accused Tran of not having a conscience.

"It's about Vietnam, isn't it? What happened there?"

Tran shook his head, and for a moment, I didn't think he'd answer.

"You know what they call unnamed babies in Vietnamese orphanages? Nguyễn Văn A, if it's a boy, and Trần Thị B, if it's a girl. A and B. The first letters in the alphabet. Except in my orphanage, they already had a boy they had named Nguyễn Văn A. So, instead, they gave me the girl's placeholder surname of Trần and the American first name of Joe, because someone thought my father might have been an American soldier."

"G.I. Joe."

"Uh-huh."

"You're older than I had thought."

He chuckled. "Good genes. Maybe that's why I'm also good at fighting. Or maybe I got good at fighting because of what they did to me."

I wanted to know, but I was afraid to push. So I waited until he was ready.

He closed his eyes and ran his fingers through his hair and pulled. "I was seven when I killed for the first time. It was another orphan, an older boy who…" Tran paused. "No one paid much attention. Then I killed a man. And that drew all kinds of attention. The nuns threw me out, and the guerilla warriors took me in. I escaped to Cambodia a few years later when I met a man with an eye for talent."

He stared at the ground as his face furrowed and twitched with memories. They must have been horrible because what I saw in Tran's expression made me want to weep. Then he cleared his throat, regained his composure, looked into my eyes, and spoke in a hard and unforgiving voice.

"Children. Should never. Be hurt."

He had answered truthfully about why he had helped me rescue Kateryna and Ilya; I was certain of it. Just as I was certain that I'd feel the same way in his position.

"What about Freddy and the others? Are their families and loved ones still in danger?"

"No. I did what Romanko hired me to do."

"For Zherdev?"

"Mostly."

"The Koreatown hit?"

"That was for Romanko."

"You, Romanko, Zherdev get to destroy lives and walk away like it's nothing?"

Tran shrugged. "Everybody pays. Maybe not in the way you want them to, but they always pay."

Chapter Fifty-Four

The last thing I wanted to do was call for another ride, but I did it anyway, just not with Kansas. I had taxed our friendship enough for one day: She deserved to chill, not fight through Friday traffic.

I locked my bike to the railing and walked to Overland to meet the driver. If I tried to ride right now, I'd keel over from exhaustion. I was that done. And yet, I couldn't leave Mia hanging, not after Tran had said Freddy and his loved ones were safe.

Thirty minutes later, I knocked on her door.

She stared at me in silence then plodded back to her living room. I closed the door behind me and followed the trail of sour sweat. Drawn blinds, strewn blankets, empty bottles, food wrappers—Mia hadn't been kidding when she'd texted that her ass hadn't left the couch.

"There's beer in the fridge," she said, reaching for one of the empty bottles that littered her coffee table and upending it over her mouth, just in case. A few drops fell on her tongue. "Get one for me while you're at it, will you?"

I did as she asked. From what I saw in the kitchen, Mia had been existing on butter cookies, pork rinds, and beer. One more bottle wouldn't hurt her. And after everything I had done and survived today, it sure as heck wouldn't hurt me.

We sipped our beers in silence until I had figured out how to begin. "It's over."

She grunted out a harsh laugh. "You think?"

"I meant your problems with Tran."

"Who gives a shit about Tran? If he wants to kill me, let him. My life sucks."

I understood. Mia had lost her job, her friends, her man. And without Freddy to help pay the rent, would probably lose the apartment. But she wouldn't lose her life. "What will you do, now?"

"Beats the shit out of me."

I sipped my beer. "Have you considered moving back to Vegas?"

"Are you kidding?"

"Why not? You must have friends there. Couldn't you get a job at one of the casinos and live with your mom until you get on your feet?"

"In the trailer park?"

I shrugged. "You'd be with family."

She scratched the edge of her soggy beer label as she considered the possibility. "I have friends. And I do know a couple of casino managers."

"See?" I wanted to ask what she had to lose, but I didn't want to make her feel any worse than she already did.

"I'm really out of danger?"

"Yep. Tran's gone. He won't bother you again."

She picked at a label and rolled the strip into a pellet. "I lied to you before. I did have boyfriend. His name was Freddy."

I nodded, as though surprised to hear the news yet understanding of her secrecy. "Was?"

She shrugged. "I'm not really upset about him dumping me. I mean it sucks—don't get me wrong—but it's not like I loved him. I just—" She shook her head and flicked the pellet across the room. "He was nice, you know? It made me feel good to think someone

294

nice could care about me."

I thought about the nice guy in my own life. Could a good Chinese son like Daniel Kwok truly care for a rebellious ninja daughter like me? And if he did, would I like it?

And then there was Tran.

Nothing about him was nice or good. And yet…as much as it disturbed me to admit, Tran had awakened something I wasn't sure could be put back to sleep. Maybe I could focus whatever that was onto Daniel. Maybe not. But I was willing to try.

"Yeah," I said. "Nice is…" I shook my head, uncertain how to finish.

Mia exhaled loudly, as if I'd confirmed the depressing state of her life. "Right? So where does that leave me?"

I shrugged. "In transition? Sometimes we have to clean house to make room for new things and new people."

"And new lives?"

"Sure. Why not?"

She chuckled. "Move back in with Mom? Wow. But, you know, I think she'd like it."

I thought about Ma and me munching gourmet potato chips and giggling about escrows. Would she want me to move back home? I had no idea—the mother-daughter dynamic baffled me. Although, if we could giggle over potato chips and tea after everything we'd been through, maybe one day, I'd find my way through the labyrinth of emotions and misconceptions.

"I bet your mom would like it a lot," I said, and believed it with all my heart. Then I put down my beer and stood. "There's a good future waiting for you in Vegas, Mia. I'm sure of it. Go home."

Ma and me. Mia and her mom. The timing felt significant—just like finding the newspaper article about Mia in Kateryna's bedroom and then getting that SMG email about Tran's preliminary trial, the next morning. They weren't coincidences; they were signs.

And a good Chinese ninja daughter always paid attention to the signs.

Chapter Fifty-Five

My phone buzzed with a text. It was from Tran. I had just returned from Mia's and had spent the car ride processing all that had happened, and now he wanted to add more? What else was there to say? How much more did I really want to know?

I opened the text.

Buy Pacific Blvd.

That's all he had written, and yet it said all I needed to know. Pacific not Santa Fe—the original route for Metro's proposed Copper Line. The message was clear: Freddy, Mayor Young, and Councilman Vasquez could vote as they saw fit.

My phone buzzed again. This time Tran had chosen a more graphic means of communication—a photo of Zherdev and Dmitry Romanko, gutted on the Mid San Gabriel Trail.

Whoa.

A new message appeared.

Everybody pays.

Then the photo and both texts vanished.

I shook my head. Leave it to Tran to send self-destructing messages.

I turned off my phone and tucked it into my pocket. Anyone who wanted to reach me could wait until morning. I was well and truly done.

Tomorrow, I'd send an anonymous message to the TAC voting members to make sure they knew the pressure was off. And another to the LA district attorney that explained the violent land-grab scheme as concisely as I could manage. Tomorrow, I would also tell Kateryna the news about Zherdev and her husband. She had a right to know. Hopefully, she would proceed as planned to Argentina where she and Ilya could live a new life. There wasn't anything for them in Los Angeles except painful memories, danger, and a mountain of debt. They deserved their chance at happiness.

I unlocked my bike from the railing and carried it up the stairs. Then I breathed in the scent of garlic and ginger. Inside, I'd find Baba in front of the wok, tossing shrimp or stirring vegetables as steam rose into his face and drops of oil splattered onto his arms. He wouldn't care. He'd squirt a long stream of soy sauce, making the hazard worse and the dish taste better. Then he'd pour the contents of the wok onto a platter that Uncle had left on the prep table and shout the order.

I opened the door and rolled my bike inside.

"Dumplings," Baba yelled.

He hadn't seen me. He was referring to the crispy jian jiao hot off the wok. While it wasn't the shrimp dish I had imagined him cooking, my stomach rumbled all the same.

"Nǐ hǎo!" Uncle said when he saw me. "Food on counter. You eat."

I smiled. "People want skinny noodles again?"

He cackled. "You smart girl. Chow fun better. I know—"

"I fix," we said in unison. Then we laughed.

A server whisked away the platter of crispy dumplings and headed out the swinging doors to the dining room. I tried not to feel envious. If I asked nicely, would Baba would fry me up another batch?

I leaned the Merida against the kitchen wall, knowing I couldn't leave it there for long, but desperately in need of food. And a hug.

Baba gaped when he saw me. I checked my jacket to make sure it was zipped over the blood-stained shirt. Had death marked me in ways I couldn't see?

As DeAndre and the rest of our staff bustled about their business, Baba wiped his big farmer hands on his white apron and marched toward me.

Tears welled in my eyes. I dropped my head and let my hair fall into my face. I felt exposed and wanted something to hide behind, but Baba wouldn't have it. He pushed my hair behind my ears and cupped my cheeks in his warm, comforting palms.

"Are you okay?" Then he folded me in his arms without waiting for an answer and murmured my nickname in a soothing drone. We stood that way, bound together by love and trust, until my tears had dried and my shuddering had ceased. Then he pushed me back and repeated his question. "Are you okay?"

I thought about that for a moment.

I was better than okay. I had done what I set out to do. Mia Mikkelsen was safe from J Tran. Kateryna and Ilya were safe from Dmitry Romanko. And hopefully all of them would find a brighter future. Metro would decide the fate of the Copper Line based on its merit and not on the machinations of a ruthless crime boss. I felt bad about the tattooed woman, but she had put her life at risk when she lay down with those wolves. She must have known they were murderers, and had probably also known about the evil things they did in that backyard house. She might have been unarmed, but she hadn't been innocent. And as for Julie Stanton and the councilman's old college flame? Well, there wasn't anything I could do for those poor women beyond the anonymous message I would send to the district attorney and my hope that the truth of their murders brought closure to their friends and families.

My life was still full of secrets, but now that some of those secrets could be shared with Baba—and to a lesser degree with Ma—my heart felt lighter. I would always have Sensei, who knew the whole truth, and friends like Aleisha, Stan, and Kansas who knew enough. But nothing filled a lonely heart as much as the unconditional support of family.

I nodded to Baba and smiled. "I'm fine. Hungry. But fine."

He puffed out his cheeks and poked me in the belly. "One order of dumplings, coming right up."

Acknowledgments

Gratitude for any writing endeavor must always begin with my husband, Tony, for his boundless encouragement, support, and patience to listen and read again and again—and again. I don't know how he does it, but I hope he never tires. He and our sons, Stopher and Austin, have encouraged my crazy journey from actress to ninja to writer with faith, love, and humor. They bless my life and fill it with joy.

This particular novel began, as we say in Hawaii, by talking story with several of my Chinese-American friends. Mahalo to Alisa Young, Kelly Lum, Emily Hsu, and Mary Qin for sharing their stories. And special thanks to Shing Hwong, who I met during Wushu training, and who not only shared her family stories but also read my early drafts. Mahalo also to all the Chinese mothers who made powerful impressions on me, especially my own dear Ma who shared her heritage unknowingly and often unintentionally but left her imprint all the same.

On my North Dakota Norwegian side of the family, thanks go to my cousin Becky Ulven and her salt-of-the-earth husband, Vern. I see his cheerful face whenever I write a scene for Baba. And, of course, my heart is full of gratitude for my dear father who proudly shared his stories and instilled in me a deep love for my

Norwegian ancestry. I'm forever grateful that Dad was able to read an early version of The Ninja Daughter and know how much he and his heritage meant to me.

I am exceedingly grateful for the training I received through To-Shin Do, the modern evolution of Ninjutsu founded by Stephen K. Hayes and Rumiko U. Hayes. My life has been enriched by all of my To-Shin Do teachers, and my ninja friends and training partners from both the To-Shin Do and Bujinkan communities. Thank you for sharing your knowledge, skill, and experiences with me. Thanks also go to my dear kunoichi beta readers, Sylvia Steere and Kim Stahl, and to my good friend Jack Hoban, ninja master and U.S. Marine, for his keen beta-reading feedback and support.

I'd also like to thank my wonderful author-editor friends Janice Gable Bashman and Patricia Gussin for their exceptional critiques. Love and thanks also to my dear friend and former agent, Cherry Weiner, for her steadfast belief and tireless effort, and to Pam Stack, cheerleader, advocate, and friend who led me to Jason Pinter and his remarkable publishing house.

I'm very grateful to be one of the launch authors for the Agora imprint of Polis Books and delighted beyond measure to be collaborating with a genius editor like Chantelle Aimée Osman. Chantelle and Jason have guided me through the debut author process with infinite patience and wisdom. To have my debut novel published by such caring and dedicated people has been a dream come true.

I'm blessed with so many supportive friends, mentors, and family. All of you have helped me stay on this path and become a better writer. All of you have enriched my life. I can only hope that as you read this, you know I'm speaking to you with fondest gratitude and aloha.

AUTHOR'S NOTES

The Ninja Daughter is an homage to my Chinese-Hawaiian mother, my North Dakota Norwegian father, and the Japanese art of the ninja that has informed so much of my life. Although not by any means an autobiography, I did draw extensively from my own heritage and experiences. The cultural perspectives and ninja interpretations belong entirely to me and my beloved protagonist, Lily Wong.

Part of my goal with this novel was to portray the ninja in a contemporary light, not as supernatural assassins or illusive mythic figures, but everyday people with skill, commitment, and a desire to do good. To this end, I set my story in a city where I've lived for thirty-five years and rooted it in as much fact as my fiction could contain. If you're wondering which is which, read on. What follows are insights to my thought process, and facts versus fiction concerning Los Angeles, Chinese language, cultural heritage, and—of course—ninja.

Of all the martial arts I've studied, Ninjutsu is by far the most comprehensive and effective. Ninjutsu practitioners fight unarmed on the ground, standing, or in the air—wherever and however is necessary. We are trained to fight with and defend against swords, spears, chains, staves, knives, shuriken, and other traditional and modern weapons, including firearms. A large part of the practice is recognizing and using whatever's at hand to distract, attack, and defend, and keeping open to new methods of fighting that we can adapt for our use.

Long weapons, like staves and spears, were a specialty of mine, and since my eldest son was competing on the UCLA Wushu team a while back, I had the opportunity to train with his Wushu master to learn Chinese spear fighting techniques. Although Wushu is very different from Ninjutsu, I found great beauty, merit, and compatibility. Naturally, I had Lily study both of these martial arts—Chinese Wushu from her heritage and Japanese Ninjutsu for her destiny.

Every fighting technique Lily executes in this book is, in fact, possible by someone with Lily's training, grit, and athleticism. I have witnessed, performed, or researched every move she makes and can attest to her effectiveness. Although I've retired from teaching and no longer actively train, I use my ninja skills every day to create a safe and harmonious life. I also maintain a daily practice of mantra, mudra, meditation, and esoteric training, some of which I describe in The Ninja Daughter.

Of course, my novel weaves fiction into fact in more ways than fighting.

I set this story in sprawling, cultural Los Angeles, where I've lived for thirty-five years, and had a blast injecting my fictional characters into real yet uncommon locales. Wong's Hong Kong Inn, Aleisha's Refuge, Paco's Tacos, and all personal residents are fiction, but the rest of the locations can be found right here in Los Angeles. If you're ever in town for a visit, I highly recommend a hike to Sandstone Peak, surfing at County Line (where I lived for twenty-three years), and a trip to Hollywood and Highlands for the novelty. You might even take a Metro rail from Santa Monica Pier to Arcadia, where Lily's parents live, with a stopover in Chinatown and Union Station for a bit of Chinese culture and Art Deco grandeur. And don't forget the epicurean delights at République, the site of Lily and Daniel's first date.

Speaking of Metro: they do have plans for expansion, but it doesn't include my fictional Copper Line. And while they do have a Technical Advisory Committee, none of my characters serve as voting members nor is Freddy Weintraub a Planning Supervisor.

The Varrio Norwalk 66 and the Ukrainian mob (as it appears in my novel) are complete fabrications. Any resemblance to any existing gangs is purely accidental. However, the LGKK and Korean Killers do and did exist.

This brings me to the complex issue of Chinese language and way too many methods of transliteration.

Lily studied Mandarin (the national language of China) in high school and college and learned Cantonese (the official language of Hong Kong) from her mother and in Saturday Cantonese class. Both of these languages (also known as dialects) can be read using the same simplified or traditional Chinese characters. However, the spoken words are completely different, not just in vocabulary but in sound—Mandarin has five tones, Cantonese has nine, and the English speaker hears…who knows what.

That brings me to my first language-related challenge: how to spell what I imagine Lily hears.

My mother's maiden name was Ching, which makes her—and me—a potential cousin to anyone with the last name Cheng, Chang, Chen, Chin, Shing, or Chung. Why? Because when immigrants arrived in the United States or—as was the case with my grandfather, pre-statehood Hawaii—the Chinese names were written according to what the registrar heard and how they decided to spell them. The discrepancies continue with Chinese words we Asian-Americans commonly use. For example, when I polled my friends—whose families all hail from Guangdong province or Hong Kong—they all called their maternal grandfathers by a common Cantonese name. But none of them spelled it in the same way. Then I searched on the internet and saw even more variations. In the end, I decided to use the spelling that most appealed to me. But, although I liked the hyphen for Gung-Gung and Po-Po, it didn't feel cozy enough for Baba. As for Ma, I spelled it the way I did for my own mother. She grew up in Wailuku, Maui. My maternal grandfather immigrated from Guangdong and died before I was born. I imagine Ma would have had me call him Gung-Gung. I never met my Chinese-Hawaiian grandmother, but since we can trace our Hawaiian ancestry to the late 1700s, I think Tutu (Hawaiian) would have trumped Po-Po (Cantonese) in Wailuku (Maui).

As the daughter of a Hong Kong-born mother, Lily grew up speaking Cantonese. However, Violet Wong also works in international finance where the universal Asian language and the national language of China is Mandarin. As a result, Violet made sure Lily studied and practiced both. Keep in mind that these are complicated languages. Once Lily moved out of her mother's home, she practiced less and forgot more until her Chinese became a hodgepodge of whatever she happened to remember or the first word embedded in her mind. This is why she calls her favorite dim sum by an assortment of Cantonese and Mandarin names.

I do the same.

I adore char siu bao and chow fun but call sticky rice dumplings zòngzi instead of jungji. To make matters even more confusing, I also throw in Hawaiian style names like manapua for char siu bao and crispy gau gee for these awesome rectangular wontons that no one from China or anywhere outside Hawaii has heard of. If you ever eat Chinese food in Hawaii, I highly recommend an order of crispy gau gee.

For simplicity, I left off the tone marks, habitually used to convey pitch and inflection, with some of the common Chinese words spoken by English speakers. I used Hanyu Pinyin with tone marks to transliterate less common Mandarin words and phrases spoken by native speakers. And when the need arises in future books, I'll use Yale Romanization for Cantonese because it has a similar appearance and uses tone marks rather than tone numbers.

I hope you enjoyed the facts, fictions, and assorted cultural morsels. If you have any questions, please feel free to drop me line. If you subscribe to my Muse-Letter, you can reply directly to me! And if you're looking for discussion topics and cool extras for your book club—like Chinese teas, recipes, decorations, fitness tips, meditations, and videos—you'll find that on my website, as well. ToriEldridge.com.

Until then... Aloha nui loa!